Gone

A HARRY STARKE NOVEL

By

Blair Howard

GONE

A Harry Starke Novel Book 5

BLAIR HOWARD

GONE
A Harry Starke Novel

ISBN-13: 978-1534673236

ISBN-10: 1534673237

GONE is a work of fiction. The persons, places and events depicted in this novel were created by the author's imagination; no resemblance to actual persons or events is intended.

Product names, brands, and other trademarks referred to within this book are the property of the trademark holders. Unless otherwise specified, no association between the author and any trademark holder is expressed or implied.

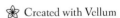 Created with Vellum

Gone

A HARRY STARKE NOVEL BOOK 5

By

Blair Howard

Dedication

This one is for
Jack Knapp
I owe you, my friend, for your support, insight, and good
advice. Thank you.

Chapter One

It had been one of those days when I couldn't wait to close the office doors and go home for the night. A rough one. I'd spent most of the morning in court being torn apart by a testosterone-deficient old man who should have retired years ago. I hadn't wanted to appear in the first place—it was a very high-profile divorce case, and very messy—but, as they say, that's what friends are for.

So there I was, all alone in my office at just after five thirty on a Friday afternoon. The staff had all left for the weekend, and I was just about to do the same. I was looking forward to some good company in the form of the inimitable Amanda Cole, star of small-screen news at Channel 7, some good food, maybe a round of golf with the old man, and some of Scotland's finest beverage to smooth the way. Yes, I was looking forward to the weekend. Little did I know it would be one of the worst weekends of my life.

I took one last look around, and then headed out into the

parking lot. I was about to lock the office door behind me when my cell phone buzzed.

Amanda?

But it wasn't her. I didn't even recognize the number. I almost rejected the call, but... well, you know what curiosity is, and what it does. I answered it.

"Hey, Harry. It's Wes Johnston. You got a minute?"

Chief Johnston? What the hell? This ain't happenin'.

But it was. Even though he was the last person I would have expected to hear from, or wanted to see that evening.

Chief Wesley Johnston, head of the Chattanooga Police Department, was an old nemesis of mine. He'd hired me on as a rookie cop more than eighteen years ago, and we'd enjoyed a somewhat bellicose relationship right up until I'd finally had enough of the political BS and quit the force. That had been more than ten years ago. Since then, I had become a successful private investigator, and things between us had deteriorated even further. Oh he tolerated me, but only because of my professional relationship with my one-time partner, Detective Lieutenant Kate Gazzara, a relationship he reluctantly, now and then, blessed in the name of closing cases. But this? This was not like him, not at all.

"I was just closing up shop, Chief. What is it?"

"I have a problem, Harry. I need... shit, I need some help. I'm outside your office. Can we talk?"

Wow, now that's a first.

Since I was already outside, I walked to the gate and looked down the street. There he was.

Oh hell. This is just what I need.

"Yeah, come on." I beckoned, disconnected the call, and went back into my outer office.

"Yeah, I know," he said as he approached. "Me, of all people, right?"

I nodded. "You want some coffee, Wes?"

"Nah. Look, Harry. I have a problem."

I'd worked for Johnston for almost nine years. He'd hired me into the Chattanooga PD right after I graduated Fairleigh Dickinson in ninety-seven. Because of my Masters in forensic psychology, I was fast-tracked, and made detective two years later—yep, and some folks did pull a string or two, hence my lack of popularity within the junior ranks of the department and... well, maybe with Johnston too. I spent the next seven years doing as I was told—most of the time— and following the rules... most of the time. I made sergeant, and then I'd had enough. I quit the force in 2007 and formed my own detective agency. My progress since then has been nothing short of meteoric, largely because of the people I know—I know everybody worth knowing in three states—but also because I'm good at what I do. I'm also discreet, thorough, and I produce results.

"Let's go in here," I said, and he followed me into my office.

My cave, as Kate Gazzara likes to call it. I offered him a seat in front of the acreage I call my desk, and dumped myself down into the leather-upholstered throne behind it.

Johnston was a big man. Not overly tall, but hefty. Out of uniform, a light blue golf shirt emphasized his slight paunch. His head was big, and round, and shaved, and polished to a shine. Hulk Hogan would have been proud of the moustache he wore, which was white and probably the reason for the shaved head. And he had an air about him. Not of arrogance, but he was certainly used to getting his own way, and he expected obedience from his underlings, a fact I could attest to personally.

"So, what's this problem? What can I do for you, Chief?"

He looked at me, shook his head, and said, "Ah, screw it. I don't need this." And he started to get his feet.

"Hey, Wes," I said. "Sit your ass back down and tell me what's on your mind."

He'd half-risen, had his hands on the arms of the chair and everything. He glared at me, balefully, then slowly lowered himself back down.

"So?" I asked.

"It's Emily. She's gone."

"Gone? Gone where?"

"If I knew that I wouldn't be here now would I?"

Emily was his eldest daughter. *Jeez, she must be... what? Twenty-one, twenty-two?*

I remembered her well. In the old days, when I was still a rookie and she was no more than five or six, she'd run riot around his office. Cute little thing... and she'd made me her special friend. Bless her, she'd even asked me to marry her when she grew up. She often visited me at my desk, full of questions, and even though I could never answer all of them, the fact that I bothered with her always seemed to be enough. *Emily, gone?*

"Okay, Wes. I'm not a mind reader. You going to tell me or what?"

He fidgeted. Wes never fidgeted. "She's supposed to be in school, at the Belle Edmondson College for Women, on Signal Mountain."

"Whoa. That's quite an exclusive school," I said. "Must cost a packet."

He looked sharply at me, but made no comment.

"As I said," he continued, "she's supposed to be at school. Thing is we—her mother and me—haven't heard a word from her in almost a week, and that's not like her. She's not answering her phone. Calls go to voicemail. Texts aren't answered."

"GPS?"

"No. It's still active, and triangulation puts it somewhere on the mountain—at the school, I assume. The school staff have looked for it: nothing."

I scribbled the details on a legal pad. "She boards up there, at the college?"

"Yes. We talked it over. It made sense. It's fine driving back and forth up there in summer, but when bad weather comes... well, you know how those roads are, and anyway, we couldn't have gotten her in there as a day student. So she boards."

"When did you last see her?"

"Last Friday. She stopped by the office for a few minutes. Last time before that was five, maybe six weeks ago. She comes and stays weekends once in a while, but mostly she stays at the college, studying or working with the horses."

"What's her major?"

"Drama, but she's also taking some other classes. English, math, and something to do with horses, as I said. She loves them, horses."

"How about friends? Could she be...?"

"We thought about that, but she doesn't have any close friends, not locally. What friends she does have are at school, and the only one I ever met was a girl named Jessica. She stayed over one weekend. Nice kid. They seemed close. Other than that, I don't know."

"Okay, so now the obvious question: boyfriends?"

He shook his head. "Not that I know of."

I stared at him hard. He didn't give an inch. Stared right back at me.

"When was the last time you heard from her?" I asked.

He sighed, sat back in his chair, and stared up at the ceiling. "Last Saturday morning. She was planning on visiting us on Sunday, but she called her mother and said she was going to stay up on the mountain and study with friends. We haven't heard from her since. I called up there yesterday morning, and they said she hasn't been seen since Saturday evening, when they came downtown to eat and party. I talked to the vice chancellor of student affairs, and she said Emily hasn't attended classes all week.... I also talked to Jessica. She said they ended up at your buddy Hinkle's place, the Sorbonne. They left there just after one in the morning. Emily caught a ride back with someone else—not... a guy. A female. Look, Harry, you might as well know now: Emily's gay, a lesbian."

This wasn't new information, hence the way I'd phrased the previous question, but I hadn't been about to let him know that I knew.

"You have a name?" I asked.

He shook his head.

"You run her credit cards, bank accounts...?"

He looked at me like I was stupid.

"Yeah, of course you did. Sorry. Nothing, huh?"

Again he shook his head.

"What about her car? I assume she has one, living up there."

"It's in the school lot. A red Civic."

I nodded. "Tag number?" He gave it to me, and I made a note of it.

"What about the friends? Do you have any names other than this... Jessica?"

He was about to shake his head again, but caught himself and said, "She never really mentioned anyone else, but there was one girl, a study partner, I think. A girl in her dorm. Lacy, I think. That's all." He looked at me sheepishly. "Yeah, I know. Not much of a father."

"I wasn't thinking that, Wes. Look, we both know it's not good," I said. "It's been almost a week without a word...."

"Yeah, I know. She'd have called if... if she could have. Christ, Harry. It's times like these I wish I wasn't a cop. We know, don't we."

I nodded. He knew what I was thinking, and he was thinking it too. It's what cops do.

"Why me?" I asked. "You have the entire department at your disposal."

He nodded. "I do, but that school is out in the county. I don't have jurisdiction up there. You can go wherever the hell you like." He hesitated, then said, "Harry, you can be an ornery son of a bitch when you want to be, but you're also the best at what you do. You know every important son of a bitch around, every mover and shaker from here to Savannah, and I know that if anyone can get the job done, it's you. Most of all, though, you're discreet, and right now that's what I need. So, will you help?"

He was right. I have unprecedented access to the rich and powerful in our fair city; most of whom I'd known since my school days, thanks to my old man, who made sure I attended the right schools and received the best possible education. His philosophy, and by proxy my philosophy too, has always been that it's not what you know that brings success; it's who you know. And I can count just about every lawyer and judge in town among my circle of friends.

"You talked to the sheriff?"

"Hands? Yeah. You can guess how that went. 'She's twenty-two,' he said, 'probably met some guy and went off partying with him.' I didn't tell him she was... you know. Wouldn't have made a hill a' beans' difference. He'd have just changed the pronouns. Arrogant son of a bitch. Told me to give it time. But that ain't good enough, Harry, because whatever she is, she's my little girl."

I wasn't surprised to hear how our erstwhile sheriff, Israel Hands, had responded. He was a politician with the insight of a donkey, and I'm being charitable.

"You know I will," I said, "but I have some conditions."

Wes raised an eyebrow.

"One: You have to agree that however it turns out, whatever

I find, you *will* let me follow it through to its conclusion, whatever that may be. Two: I want access to your facilities—labs, forensics, everything. Three: I want you to turn Kate Gazzara loose to work with me and act as a liaison between me and your department. Four: Stay off my back. I don't need you looking over my shoulder, hounding me for minute-by-minute updates. I can't give you that. Agreed?"

He nodded, staring at me. I could tell he wasn't happy, but it was his call, and he made it.

"I'll have Gazzara take some leave. God knows she's got plenty owed her. Discretion, Harry. Until we know what's happened to my daughter. You good with that?"

"Yes, of course. Not even Kate."

"Ah. She already knows, about the gay thing."

"Mm. You got photos?"

"Yeah." He took them from the inside pocket of his jacket and handed them to me. "The one on top is the best. It was taken on her birthday. The others...." He shrugged.

"Call Kate. I want to talk to her this evening. Put her in the picture; make sure she understands that it's my investigation, that she's to work with me, and keep everything to herself." I told him I'd stay in touch, and call him as soon as I found anything, and then he left.

I sat for a moment, staring out through the open door into the outer office. *Emily. Little Emily. Not good. Six days. Not good at all.*

I was startled out of my daydreams when my iPhone buzzed and began to travel across my desk. I picked it up and flipped the lock screen.

"Hey, Kate. Yeah, he just left. You good with this? Good. We need to talk. You busy tonight? Can you stop by? Amanda's cooking dinner.... No, she'll be fine with it." I looked at my watch. It was after six. "Shall we say seven thirty?"

Chapter Two

I arrived home at six thirty to find Amanda busy in the kitchen.

"So," she said, an enigmatic smile on her lips, "we have a guest, do we?"

She was wearing a simple form-fitting gray dress cut just below her knees, and she was barefoot. I crept up behind her, slipped my arms around her waist, and nuzzled her ear.

"Stop it, you ass. Tell me why Kate's coming over."

There wasn't much to tell yet, but I filled her in on what I did know, and how Kate and I would be working together for a couple of days.

Now, let me put something on the table. Amanda is a very special, strikingly beautiful woman, and the love of my life. She's tall, five feet nine, with a figure you can't buy anywhere, and wears her strawberry blonde hair bobbed, elfin-like. Her heart-shaped face is sharply defined by high cheekbones, a small, slightly upturned nose, and wide-set, pale green eyes. She's the star of the small screen owned by the local Channel 7, and she's smart: she has a bachelor's degree in broadcast journalism from Columbia. Yeah, she's quite the package.

Kate Gazzara is also quite special and was, until a couple of years ago... well, you get the idea. So you can understand Amanda's question. I've known Kate since she was a rookie cop, more than fifteen years, and until I quit the force in 2007, she was my partner. Now she's a lieutenant with the Chattanooga PD, a homicide detective in the major crimes unit. She's almost six feet tall, and she works out. A lot. She has a high forehead and long, tawny blond hair. She and Amanda get along. Well. Sort of.

So, that was the situation. While Amanda finished getting dinner ready, I showered and changed, and when I returned to the kitchen, Amanda had three fingers of my favorite beverage waiting for me: Laphroaig scotch, poured over a single ice cube into a Waterford Baccarat crystal glass.

I went to the living room and looked out over the river. The light was fading fast, but my gaze was drawn inevitably to the tree stump on the far riverbank. My longstanding love affair with the great river was over. Mary Hartwell had ended it for me back in June, when she crouched behind that tree stump with a rifle and tried to kill me. She only succeeded in shooting out the window, but I used to sit for hours in front of that window, enjoying the view. Not anymore. Now I'm always... wary. Looking for something that isn't there, wondering when it *will* be there. That's no way to live....

"Hey," I said, as I wandered back into the kitchen. "You have any luck with the realtor today?"

No, Amanda doesn't live with me, at least not yet, though she might as well. She spends more time at my place than she does at hers.

"As a matter of fact I did," Amanda said. "She has a place on East Brow Road she wants us to look at."

"East Brow? That sounds expensive."

"Probably, but it needs some work, so if you like it maybe you can cut some sort of a deal. When do you want to go look at it?"

"I don't know. Maybe tomorrow afternoon, if I get done with the Johnston thing...." It was then that the doorbell rang.

Amanda raised an eyebrow at me. "I thought she had a key." It was lightly said, but there was no mistaking the undertone.

"I got that back eighteen months ago, as you well know."

She smiled at me, but there was little humor in it.

I went to let Kate in, and as soon as I opened the door I knew I'd made a mistake. She was dressed to kill.

When are you ever going to learn, Harry?

She had her hair tied back in a ponytail and wore a sleeve-less white top, a black skirt cut above the knee, and three-inch heels.

"Hey, come on through," I said, leading the way into the kitchen.

"Hi Kate," Amanda said, coming around the breakfast bar and giving her a hug. "Wine, or something stronger?"

"Wine please. Anything red will work."

"Dinner's ready. Nothing fancy, I'm afraid. Just salmon, baked sweet potatos, and asparagus. I'm on a diet."

Diet, my ass, I thought. *You could eat an elephant and not put on a single pound.*

We ate quickly and in silence; the whole meal couldn't have taken us more than ten minutes. When we were done, I cleared the table and made coffee, and we talked.

"So you're all right with this, Kate?" I asked. She nodded. "How much did Johnston tell you?"

"Not much, just that I was going to take some vacation days and spend them working with you. What the hell is this all about?"

"Emily."

"Emily the chief's daughter? What about her?"

"She's missing. Five days, six if you count last Sunday, which was the last time anyone heard from her. She was last seen leaving Hinkle's place around one in the morning."

"Shit. I was talking to her only last Friday. She'd just come out of Johnston's office. She was all smiles. Happy."

"Well, from what he's been able to discover, she was last seen outside the Sorbonne getting into a car. The driver was female. Her friends said she hitched a ride back to school, but... well, she never made it."

"What school?" Amanda asked.

"Belle Edmondson, on Signal Mountain."

"Ahhh."

"What?"

"Well, I know it. It's... exclusive, and very, very expensive. I did a story on it years ago. Weird place. Liberal arts college, emphasis on the liberal. Small. No more than five hundred or so students, and a small faculty too. I think it's more a finishing school than anything else. They have classes, of course—acting, music, dance, history, journalism, and so on —but I think they focus more on the social graces than on academic excellence. I found them to be an affected, catty bunch, the girls and the faculty both. The students come from all over the world. It's very difficult to get accepted, too, and I'm not talking about grades. From what I could tell, they tend to choose from a certain... shall we say, elite class of people."

"How the hell did Emily get in then?" Kate asked.

I'd been wondering that myself.

Amanda shrugged. "You'd be the best person to answer that, Harry. It's not what you know, right?"

"It's like that, huh?" I said. "But who the hell does Johnston know with that kind of pull, I wonder? Any idea what it costs?"

"About the same as one of the Ivy League schools. $55,000 a year, plus another five for personal expenses, books, etcetera."

"Jesus." Kate said. "Where the hell is Johnston getting that kind of money? Must be up to his ears in debt."

I opened my legal pad and scanned the notes I'd taken while talking to Johnston. I shook my head. It was little enough.

"I have two names. Jessica, no last name, who's a friend from school, and a girl named Lacy. I don't know if she's a friend or not; her name was all Wes had. Kate, I need you to check and see what security cameras there are downtown, close to Hinkle's place. If there are any, we might get lucky. If not, it's back to good old-fashioned footwork. Hinkle has cameras; I do know that. We'll check those. We need to find out who she was with that night, what they saw, and we need the make, model and tag number of the car she got into.... Shit. I don't like it. Not one bit."

"You know she's probably dead, right?" Kate asked. "People don't just drop off the map like that, not unless they want to get lost, and Emily didn't give me that impression. So...."

"Come on now, Kate. Let's try to be a little optimistic." I

said it, but I knew she was right. I'd seen it before, and all too often. I had a bad feeling, and those feelings were rarely wrong. *Damn it.*

"Do you want me to start at the Sorbonne?" Kate asked.

"I'll go see our friend Benny Hinkle. You check the other bars. There would have been plenty of places open at one in the morning on a Saturday. Here, show those around. See if you get any hits." I handed her copies of the photos Johnston had given me. I'd run them off on the office copier before I'd headed home. "We can meet up there when we get done."

"What about me?" Amanda asked.

I looked at her quizzically.

"I'm coming with you," she said.

I opened my mouth to object, but the look on her face told me not to bother. So I didn't.

I looked at my watch. It was a little after eight thirty; still early, which was good, because I didn't want to be in the Sorbonne on a Friday night when things started jumping. I'd always thought that if I were to be given a choice between going to Hell or the Sorbonne, Hell would win out every time.

The Sorbonne. With a fancy name like that you'd think it would be one of those ritzy places society folks like to inhabit. But you'd be wrong. Oh so wrong. Sorbonne is a fancy name for what can only be described as a boil on

Chattanooga's ass. Benny Hinkle, the proud owner, likes to call it a nightclub. It is not a nightclub. It's a dump and a place of ill repute, the last refuge of every lowlife that can afford the price of a watered-down drink and stand the soul-destroying cacophony Benny likes to call music. I knew the place well, and knew its owner even better. I'd spent more time in there than I probably should have, sometimes just to jerk myself out the lethargy brought on by the daily grind—it can be quite an entertaining experience—but mostly to keep an eye on the lowlifes that inhabit the place.

Kate also knew the place well. Amanda, not so much. But I'd taken her in there a couple of times and, to my utter amazement, she'd hit it off not only with the fat smear of humanity that was Benny Hinkle, but also with his sidekick, Laura. Don't ask me her last name. I don't know it, and I don't want to.

Laura is Benny's longtime partner, a big, blowsy blonde, usually dressed in a tank top that barely covers an amazing pair of breasts, cutoff jeans that barely cover her even more amazing ass, and... cowboy boots. Unbelievable. She is the epitome of the stereotypical Southern barkeep, and that in itself is worth a fortune to both of them.

So I gathered up my pad and the photos and, with healthy enthusiasm, we all headed out the door.

Chapter Three

W e parked our cars—Amanda and me in my Maxima and Kate in her personal Accord— in the Unum lot just off East Third and from there went our separate ways. We'd arranged to meet at the Sorbonne at ten thirty; it was almost nine when Amanda and I walked into Hell that night. Satan himself, in the form of Benny Hinkle, spotted us the moment we crossed the threshold.

"Goddamn it, Starke. I told you to stay the hell out of here. Oh hey, Miss Cole. Nice to see ya. What will you have?"

"I'll have a gin and tonic, Benny," I said, "heavy on the gin, light on the tonic." That was supposed to get me something that might, on a good night, be close to drinkable.

"Screw you, Starke. I was talking to the lady, an' that is what you ain't. So zip it. Better yet, get the hell out of my club."

I leaned over the bar and grabbed him by the front of his beer-stained shirt and pulled, and he yelped, and the customers on either side of us scattered, most of them heading for the door.

"You gonna get me a drink, or do I have to come around there and get it myself?" I said it, and then literally gasped as he choked and hit me with a blast of fetid breath. It was too much. I dropped him and took a step back. Hell, I almost lost my salmon.

I looked sideways at Amanda. She had a hand to her mouth and was laughing silently.

"One more time, Benny," I said. "A gin and tonic for me and another for the lady."

"I'll get 'em," a voice said, just off to Benny's right.

"Hey, Laura," I said. "You're just in time to save his miserable skin, yet again. How the hell are you?"

"What do you think, Harry? I'm just *peachy*." And then she leaned forward over the bar to show them to me. I shook my head. They really were amazing.

"Hello, Amanda," she said, sliding her gaze to my right. "Big boy here treating you proper, I hope."

"Better than I deserve."

Laura turned again to look at me. Her gaze travelled down, paused a lot longer than was necessary, and then came back up. She looked me in the eye, smiled—she reminded me of hungry barracuda—and winked.

"Yeah, I'll just bet he is." She never took her eyes off me.

"Drinks, Laura," I said. "Pour the damned drinks." And she did. When she was done, I turned to Benny. "We need to talk," I told him.

"You need to talk; I need you gone. Every time you come in here you cost me money. Five customers just left, and it's down to you. What do you want this time?"

"Let's go to your office. I need to be able to hear myself think."

Benny's office, if you could call it that, looked no different than it had the last time I'd been in it, and that was almost a year ago. An open pizza box on the desk held the remains of a half-eaten slice that could easily have been the same one I remembered. The desk was inches deep in papers, bills, delivery notes, newspapers—not an exaggeration. The iron bed under the window sagged in the middle, and the bedsheets were crumpled in a pile at one end; a large calico cat lay on top, contentedly licking its paws. Two more cats stared down at us from the top of a rusty file cabinet. The number of beer crates, soft drink crates, and cardboard boxes full of empty wine and liquor bottles stacked against the walls had increased two-fold. The place was a pigsty. A literal health hazard.

"Sit," he said, as he flopped heavily into the chair behind his desk. "Tell me what you want and then get outta here. I got a bar to run."

Amanda looked at the two folding metal chairs and shuddered—she did, she really did—and remained standing. I can't say I blamed her.

I took the photos of Emily from my inside jacket pocket and laid them out in front of him.

"She was in here last Saturday night. What time did she come in, who was she with; what time did she leave, and who did she leave with?"

"Shit Harry. You ain't asking for much."

"Sarcasm, Benny, is what I don't need. Just take a look and tell me."

He picked up one of the photos, stared at it, spread the other three a little with his fingers, nodded again, then looked up at me. "Yeah she was here. I remember. There were five... no, six of 'em. Nice kids, but loud, and drunk. Four girls and two guys. They came in around ten thirty and left sometime after midnight. What time exactly, I don't know. I don't keep tabs on my clients."

"Names, Benny."

"Hell, I don't know. I don't even know her name. Who is she, by the way?"

"She's Chief Johnston's daughter, Emily, and she's missing, so think. Give me something."

"Whoa! Phoo-eee, the chief's kid, huh? Emily? Yeah, I heard that name... and... Jess, I think, but that's all."

"You sure, Benny?"

"Yeah, Harry, I'm sure. You know how it is out there, especially late. Can't hear much of anything."

"The chief seems to think she left with a girl. Did you see them?"

"It wasn't no girl; at least, not a kid like the rest of 'em. She had to be at least thirty-five, maybe more."

"She was with them?"

"Nah. She was on her own. Sat most of the night at the far end of the bar, nursing her drinks. Tight-assed bitch. She and this... Emily, you said? They were eying each other most of the night. It was late. I didn't see 'em get together, but I did see 'em leave."

"She been in before?"

"Three, maybe four times over the last three months. Always on her own."

"She meet anyone in the bar?"

"She always came in alone. Only hooked up once, and that was last Saturday. High dollar, that one. Class."

"And you didn't get a name?"

"Nope."

"Would you recognize her if you saw her again, this woman?"

He nodded, "Yeah, I think so. Prob'ly. Yeah."

"Did you see the car?"

"Yeah. It was parked out front, a late-model Merc SUV, white."

"Anything else, Benny?"

He shook his head.

"How about Laura?"

"Maybe. She was here. You'll have to ask her."

"Okay. We're done, for now. Would you mind asking Laura to join us, please?"

"Screw you, Starke.... Okay, okay!" He held up his hands as I reached for his neck. "I'll send her back, jeez."

"Hey, one more thing. Make copies of your security footage for me, say from nine until two. She'll be on them, right?"

"Yeah, I guess." And with that he shuffled on out the door.

"So, Harry. What can I do for you?" Barely twenty seconds later, Laura parked herself on the corner of Benny desk in front of me and folded her arms. I blinked. That was some pair of legs. Amanda smiled and dipped her head.

I handed Laura the photograph of Emily. "She was here last Saturday."

She looked at it, nodded, said, "Yeah, and late. Left with a pickup. At least I think that's what she was."

"The pickup, you seen her before?"

"Yeah, she's been in several times. Nice woman, friendly, well off, I should think, judging by the way she was dressed."

"How was she dressed?" Amanda sked.

"Dark colored silvery cocktail dress, more metal than cloth. You know the kind of thing I mean, right?"

Amanda nodded.

"And a short, dark green jacket."

"How did the two of them hook up, did you see?"

"Oh yeah. She sent the girl a drink, gin and tonic. I took it to her. Next minute, she, the girl, had joined her at the end of the bar and they had their heads together, talking, laughing."

"Anything else?"

"Not that I can think of."

It was at that point that Benny came back in and dropped a disk on the desk in front of me.

"Got 'em both on there. Got 'em all, all six of the kids. Good shots of the woman. Now I need Laura back behind the bar, and you gone."

"Thanks, Laura," I said. "You'd better do as he says."

She slid off the edge of the desk. "Keep him honest, Amanda." And she left.

I picked up the disk and slid it into my inside jacket pocket with the rest of the photos. "Benny, we're not leaving just yet. I arranged to meet Kate in the bar. Oh, don't worry," I said as he opened his mouth to object, "we'll stay out of the way. Thanks for the disk."

Kate arrived less than thirty minutes later. She had security footage from four different locations. She dumped them on the table, sat, then turned and waved to get Laura's attention.

Orange juice. She mouthed the words.

"So," I said. "What did you find?"

"Not a whole lot. It was Saturday. Everywhere was busy. Nobody remembered seeing the girl. I'm sure she was out and about, though. There were plenty that were. The footage on those disks runs from six until two. We know she was here, so maybe we'll get lucky. How about you?"

I filled her in on what we'd learned from Benny and Laura. By the time I'd finished it was almost eleven, and I'd had enough of the noise. We made arrangements to meet at my office the following morning and run the footage, and then we all headed home.

Chapter Four

I try not to work on weekends. That was one of the reasons I quit the PD in the first place: no time off, ever, so it seemed. That Saturday, however, was different; I was doing it for Emily. Those true crime shows on TV make much of the First Forty-Eight Hours, and it's hard to argue with the tenet. Now, there we were, seven days since Emily had disappeared. Time had already run out for her. I was sure of it. But I could still hope.

Amanda and I were already there when Kate arrived at my office. Tim Clarke, my computer geek, and Bob Ryan, my second-in-command designate, arrived a few minutes later; Jacque, my PA, arrived a few minutes after them. A little small talk and a few minutes later we were all settled in the back office in front of the four huge flat-screen monitors—two over two—that were the focus of Tim's world. A world that had just set me back more than eighty-five grand: a very fancy and very expensive Haswell dedicated private server, three Dell 7910 towers, and a whole bunch of extras I didn't, and didn't want to, understand.

Tim is a member of that rare breed of weirdo that lives only to sail the binary ocean. He's been hacking since his dad bought him his first IBM PC back in 1998. He never got caught, although to hear him tell it he came close a couple of times. Now he's reformed. At least I think he is. I found him in an Internet café less than a month after he'd dropped out of his second year of college; he'd only been seventeen.

I said he was geeky, and he is. Tall, skinny, less than 150 pounds even with his glasses on, he speaks in tongues, a language known only to himself. He's also the busiest member of my staff, hence his new baby.

"So lemme see it," he said, adjusting his seat with one hand and flapping his fingers at me with the other.

I handed him the first disk, the one we'd gotten from Benny Hinkle. He slipped it into one of the drives and opened the file.

"Okay, what am I looking for?" he asked as he scanned through the footage. No sound, but the quality was surprisingly good. Benny must have upgraded to HD cameras.

The time log running at the bottom of the image gave the date and time as 10/1/2016, 22:16, that would be ten-sixteen p.m. The footage ran slowly, jumping from one camera to another to give an almost 360-degree view of the bar. I saw a few familiar faces, but not the ones I was looking for.

"Stop," I said, pointing at the screen. "That one, can you pull it up?"

He could, and he did.

It had to be her. The woman Emily had left with. She was seated at the far end of the bar on a stool, legs crossed at the knees, in a short silvery dress and green jacket, with dark brown hair and a drink in her hand. Just like Laura had described. It was hard to make out her features, though; the angle wasn't quite right.

"Okay, Tim. Start it up again. See if we can get a better look at her."

Five minutes later, we had her. She'd leaned back on the stool and turned her face toward the camera. She was obviously casing the room.

"Stop. That's it. That's what I need. Can you enlarge it, enhance it a little? That's it. That's good. Get me six copies of that, would you? Okay. Now let's move things along a little. Fast forward to ten thirty and let it run."

And there they were. Benny had been right. There were six of them, including Emily. They came bustling in, obviously talking loudly, laughing, and generally being the obnoxious bunch of students out on the town that they were.

"Okay, Tim. I need a half dozen sets of prints of those faces." That took a few minutes.

"Okay, now let it run," I said. "Let's see what happens...."

Can you speed it up a little? Whoa. Stop right there. Back up a little... there. Good."

The screen froze. Emily had her back to the camera and was facing the woman, who was obviously making eyes at her: her chin was down, her eyebrows raised, and even from the high angle of the camera, I could see the tip of her tongue.

"That's plain enough," Kate said. "A bit in-your-face, in fact. I wonder if they know each other."

"Okay, Tim. Let it run, but slowly. No, hell—not slow motion, real time, damn it."

I heard Bob snigger. I ignored him. *Damn, I wish I could do this shit myself.*

The images continued to jump around, seemingly in random order, from one camera to another. We almost missed Laura when she delivered the drink to Emily, then turned and pointed to the woman at the end of the bar, and it jumped again just before she reacted. Five minutes later it jumped back again. The timestamp at the bottom of the image read 00:32, half past midnight, when we saw the woman beckon for Emily to join her.

"Damn," I was frustrated. That kind of jumping around is for the birds. The next time the camera scanned that end of the bar, the two of them were together. The woman was still seated and Emily was standing close to her, well inside her personal space. It looked as if maybe their thighs were touching. Their heads were close together—talking, I assumed. And that was how they stayed, heads sometimes dipped, sometimes thrown back, laughing.

Finally one of the girls in the group looked around at Emily, shouted something, and beckoned for her to rejoin them. They were, so it seemed, about to leave. I looked at the time-stamp: 01:07. Emily smiled, shook her head, then said something and waved a hand, indicating for them to go on without her. At least, that was what it looked like. And that was what they did. They left. Emily stayed with the woman. By now, they were discreetly holding hands.

It was 01:32 when the woman beckoned for Laura and paid the tab. They left the bar right after, the woman leading by perhaps a couple of steps. A few seconds later, the footage switched to an outside camera, just in time to catch the passenger door of a white Mercedes M-Class SUV closing. It was too late to see the passenger, but I had to assume it was Emily. Fortunately, the license plate was visible. The number was JEPSON2.

"So where the hell did they go?" I was asking myself more than the group, but I didn't get an answer either way. "Run the plate, Tim. Let's see who she is."

It wasn't a she. It wasn't a he, either. It was a company: the Jepson Animal Clinic on Taft Highway, Signal Mountain.

"Well, I suppose that's something," I said. "Tim, I want you to run through the rest of these disks. You know what we're looking for: anything with any of these people, especially the woman or Emily. Questions?"

"Er... no, sir."

"Good. Call me if you find anything. We'll be in the conference room."

"So," I said, after everyone had refilled their coffee cups and we were seated at the table. "Anybody have any thoughts or comments?"

"She's gay, right?" Bob asked, his voice a low growl.

Bob Ryan is a quiet man, most of the time, and deceptively easygoing. He's my lead investigator, been with me almost since the first day I opened the agency. Like me, he's an ex-cop—Chicago PD. Also like me, he's six foot two, but there the similarities end. He's an ex-marine and a lot heavier than I am: 240 pounds, all of it solid muscle. He carries a Sig Sauer, 1911 compact .45, but he also has a fondness for baseball bats. He's quiet, dedicated, and not someone you'd want to screw around with.

His question didn't surprise me. That Emily was gay had been obvious to anyone who watched the security footage, but I looked at Kate quizzically. She merely shrugged.

"Come on, Harry," Bob said. "Anyone with half a brain can see it was a pickup, if not a damned prearranged date."

"Well, yeah," I said, grudgingly, "but keep it to yourself. Johnston doesn't want it getting around."

Bob nodded. "If she's gay, I'd say it isn't much of a secret. Not among her friends, at least."

"Yeah, well. Let's move on. Kate?"

"I'm thinking she already knew the woman," she said, "and

that the meeting was prearranged. It looks like a pickup, but if so, they got real close real soon, and that I don't buy. The woman's obviously well off. I'd say they're probably on a beach somewhere having a good time. She'll be back."

"I dunno," I said, shaking my head. "Johnston swears it's not like her not to be in touch with her mother. It's never happened before, he said."

Amanda shook her head. "How old is she, twenty-two? Come on, Harry. You know how kids are at that age, especially when they're away from home at college."

"If that were the case, she'd have her phone with her, and we'd be able to track it. Johnston says it's still active and up at the school somewhere. Kids never go anywhere without their phones."

That swept a gloomy cloud over our little gathering. We all knew time was running out—no, I had a bad feeling that it already *had* run out, and by the looks on their faces, so did the rest of my crew.

"There's not much we can do today, it being the weekend, and tomorrow is Sunday. We need to find that woman and talk to those kids. Jacque. Give the Jepson Veterinary Clinic a call. I doubt you'll get anyone, but it's worth a try. Then try the college. We need to talk to her friends, professors, her councilors if she has them. I'd like to get started on it today, tomorrow at the latest. See what you can do."

She left to make the calls, but was back just a few minutes later.

"Jepson's is closed until Monday. I got their answering service. I did get a number for a Dr. Henry Jepson, but he's not answering. The calls just go straight to voicemail. All I got at the college was a recorded message giving the office hours. We won't be able to get through to them until after nine on Monday."

"Shit," I muttered. "That's not good. What the hell...?" I looked at Kate, then Amanda. "We can't wait that long. She's been gone almost a week. We have to get moving."

"Uh, you're right," Bob interrupted me. "She's been gone too long, and whatever's happened, if anything, probably happened within the first twenty-four hours. A day and a half more ain't gonna make a difference."

"So you say, but I can't spend the rest of the weekend twiddling my damn thumbs. I'm going up there. Kate, you can go with me or not. Amanda, can you manage on your own this afternoon?"

Stupid question. Need to think before I open my mouth. Of course she can.

"We have an appointment to view the house on East Brow Road at three, but I can handle that myself."

I nodded. "Sorry. I'll call you later. Bob, what about you? There's no point in all us of heading up there. I'll see you here on Monday morning, unless something comes up. In which case, I'll give you a call, okay?"

He nodded, and got to his feet.

Next I went to check on Tim. The rest of the security disks had produced nothing new, other than showing the group doing the rounds of the downtown bars. Cameras caught them going into and then coming out of the Mellow Mushroom, and then the Big River Grill, both on Broad Street. Of the woman there was no sign. She must have begun and ended her night at Benny's. She'd entered around nine thirty and, except for Emily, had spent the evening alone, as Benny had said, nursing her drinks.

Damn!

Tim had keys to the office, so I had Jacque lock up and left him to it. Amanda went to her apartment in Hixson; Kate and I headed for Signal Mountain and the Belle Edmondson College for Women.

Chapter Five

B elle Edmondson College was a throwback to the days when military academies were in vogue, which was hardly surprising because, back in the 1850s, that was exactly what it had been. Today, the old stone perimeter wall was just as imposing as it must have been back in the day. Even the massive, ornate iron gates flanked by two even more massive stone pillars were still intact, a relic of a once-grand era, though they now stood open and were in sore need of a good coat of paint.

We followed the signs, and I parked the Maxima in the gravel semicircle in front of the administration building, a smaller but just as imposing version of the Citadel in South Carolina. The parade grounds were long gone, but vast stretches of immaculately manicured lawns separated maybe eight or ten three-story buildings of tan limestone. Here and there stood old-growth oaks and loblolly pines. But as imposing as the buildings were, there was a certain bleakness about the place.

We walked into the administration building, our footsteps echoing around the vast lobby. It was only then that I realized the place was just about deserted. We'd seen maybe a dozen students walking the grounds, but here inside, just a single clerk—at least I thought she was a clerk—sat pecking away at a computer keyboard, squinting so close to the monitor that her glasses were almost touching it.

"Good afternoon," Kate said.

"Be with you in a minute," Glasses said. She didn't even turn her head. She just kept pecking away. Finally she rose slowly from her seat, still typing, leaning farther and farther back as she became unglued, eyes still on the screen as she stepped away. It was quite a performance.

"Sorry about that," she said brightly. "Trying to write my thesis. Not too good at it, I'm afraid. Never mind. What can I do for you?"

"My name is Lieutenant Catherine Gazzara. This is my associate, Mr. Starke." She flashed her badge, quickly enough that the woman could see the shield, but probably not much more.

"How can I help you, Lieutenant?"

"We're looking for a missing person, Emily Johnston. She's a student here. She was last seen in the company of these people." Kate laid out the six headshots across the counter. "The three girls are also students here. This one, probably not," she tapped the image of the woman at the bar. "We need to find out who they are. Do you know any of them?"

"Emily is missing? Oh my God. I didn't know. When...?"

"She was last seen early Sunday morning, leaving the Sorbonne in Chattanooga with this woman here." She tapped the photo again. "Can I get your name, please?"

"I'm Christine Hammond. I get extra credit for being Edna Morgan's secretary. She's the vice chancellor of student affairs. Are you sure Emily's *missing*?"

"Would you mind looking at the photos, please?" Kate asked.

She looked at each one in turn. I watched her eyes and mouth, looking for tells. I saw none.

"This is Autumn Leaf," she said, and picked up one of the photos and handed it to Kate. "She's a senior, a drama major. Her parents must have a sense of humor. Nice name, though, Autumn."

Kate turned the photo over and made a couple notes on the back, then opened her iPad and made some more.

"And this is Marianne Siddons, and this is Jessica Henderson. They're all drama students, Emily too. I don't know who the boys are."

"Her father mentioned a girl called Lacy. Do you have any idea who that might be?"

"Lacy McMillan. She's also a drama major. I told you: they all are."

"How about her?" Kate asked, pushing the photo toward her.

She shook her head. "I think I may have seen her before, but I can't place her. She doesn't work here.... No, I don't know. She looks familiar, but.... I can't remember."

"Please," I said. "Try a little harder. This is the last person Emily was seen with."

"I'm sorry. She does look familiar, but I just don't know." She shook her head again, but after a moment her eyes brightened and her head came up. "Oh wait, no. She's a vet. She was here a couple of months ago. One of the horses went down with colic, but Dr. Jepson wasn't available for some reason, so she came instead. Now that I think of it, she's been here several times—with Dr. Jepson, mostly. Wow."

"Wow?" I asked. "Why wow?"

"Oh nothing. She's... well, she's not quite what you'd expect. That's all."

"How do you mean?" Kate asked.

"Well, she's just not the sort of person you'd imagine being a vet, is all. Arrogant, a little snobbish. She didn't dress like a vet either: short skirts, tight sweaters, heels. Most vets that I know, not that I know many, wear jeans and boots, but not her."

"Do you know her name?"

She shook her head. "Sorry. I never spoke to her."

"So," I said. "Where can we find the girls?"

"They all live together in the Huddleston building. That's one of the dorms. It's over on the north side of campus. I doubt you'll find any of them there, though. There's nothing to do on campus over the weekend; it's too remote. Most people go into town. Still, there's no harm giving it a try. Just follow the road around to the right. Eventually it'll make a sharp left. Huddleston will be the building on the right. They're in, hold on...." She turned to her computer, clicked the mouse several times, then said, "Rooms seven, eight, and nine, adjoining."

"And Emily's room?"

"Seven. She has... had it to herself. Her roommate dropped out, as I recall, just a couple of weeks after they returned from summer break. You'll need a key. I'll get it for you." And she did.

Kate took the key from her, gathered up the photographs, and told her thank you and goodbye. And then we left.

We paused just outside the door, at the top of the steps. A campus security cruiser was angled across in front of the Maxima. Two uniformed security officers were leaning, side by side, arms folded, legs crossed at the ankles, against the side of my car.

This could get ugly very quickly.

"Let me deal with this, Harry," Kate said quietly as she started down the steps. I followed, two steps behind.

They were both big guys. Not big as in 'I work out four hours a day.' They were both overweight, and kind of frowsy. The taller of the two wore mirrored, wrap-around sunglasses, the other aviators. The guy with the mirrors was bald, his head shaved and shiny. He had a big, round face, florid, fat lips, and a nose that would have... well, let me put it this way: you wouldn't get very many of them in a pound. He was a little over six feet and weighed at least 250 pounds. His partner was slightly smaller, though not by much. His hair was cut like a marine's. His face was leaner and tanned, with a mouth that reminded me of one of those talking fish you see hanging on the wall in bars. And they were armed. They each had a Glock 17 holstered at their hip.

Now why would that be necessary?

Tough, both of them—at least that's what they thought.

"This is private property," the guy with the mirrors said. "What y'all doing here?"

"I'm a detective with the Chattanooga PD. This is my associate. We're following up on some inquiries." She flashed her badge. They both looked at it, but neither of them moved, or even looked impressed.

"Y'all don't got no jurisdiction up here," Mirrors said, his head cocked to one side.

"That's true," she said, "but we're looking for a missing girl. She's a student here. We're just about to head on around to the Huddleston Building to see her friends."

"Is that right? Well, I'm not sure we can 'low that. Like I said, y'ain't got no jurisdiction. Y'all are trespassing." He said it easily, but there was an edge to his voice. I took a step forward; Kate put her hand on my arm; I stopped.

"Oh," she said. "I'm sorry. We were hoping for a little cooperation. After all, we're in the same line of business, right?"

The hell we are.

"Yeah, well," Mirrors said. His head was still tilted, but now he was feeling sure of himself, cocky, and he had a nasty grin on his face. "Can't let you loose on campus. Got the ladies privacy to protec'. You'll need to go get Sherriff Hands, him an' a warrant. Either that or an invite from one of the biggies here at the college, an' there ain't none o' them here right now that I know of."

"Look," I said. "The girl is missing. She could be in real trouble. I'm sure you can appreciate that time is of the essence. We need to talk to her friends—now. We can get a warrant, but it will take time. Come on, friend. Let us go see the girls."

He grinned at me, shaking his head. "No can do, bub. Come back with a warrant. Oh, an' I ain't your friend."

I took another step forward; again Kate put her hand on my arm. They both came up off my car, stood side-by-side, feet apart, stuck their thumbs into their belts, and rocked gently back and forth on the balls of their feet, waiting.

"We'll be back," Kate said. "Let's go, Harry."

Reluctantly, I nodded, then walked down the remaining two steps and got into my car. Kate got in on the passenger side. Mirrors grinned at me through the windshield. Aviators didn't. He just stood to one side, his arms folded.

I backed out from behind the cruiser and headed back along the drive, out onto the highway. The cruiser followed, but stopped at the gates.

"Kate, you should have let me handle it," I growled at her. "We could have been talking to the kids right now."

"Yeah, probably. You could have handled both of them, of that I have no doubt, but the fallout: that you couldn't handle. He was right. We had no right to be on the property. Those two rent-a-cops would have called the real thing, and that would have been Israel Hands' people. You —no, *we* would have been arrested for assault, and the two bruisers would have sued you, and they would have won. Is that what you want?"

Well, of course she was right.

"Ah, fine, fine. And a warrant's out of the question, at least today. We'll need permission from someone to visit and question the kids. I'm not sure we'll be able to get that sooner than the day after tomorrow, but we have to try. Time is not on our side, and I hate to say it, but we may need help from Israel, or at least his two lackeys. Damn it, Kate. What the hell are we going to do? We don't have time for this bullshit. Emily sure as hell doesn't either."

"Take me back to your office. I'll pick up my car and head home. I need some time off, but I'll make a few calls, see what I can do about getting us access. You need to head home too. You're wired. I thought you were going to come unglued up there."

We drove up the ramp, off Signal Mountain Boulevard onto Highway 27. From there it was no more than a few minutes to my offices on Georgia. I dropped Kate off, then headed home. It was just after two. There was still time.

I called Amanda.

"Hey," I said when she answered. "You haven't left to meet the realtor yet, have you? Okay, good. Where are you? I'm coming with you."

Chapter Six

The house on East Brow Road on the side of Lookout Mountain was a mess, but as my stepmother Rose would have said, it had potential.

Built in 1932, it was set back from the road on almost two acres of some of the most expensive real estate in Tennessee... well, almost. A rambling, five-bedroom rancher in dire need of renovations, it came complete with what once had been a pool with a built-in hot tub; the bottom was covered with several inches of thick green sludge: nasty. Its best attraction was the extensive rock garden that stretched from the patio down the slope for almost a hundred yards, with tiny pathways that meandered this way and that among what once must have been a riot of color: the flower beds now were sadly neglected and, for the most part, denuded. Sad times had fallen upon the old home, but the view of the city and the river was spectacular. The house? I could see it would cost a fortune, and God only knew how much time it would take to drag it into the twenty-first century, and much as I liked it, I hesitated. Money I had; time I did not.

"What do they want for it?" I asked the realtor.

"They're asking $1.25 million."

"Hmmm. And I'm thinking it will take almost half that much to renovate the place. It still has the original wiring and plumbing, for Pete's sake."

I looked at Amanda. She smiled. I took her hand and led her a little way down one of the pathways, where we could talk privately.

"What do you think?" I asked.

"Oh, Harry. I love it. It's beautiful."

"Hah. You mean it used to be. Now it's a money pit waiting for a sucker to fall into it. I dunno. The money isn't a problem. I figure it will cost at least half a million to renovate. But it's the time to do it that I don't have."

"You don't need to. I'll see to it. My hours at Channel 7 are flexible. It's up to you. If you like it, do it. We'll figure it out somehow."

I wasn't sure I liked that last word, 'somehow,' but I sure as hell wanted to get away from Lakeshore Lane.

"Let's go talk to her," I said.

She was waiting on the patio.

"$1.25 million?" I asked. "You think they'll take less?"

She smiled. "They might. Would you like make them an offer?"

I thought about it, then said, "If it was in peak condition it would probably be worth that much, but it's not. It's far from it. I figure it will cost close to $500,000 to put it right. That being so, I'll pay $900,000, cash. Tell them it's non-negotiable."

She nodded. "If you'll give me just a minute, I'll let them know." She smiled, took out her phone, and went into the house. She was gone for just a few minutes. When she returned, the smile was still on her face.

"Congratulations, Mr. Starke," she said, extending her hand. "You have a deal."

Damn. I was stunned; I hadn't thought they would take it, not really. There was a sudden hollow feeling in the pit of my stomach. *What the hell have I done?*

Amanda was ecstatic.

Maybe, I thought, *I should have offered less.*

Chapter Seven

I woke early that Sunday. Amanda had gone home around nine the night before, so I was alone. And according to my bedside clock, it was just after five thirty.

I tossed. I turned. By six, the bed was a pile of tangled sheets, and I could stand it no more. Reluctantly, I heaved myself out of bed and hit the shower. After more than ten minutes under multiple streams of blistering-hot water, I finally felt ready to face the world.

The plan was that Amanda and I would meet around eleven thirty, and then join my father and stepmother at the club for lunch.

Stepmother! I'll never get used to that. She's barely older than I am.

I looked at the kitchen clock. Still only six thirty. Still dark outside. I looked at the Keurig, trying to decide if I wanted a single-serve coffee or something better. I decided on something better. I made a full press of Jamaican Blue Mountain —not a blend, the real stuff—and, wearing nothing but boxers, flopped down on the sofa in front of the window.

The sky was clear, and the first faint hint of a promising dawn was just beginning to appear above the treetops to the east. The lights on Thrasher Bridge spread across the surface of the Tennessee like glittering golden fingers. The homes on the crest of Lookout Mountain shone like stars against the still-dark sky. I savored the first cup of coffee, got up, poured another, returned to my reverie and sipped the delicious, full-bodied liquid. It was good. *Hell, at sixty bucks a pound it had better be.*

I was at such loose ends, I actually sat and watched the sun rise. But the truth was, I was missing Amanda. I'd gotten used to having her around, which lately had been most of the time.

By eight o'clock I'd had it. I almost called her, but thought better of it. So I dressed in sweats and running shoes and headed out around the Lake Resort loop at a fast clip. I ran the last half mile almost at a sprint, and by the time I got home, I was breathing hard but feeling a whole lot better.

I showered again, dressed in a pair of lightweight tan pants, black golf shirt, and ECCO Golf Street shoes. I scrambled three eggs with a little white cheddar, and reheated what was left of the coffee in the press: a somewhat Philistine thing to do, but it was so good I hated to waste it. I ate breakfast, cleaned up the kitchen, and... looked at the clock. Nine-thirty, whew. *Okay, now what?*

It was at that moment that my iPhone buzzed on the kitchen table. *Amanda! Thank God for that.*

But it wasn't her. It was Chief Johnston.

"Harry, they found her.... She's—she's dead."

I was stunned. I shouldn't have been. We all knew it was likely. But the reality... well, it came as a shock.

"Oh my God. I'm so sorry."

"Yeah." I heard his voice shudder. No, it was a half-controlled sob. "Yeah...."

"Where, Wes?"

"Signal Mountain. In the woods. Hick's Branch, in the county just off Wicker Road, that old track that runs past the small lake, pond, whatever. You'd better come on up. Doc Sheddon's already here. So's Israel Hands, a county crime scene unit, and a whole mess of deputies. I've told them I want the scene preserved until you get here, but you know what these people are like, and I have no clout up here. Kate Gazzara is on her way now. How long will you be?"

I looked at my watch. "Thirty minutes at best. Can you hold everything for that long?"

"You bet your ass I can. I will. See you in thirty. And... thanks, Harry."

Roberts Mill Road is a pig to drive fast, even in good weather. Still, I hauled the Maxima around one tight bend after another until finally I turned off onto Cooper and then onto Wicker and saw the flashing blue and red lights. I'd made it in twenty-nine minutes.

Wicker Road was no more than a one-lane track that dead-ended at an iron gate, chained and padlocked, with notice proclaiming it to be a "Private Drive." *To what?* I wondered. Beyond the gate the road became an unpaved, overgrown track that led into unadulterated forest.

About a hundred yards from the turnoff for Cooper Drive, the road was cordoned off with yellow tape. Just beyond the tape lay an open area with room for two or three cars to park, which was occupied by a crime scene unit and two country cruisers. Doc Sheddon's black SUV stood off the road in the grass with two more cruisers and a white Toyota SUV I knew belonged to Johnston. Kate must have been the last to arrive, because her Accord was parked closest to Cooper Drive. I parked behind it, then called Amanda. I told her what was happening, and that I doubted I'd make it back by eleven thirty. I also asked her to call my father and let him know we'd be there as soon as we could. Then I got out of the car and walked north on Wicker toward the lights.

Kate was there, talking to Johnston, Hands, and two of his detectives. *Oh hell, Heart and Sole.*

Heart? His name is Detective Anthony Hart. Sole? He looks like a damned fish, but his name is Alex McLeish. They're two of Israel's best, which isn't saying much. We bump into each other once in a while and for the most part we get along, but friends we are not.

The county Mounties I could tell were not pleased to see me. Me? I could not have cared less.

"How you holding up, Wes?" I asked the chief. He wasn't doing so well. I could see it immediately, when he just nodded and turned away.

I turned to the others. "Kate, Hart, McLeish, Israel."

"Starke," Hands said. He wasn't pleased to see me. I could tell by the look on his face. I knew I had to do something, or the next words out of his mouth would be to try to kick me off the scene.

"Israel, walk with me a little way, yeah? Indulge me." I put my hand on his shoulder and steered him a few yards down the road, where we couldn't be overheard, and then I turned to face him.

"Now let me tell you how it's gonna be," I said quietly, my hand still on his shoulder.

Hands was a most unlikely-looking sheriff: he was sixty-two, of average build, and balding; what little hair he had left was pure white. His long face, prominent cheekbones, and thick lips put me in mind of that ancient Egyptian pharaoh, Akhenaten. The white scar across the tip of his chin, the result of a collision during a high-speed chase, pulled at the corners of his mouth and imparted a permanent look of reproach. He'd been sheriff in Hamilton County for two terms and was up for reelection in November.

"Chief Johnston," I continued, "asked me to investigate his daughter's disappearance, now death, and I intend to do just that. I don't need your approval, Israel. I have a private investigator's license that allows me to work anywhere in the state, which also means out here in the county. Now, if you have a problem with that, I can bring some pretty heavy pressure to bear, including the DA, two Federal judges, and the state's commissioner of public safety. I'll cooperate with you and your two... two..." I turned and looked at them, shook my head, and continued, "*detectives* as best I can, but I'm doing this my way. Capiche?"

He took a half step backward, stuck his thumbs in his belt, and said, "I don't like you, Starke. Never did. I know how much pull you have around here, but I don't give a shit; you're one arrogant son of a bitch. Now I'll tell you how *I* see it. You go right ahead and investigate. So will my team. Out of respect for Chief Johnston, I'll instruct them to coop- erate with his department, but out here...." He waved his hand in a half circle. "This is my world, and I'm king, so I'll be watching. You put one foot out of line and I'll—"

"You'll nothing. You're up for reelection next month. Need I say more?"

"Screw you, Starke. One of these days you'll go too far, and I'll be waiting, you egotistical piece a' shit." With that he turned and walked to his cruiser, climbed in, backed all the way up the road onto Cooper, and then roared away in a cloud of dust.

"What the hell did you say to him?" Kate asked when I rejoined the group, now less one.

"I told him I'd cooperate with his team," I said with a grim smile.

"Oh, yeah. The hell you did."

"It'll be fine, Kate. Don't sweat the small stuff. That's what they say, right? Now, Wes, where is she?"

"This way." He walked a few yards down the road, hands in his pockets, head down, and turned left into the trees and started down a steep slope into a gully just to the south of a small lake; we followed, me leading the group.

We didn't need to go far, not more than a couple dozen yards. The scene was cordoned off with yellow tape. Doc Sheddon, the Hamilton County medical examiner, was sitting on his big black case, still dressed head to toe in white Tyvek. He had his hands together, elbows resting on his knees, his chin resting on his knuckles. He looked up when he heard us coming, stood, and walked to where we waited outside the crime scene perimeter.

"Hey, Harry. How's it hanging?" He greeted me as usual, though he sounded bone weary. "Put on some covers and come take a look."

We helped ourselves to Tyvek coveralls from the box at the edge of the scene, all but the chief, who stood, hands in his pockets, staring off into the trees. He held the tape up, and we ducked under.

"Stay in line and follow me," Sheddon said, stepping out into the trees. "The techs still have a lot of ground to cover."

Doc Sheddon was a small man, overweight, almost totally bald, with a round face that usually sported a jovial expression. But not today. Eventually he stopped, stepped aside, and pointed. "There. She's just there."

I took a few more steps forward, to get a better view, and immediately wished I hadn't. *Oh for Christ's sake.... No.*

She—what was left of her—was lying facedown, legs spread slightly, arms by her sides. She was naked. She'd begun to decompose, but even I could tell she hadn't been there for six days.

"You know, Harry," Sheddon said as he stood beside me, looking down at her. "Sometimes, like now, I wonder why I don't just quit. I'll never get used to it. I should, but I don't. I see these kids as their parents never will, thank God.... Well, in this case, that's not quite true. Wes has already seen her. It's bad enough when the body is a stranger, but this.... I've known Emily since she was a baby, and it hurts, Harry. It does."

I listened to him, and I heard him, and I knew what he meant, but I couldn't take it in. It was too horrible. I looked down at her and saw the little girl who'd played around my desk, the little girl who'd told me she would marry me when she grew up, and the tears came. I couldn't help it. I felt Kate's hand on my arm, pulling me away. I shrugged it off angrily, shook my head, wiped my eyes on the sleeve of my covers.

I knelt down beside her and stroked her hair. It was... just a gesture. I couldn't feel much through the latex, but....

"I'll find them, Emily," I whispered. I felt rather than heard Sheddon turn toward me. "I swear it, and when I do...." And then I stood, turned away, and walked back up the slope to the taped perimeter, anger and grief eating at my gut.

"I'll get them, Wes," I said, putting a hand on his shoulder. "I promise, and then you and me...."

He nodded, his eyes watering. "I'm counting on it." He turned and walked off through the trees, slowly, head down, hands in his pocket. He'd aged ten years in less than ten minutes.

I watched him go, and waited for Doc, Kate, and the two county detectives to join me. Together we stripped off our covers and bagged and labeled them for processing. That done, I turned to Sheddon.

"Who found her?"

He jerked his in the direction of the road. "Over there. The woman with the dog. She said the dog stopped, wouldn't move. It was staring down into the gully. She spotted something white and climbed down to take a look. Saw what it was and called 911."

"What time was that?"

"I got the call about quarter to nine and came right on up. Hands and his crew were already here and had the scene taped off."

"Any idea how long she's been here?"

"Well, there's dew on the grass, but the ground under the body is dry, so last night sometime. She must have lain like that, face down, somewhere else for... I dunno precisely, but lividity is complete, so thirty-six, maybe even forty-eight hours. Then she was dumped here. Strange, though, because whoever brought her here laid her out the same way, facedown. Weird."

"Not if she was stiff."

"Rigor, you mean? Yes, that would account for it."

"Any ideas on cause of death?"

"Come on, Harry. You know better than that. You saw what I saw."

"When, Doc?" I asked.

"The autopsy? Tomorrow morning, early. You'll be there, of course."

"Oh yeah. I'll be there. So will Kate." I hadn't bothered to ask her; I just assumed she would be. "How about you guys?"

Hart looked quizzically at McLeish, who shook his head. "Me neither," Hart said. "We'll get the report from Doc, and then we'll talk, all right?"

"Yeah, we'll talk," I said. *The hell we will.*

"You'll need to get a recovery vehicle up to the school," I told Hart. "Her car will have to be processed. Can you do that today?" I wrote the make, model, color, and tag number on the back of one of my cards and handed it to him. He looked at it, hesitated, seemed about to say something, but eventually nodded and stuck the card in the breast pocket of his jacket.

"Today, Tony. It needs to be done today."

"I heard ya the first time, Harry. I'll see to it, okay?"

"I'll check in with you later."

He walked away without answering.

"Any thoughts on time of death?" I asked Sheddon.

"Two, maybe three days at most, as I said. Putrification is still in the early stages. I'll know better when... well, you know the procedure. Look, I've had enough for today. This is a tough one. I've told them to remove her. I'm going home, but I'll go with her to the lab before I do, see her settled in, so to speak. It's the least I can do for her. Tomorrow, Harry, Kate. Nine o'clock. Don't be late. If you are, I'll start without you." And then he left. Hart and McLeish followed him.

"Two to three days. What the hell is that?" I asked Kate. "She's been missing for almost a week. Where the hell has she been?"

She shook her head. "It makes no sense. Why would they keep her, and where? You kill someone, you get rid of the body, fast. You don't keep it around. Unless...."

I knew what she was thinking, and I didn't like it. Necrophilia is a bitch.

"We'll know tomorrow, I guess. Not much we can do here. Let the techs have at it. Maybe they'll find something. In the meantime, let's go talk to the lady who found her. You want to talk to her, Kate?"

She was maybe thirty years old, the outdoorsy type, a big woman, maybe 200 pounds, full-figured: she was wearing a white sleeveless crop top and cut-off jeans. Her face was already showing the effects of too much time in the sun. The dog, a small terrier, sat patiently at her feet.

"Hello, Mrs...."

"It's miss. Kimberly, Kim, Watson. I live just over there." She pointed toward Cooper Drive. We both looked around. I could see the roof of a small two-story house through the trees. "This is Merry, and you are?"

"Lieutenant Catherine Gazzara, Chattanooga PD. And this is my associate, Harry Starke. I have a few questions, if you wouldn't mind."

Watson nodded. "Of course."

Kate opened her notepad. "You found the body, correct?"

Watson nodded again. Her face was pale beneath the tan.

"And what time was that, can you remember?"

"I'm not really sure. It must have been a little before eight, I think. I usually take Merry out around seven thirty in the mornings, so that I can get back in time to go to work. It's the same every day, even on weekends. Habit, I suppose. I walk her the same route again after dinner."

"So you were out here last night, then. About what time would that have been?"

"Well it was still light when I left home so, maybe seven, a quarter after. I like to get back by eight so I can watch the English comedy shows on TV."

"Did you see anything? People, parked cars, anything like that? Especially in the parking area."

"No, nothing like that. Just a couple of students from the college on bikes. They often go down to the lake to, well, you know. Can't think why, though. The place is a mosquito trap."

"This is a pretty remote spot. No traffic at all, right?"

"No. No through traffic. The track dead ends at that iron gate, and there's no room to make a turn. The road is way too narrow. We get hikers, but not many, and I saw only the two girls on their bikes last night."

"Okay, so this morning you're walking the dog, and you're on your way back home. Tell me what happened, how you discovered the body."

All through the conversation I was watching the woman's face, looking for the slightest hint that she might be lying, or at least not telling us everything. She seemed a little nervous, but that was about all, and that was to be expected considering her recent experience. No, she was telling it like was. I was sure of it.

"Well, we were walking slowly. Merry, just like she always

does, was sniffing at every blade of grass and rock—we do get other dogs down here, you know—and suddenly she just stopped. She tilted her head up and was sniffing and sniffing the air. I pulled her leash, but she wouldn't move. She just stood there, her legs spread, looking away into the trees, and then she leaped forward. You can see she's not a big dog, but she's very strong and she dragged me off the road and down into the gully, and that's when—when—I saw it. I called 911 right away, and they told me to stay here and wait until the police could get here, and... well, that's what I did."

"Kim. This is important. How close to the body did you go, and did you touch anything?"

"Oh no. Absolutely not. Nothing! Neither did Merry, because I picked her up and came back here. No, no, I didn't touch anything. I was about six feet from her. I could tell she was dead. I've never seen anything like it before, but you can tell just by looking, can't you?"

We both nodded. She was right. You can tell. There's nothing else that looks like a body two days dead. Unfortunately, the poor woman would remember it for the rest of her days.

"Okay," I said, nodding. "Let's go back to last night."

"What about it?"

"Well, there are no other houses on Wicker that I can see, not down there beyond the lake, and there are no lights, so it must get very dark. Your house is way back there. Would you have seen lights, vehicle lights?"

"Well there is one more house, back in the trees, but I don't think anyone's been living there for a while. I didn't see any car lights last night, but... well, Merry did get a bit excited, barked for a few minutes. She jumped up on the back of the couch and almost pulled down the drapes. Do you think...?"

"What time was that, Kim?" I asked.

"Ten. Maybe a little after. I didn't take any notice. She gets that way about anything: stray cats, foxes, coyotes. I didn't look at the time, but only because *Call the Midwife* had just come on."

I nodded. Kate made notes.

"I need your full name, address, and phone number please, Kim." She noted it down, smiled and said, "Thank you. I know it's been rough, but... well, that's it for now." Kate closed her iPad. "I'm sure we'll need to talk to you again. If you remember anything that might help, or if you just need to talk, please give me a call. This has my cell number, so you can reach me anytime."

Kim took Kate's card, smiled at her, and walked away, talking quietly to her dog. There was no telling what was going on inside her head, but I knew it wasn't good.

"Ideas?" I asked Kate as we watched her go.

"Yeah, one. Whoever dumped her was familiar with the area, knew these woods. This is not the sort of place for a random drop off."

"I agree. That parking area is the only place on this track

where a vehicle could park and not be seen, so whoever it was knew what they were doing. Except... she said there's another house down there, right? If there is, the driveway is probably overgrown. Let's go take a look at it."

The driveway was indeed overgrown. The vegetation was dense, and there was no sign that it had been accessed anytime in the last several weeks.

"We need to get the techs to check it out," Kate said. "You never know."

I nodded, looked at my watch. It was already eleven. "There's nothing more we can do today, not with the techs still working. I'll see you tomorrow morning."

She nodded. "Yeah, I'll have a word with them before I go. See you tomorrow."

I usually enjoy my Sunday afternoons, but not this one. I drove down the mountain a whole lot slower than I'd come up it. I picked Amanda up at her apartment, and from there we went to the country club to join my father and Rose for lunch and a couple of drinks the way we always did. It was usually a relaxing way to finish out the week. We arrived more than an hour late, and the place was bustling. Lunch was already well under way, and my father was getting antsy. You wouldn't think it, with the kind of life he leads, but my father is a man dedicated to his routines; it took two large Bombay Sapphire gins and an extended explanation of why I was late to turn him back into his usual affable self.

Me? I never did get over my feeling of utter despair. Emily had been a very special kid, and I brooded over the loss—and several glasses of scotch whiskey, and a very fine lunch, which I only played with. I couldn't wait to get out of there and go home.

Halfway through the meal I called Kate, but got only her voicemail. I then got through the first four numbers of Wes Johnston's number, but thought better of it. In the end I excused myself, left the table, and went out onto the patio to think, but I couldn't get the image of Emily's body out of my head. Two more large scotches later, Amanda had to drive me home. Hell, it was where I should have stayed. Amanda had to put me to bed that night, or I would have fallen asleep with my shoes on. I woke up the next morning feeling and looking like shit. Even thirty minutes in the shower didn't help. I hadn't been on a bender like that in almost twenty years.

Chapter Eight

Monday started badly. It was raining, miserable, a portent of what was to come. Kate was already in scrubs when I arrived at the forensic center that morning.

"Hey," she said. "You don't look so good. How are you doing?"

"I feel like a sack of... well. You?"

"I've been better." She glanced toward the autopsy room door. "Before we go in there, I should tell you I've made us an appointment at the college. We're seeing the chancellor, a Mrs. Jones, at two o'clock. You all right with that?"

"Yeah. Maybe this won't take too long." *Who the hell am I kidding.*

The mood in the autopsy room was all doom and gloom. Even the usually bubbly Carol Owens—Bones, as Doc

Sheddon insists on calling her—had a grim look on her face. And no wonder: we all knew Chief Johnston, and we'd all known Emily too. Now here she was, her body laid out on a stainless steel table, about to undergo one of forensic medicine's most horrendous procedures.

"Carol hasn't cleaned her yet," Sheddon said, leaning with both hands on the edge of the table. "She'll do that when I get done going over her skin."

Emily's body lay face up on the gleaming table. The skin of her legs, chest, and face were creased from lying facedown in debris on the woodland floor, bits of which were stuck to her skin, and lividity and early putrifaction had turned her the color of rotten plums.

I've seen some god-awful things in Doc Sheddon's house of horrors, but this.... Probably because of who it was—who it had been—this was the worst ever.

Kate and I stood back from the table at Sheddon's right. Carol was at the head, just to his left. The doc's face was grim. There was no sign of his usual gallows humor. Carol's face was white under the surgical mask, as was Kate's. Me? My guts were churning, though more from anger than from the appalling ordeal we were all about to undergo.

"Well," Sheddon said quietly, "let's do it." With a large magnifying glass in one hand and an ultraviolet light in the other, he began to examine the body. He inspected every inch of her, searching for anything that might offer a clue to where she'd been or what had happened to her: fibers, hairs, dust particles, paint or other deposits; bruises, cuts, ligature marks, injuries, anything. While he was doing that, Carol took swabs. She took hair samples, nail clippings, and scrapings from under Emily's finger and toenails. Everything was bagged and labeled. And Doc Sheddon droned endlessly into the microphone clipped to his lapel, pausing to bag and label small pieces of what looked to me like debris, several hairs, and flakes of what might have been paint, and to make notes on a body diagram.

"You find anything, Carol?" he asked eventually, taking a step back.

"There appears to be blood and tissue under the nails of the first, second, and third finger of the right hand, and under the first and second of the left. Looks like she put up a fight."

He nodded. "Yes, that's consistent with what I'm thinking. You can go ahead and clean her up now, Carol.

"At this point," he continued, "I'd say the cause of death was strangulation, possibly due to the incorrect application of a sleeper hold."

My gut knotted. "You're talking about a choke hold, right?"

"Hmmm, yes... and no. A carotid sleeper hold is applied by using the forearm and upper arm. In which case the v—the antecubital fossa or crook of the arm—is centered at the midline of the neck, so the trachea is not compressed, only the carotid arteries and jugular veins. Such an application is designed to render the victim unconscious in a matter of seconds by restricting the flow of blood to the brain.

Relaxing the hold would restore consciousness quite quickly, leaving the vic virtually unharmed. That would be the correct way, if there is such a thing, to apply what you call a choke hold, and if that were the case there would be bruising here, and here." He indicated either side of her neck. "As you can see, that's not the case. The bruising is here." Now he pointed to the front of her neck at the underside of the chin.

"Unfortunately, a less-than-skilled application of such a hold would be the 'bar,' or choke hold proper, in which case the forearm lies across the center of the throat and does in fact crush the trachea, as I'm sure was the case here. This would cause asphyxiation and... most probably, death."

It was at that moment that Chief Johnston walked in. He was wearing a full set of scrubs. I turned toward him and held up my hand. "Chief—"

He brushed me away. "Get out of the way, Harry. This is my child."

"Chief," Sheddon said, "I've barely started. You don't want to be here for the rest of this."

"You know the cause of death yet?" Johnston asked.

"Maybe. My gut feeling is that she was strangled, but that's not all. You need to leave, Chief. Harry, take him out. I will not continue as long as he is present."

I took Wes by the arm, turned him around, and led him out into the waiting area. He slumped down in an easy chair, his elbows on his knees, head in his hands. He was shaking from head to toe. I laid a hand on his shoulder and squeezed, but he didn't respond.

"I'll be back when this is done, Chief, and then we'll talk. Okay?"

He didn't answer.

I returned to the autopsy room and to my place at the table.

"You said there was more," I said to Sheddon.

"I want to take a look at her organs and stomach before I say anything else."

"Shit."

"You all right, Harry?" Kate asked.

I looked at her. Her face was the color of cookie dough.

I nodded, took a deep breath. "Get on with it, Doc."

"Okay. Carol, if you please?"

Together they wrestled the rubber block under the torso to extend the ribcage and, when he was satisfied with the positioning, he picked up a scalpel, looked at me, then at Kate, then shook his head and made the first incision, down from the left shoulder joint, under and around the left breast to the center of her chest. The skin and flesh, already in the early stages of decomposition, split open like an over-ripe banana. He repeated the incision from the right shoulder, and then completed the y by cutting from the join of the first two cuts down to the pubic area. The now-exposed flesh was a deep, blueish violet color, which I knew indicated asphyxia.

He's right. She was strangled.

It went on. He pulled the flaps of skin back, cut the ribs with an instrument most folks use for pruning trees, removed the breastplate, and inspected the internal organs: the liver, kidneys, lungs, stomach, and finally the brain. The stench was overpowering.

"I need a drink," Sheddon said.

"Shit, so do I," I said. "In the worst way."

He smiled wanly. "That's not what I meant, Harry. I'm thirsty. You probably need something a whole lot stronger." He went to the refrigerator, got a bottle of water, unscrewed the cap, and took a long swallow.

He was right. I looked down at the now-broken body of Emily Johnston and I did need a drink, and I sure as hell would get one just as soon as I could get out of this hellhole.

"Okay," Sheddon said, returning to the table. He set the water bottle down next to the pan containing Emily's brain. "Here's how I see it. She died sometime between eight o'clock on Thursday evening and two o'clock in the morning on Friday. That's as close as I can get it. The cause of death was, as I said, asphyxiation, undoubtedly caused by strangulation. The larynx and windpipe are crushed, probably by the application of a bar chokehold. The blood and tissue under her nails probably came from the arm that did the damage...." He paused, looked first at Kate then at me. "But, as I said, there's more. And that's why I didn't want the chief in here. I'm quite certain that what we have here is the result of BDSM, sadomasochism, pushed beyond the point of no return."

I was horrified. "Christ, Doc. What are you talking about?"

"First, there are signs that she was restrained, and I don't mean locked away, though I'm sure she must have been. See these marks on her wrists and ankles? They were made by straps, but this is what's really interesting."

Interesting?

"These marks here and here.... They also were made by straps and, from the positioning of the bruises—see? They are mostly on the inside and rear of the thighs—I think the restraint was a sex swing."

And I knew exactly what he meant. I'd seen the apparatus he was talking about, and so had Kate. Back when I was a cop, we'd been called to the scene of a sex party gone wrong. In that case the poor woman had still been hanging there, naked and gagged, legs and arms spread for all to see. Her death was an accident, but this—

Jeez.

"Now for the tough part. Her breasts were tied with, I'm almost certain, nylon electrical ties—zip ties. You can see the marks where someone cut them off. They were circled around the breasts and tightened: extremely painful. There's trauma to the nipples, possibly caused by the application of electrical clips. Even worse, there are injuries to the vagina: the vulva and labia both show signs of blunt force trauma. I think someone beat her genital area, probably with some sort of flat instrument, maybe just a piece of wood, or maybe some sort of whip. There is also trauma to the interior of the vagina consistent with the insertion of a foreign object, something too big for the poor girl to handle. What, I have no idea."

"Oh shit." I shook my head.

"I found five human hairs," he continued, "one with the follicle attached. That'll be good for some usable DNA, as will the tissue under her nails. There are also some other hairs, short, white, coarse, not human. I found two small flakes of what I think is white paint—old paint, possibly lead —with traces of mold on them and some dust particles, all of which will need to be analyzed. And... that's about it, at least for now. The rest will have to wait until I get the tox screen and the hair and DNA results back. That could take a couple of weeks."

"We need to do better than that," I said. "Can you put a rush on it?"

He began to shake his head.

"Oh no, Doc. We have to move on this. If you can't get it rushed, I can. Do you have enough material to let me have samples?"

"Can't do that, Harry. This is evidence we're talking about. Chain of custody and all that."

He was right, of course.

"Let me see what I can do," he said after a moment. "The big problem is cost, of course."

"Cost my ass. This is the chief's daughter we're talking about. It's *Emily*, for Christ's sake. Look, give it a try. If you need cash... hell, I'll pay for the tests, just get 'em done as fast as you can."

"I'll give it my best shot, Harry."

I shook my head in frustration, looked again at the mess on the table, then turned to Kate and said, "Let's get the hell out of here. I need to get drunk, again."

"Wait," she said. "What about the chief?"

"He's waiting outside."

"What are we going to tell him, Harry?" Oh she was pissed. "You going to lay all that crap about BDSM on him? Because I'm sure as hell not."

"I don't see how we can't. It will be in the record, right?" I looked at Sheddon. He shrugged and nodded.

"I'll tell him she was sexually assaulted, for now. That's the best I can do. If he asks how, I'll have to tell him. I'm not going to lie to him."

As luck would have it, I didn't have to do it either. When we arrived in the waiting area, Johnston had already left. I heaved a sigh of relief, then glanced at my watch. It was just after twelve thirty.

"I said I needed a drink, and I meant it. The Boathouse okay with you? It's the nearest decent place I know."

"That's fine with me," she said.

Less than ten minutes later we were seated in a booth alongside the window, overlooking the river. It was not the pleasant panorama it almost always was. Today the driving rain had turned the river into a vast bed of nails. Oh happy day.

Chapter Nine

I sure as hell needed a drink, and a single shot of Glenlivet would have cut it, but I was driving and didn't want alcohol on my breath. Cops tend to take a dim view of it. And besides, I never drink when I'm working. So no Glenlivet. Instead, I had black coffee. Kate had a single glass of house white. Neither of us felt like eating, or talking, so we sat there in silence like two zombies, staring out over the turbulent river. There was no sky, just an impenetrable gray mist... and the rain. A driving, almost horizontal torrent that hammered against the glass.

Our appointment was set for two o'clock. We left the Boathouse at 1:15. Usually it would have been a drive of twenty or thirty minutes, but not that day. I'd allowed a little extra time because of the weather—it wasn't enough. Signal Mountain Road was a virtual river. We arrived outside the administration building at Belle Edmonson at ten after two. A little late, but what the hell.

The chancellor's PA showed us into the office, and the

chancellor herself came around from behind her desk to greet us. She quite beautiful. Not tall, maybe five foot six; perhaps forty-five years old, but she looked younger. Her red hair was cut very short and showed off her long neck and near-perfect ears, accented by ruby studs that looked to be all of two carats apiece.

She extended her hand to Kate, who made the introductions, and we sat: Kate and I on one side of a heavy, carved coffee table, and she on the other, facing us.

"Before we begin," she began. "I would like to say how utterly devastated I was to hear about poor Emily."

Wow. That's some accent. Victoria Mason-Jones was English. But with a name like that, she had to be, right?

"Now," she continued. "How may I help you?"

Kate lifted a small digital recorder. "Do you mind?"

"Not at all."

Kate turned on the machine and noted the details of the meeting for the record: time, date, present, etc.

"We have some questions about Emily, but before we begin, you should know that we are investigating her death on behalf of Chief Wesley Johnston."

"I thought the sheriff's department was investigating her death. The detectives didn't mention anything about your department being involved." She reached for the phone and punched in a number.

Why doesn't that surprise me?

"How will your investigation affect the one being conducted by the sheriff's office?"

"It's a combined effort. The two departments are working together." I could almost see her tongue in her cheek.

"Very well... and...? Oh, just give me a minute," she said to Kate. She tapped another number into her cell, and then said, "Could I speak to Sheriff Hands, please?" There was a moment of silence, and then, "Sheriff Hands. This is Victoria Mason-Jones at Belle Edmondson. Thank you for taking my call. Yes... yes.... I'm sure, but that's not what I called about. I have a Chattanooga police office here, a Lieutenant Catherine Gazzara, and a private investigator, Harry Starke. I was wondering if you were aware that they are conducting an investigation into the death of Emily Johnston. Hmmm. Yes.... I understand. So it's all right for me to talk to them? Good.... Thank you, Sheriff. Yes, I'll see you then." She disconnected and hung up the handset.

Okay, I thought. *That sure as hell lays out the ground rules. Yours, anyway....*

"Very well," she said to Kate. "It seems everything is in order."

"That's good to hear," Kate said dryly. "We'll need to talk to you, of course, Ms. Mason-Jones, and your staff, which means we'll need their cooperation, especially your security people. We'll need access to the college, the dorms, and the grounds, and we'll need your permission to talk to the faculty and students, especially Emily's friends. I will also need a list of the faculty members she's involved with. And we'll need it all in writing, please."

"You have my full cooperation, and that of my staff, of course. Give me a minute and I'll organize the lists and written permissions. I'll also have extended passes made up for you." She got up, walked to the door, and gave the necessary instructions to her secretary. "My assistant will have something ready for you when you've finished here," she told us. She looked pointedly at her watch—a slim gold Rolex—and then expectantly at us.

"You said detectives from the sheriff's department were here. Hart and McLeish," I said.

"Yes. This morning. They weren't here very long; they said they had an appointment in town, but would be back later today."

"Did they look at Emily's room? Talk to her friends, staff, anyone other than yourself?"

"I don't think so. They seemed to be in a hurry."

Okay. They're not Hamilton County's finest by any means, but this is a murder investigation. They should have had that room locked down. What the hell are they thinking?

"What can you tell us about Emily?" Kate asked. "What kind of girl was she?"

"I can't tell you very much, I'm afraid. My job here is almost entirely administrative, and I have very little interaction with the student body. I do know she was a good student, well-liked and active in sports, predominantly show jumping. I've also been told she was quite a golfer. But you should talk to Edna Morgan. She's the vice chancellor of student affairs."

"Ms. Jones," I started, but she interrupted me.

"It's Mason-Jones." She gave me a tight smile.

Now that pisses me off. Arrogant....

"My apologies, ma'am. Ms. Mason-Jones. We know she was out with friends Saturday evening. We also know she hitched a ride back here with this woman." I pulled up the image on my phone and handed it to her. "We're told she's a vet. Do you know her?"

"Yes, of course. That's Erika Padgett. She works with Dr. Jepson. There's not much I can tell you about her, though, other than that she visits on a fairly regular basis. We have an equestrian center here, and a large number of horses."

I made a note of the name.

"When we were here on Saturday," I said looking her in the eye, "we ran into some very aggressive and uncooperative campus police officers. If I hadn't known better, I would have thought they were paramilitary."

She smiled. "Actually, they are not police per se. We are not a large enough facility to warrant having such a department. They are private security contractors. Our Captain Rösche is somewhat zealous in his approach, but he runs a tight ship, I'm pleased to say. He keeps us safe." The smile was gone. "If he gives you any trouble, you may refer him to me."

"It seems a little excessive," I said. "This is not Chicago; it's a women's college, and you're not lacking law enforcement up here. You have the local Signal Mountain Police Department, as well as the sheriff's department. Why would you need a bunch of heavies patrolling the campus?"

She shrugged. "Why not? We are indeed a college for women, and I am charged with their safety, a responsibility I don't take lightly. Now—" she looked again at her watch —"if there's nothing else, I have a very busy schedule." She rose to her feet and offered Kate her hand.

"Please," she said, "feel free to visit and explore the college as you see fit. Everyone, including Captain Rösche, will cooperate."

I had more questions, but I also had the feeling that I'd somehow stepped on her toes. She didn't offer me her hand. Instead, she stepped to the door and opened it. We were getting academia's version of the bum's rush.

Okay. That's cool. I'll getcha next time.

"We'll need your personal phone number; in case we need to contact you," Kate said.

"Of course. Here's my card. It has my office number on it, but I'll write my cell number on the back for you."

She handed the card to Kate, and we said our goodbyes.

We collected the paperwork and visitor's badges from Jones'

secretary and stepped out of the building into watery sunshine. The rain had stopped, and the sky was a fast-moving field of blue and white.

They were there again, the same two security officers, Mirrors and Aviators, leaning casually against the side of their cruiser, arms folded across their chests.

We walked down the steps, past the cruiser to my car. They said not a word. And they didn't move.

I opened the car door for Kate, and then got in behind the wheel.

"Well. That went well," she said.

I nodded. "What is it with women like that? I got the distinct impression that, as far as she's concerned, the rest of humanity is beneath her notice."

Kate rolled her eyes. "That, I think, comes with the PhD. I hate academics, especially the high-minded ones." She sighed. "What now?"

"Now we go take a look at Emily's room and, I hope, talk to Jessica Henderson. And what the hell is it with Hart and McLeish?"

She shrugged. "You tell me. Might be for the best if they stay the hell out of the way."

I put the car in reverse, backed away from the cruiser, and then pulled out of the lot. Only then did the security guys get into their car and follow us.

Chapter Ten

I pulled into the gravel parking area to the left of the Huddleston Building. The cruiser followed me in and parked some fifteen feet away.

I turned off the engine, looked sideways at Kate. "Okay. Stay here. I need to handle this."

"Harry...."

"I know, I know. I'll be nice."

I got out of the car and walked across the lot to the passenger side of the car.

"Good afternoon, boys. Is there a problem?"

Aviators grinned up at me through the open window. "No sir."

"Then why are you following us?"

"Boss's orders. Told us to keep an eye you, is all."

"That would be Rösche, right?"

"*Captain* Rösche. Yessir. That would be him."

"Then I suggest you head back to whatever sty he's holed up in and tell him we'll be around to see him as soon as we get done here. Go on. Off you go."

I walked back to my car. Kate was already halfway up the steps to the dorm, waiting.

"What did you say to them?"

"I just told them to let their boss know we'd be around to see him shortly."

"Yeah, I'll just bet you did."

I grinned at her, and we entered the building. The cruiser hadn't moved.

Just beyond the front door and to the left, half a dozen young women occupied a large, somewhat sparsely furnished sitting room, most of them sitting cross-legged on sofas with books, laptops, or tablets open in their laps. To the right, opposite the sitting room door, a wide staircase led to the upper floors.

Kate knocked on the doorframe. They all looked up; they all looked down again.

"We're looking for Jessica Henderson," Kate said loudly.

A young woman seated by the window looked up, closed her book, stood, and walked over to us. I recognized her immediately as one of the girls at the Sorbonne that night.

She was of medium build, and her body was exquisite. She was wearing skin-tight yoga pants and a sports bra that left little the imagination. Her hair was curly, and dark brown, as were her eyes. Her face would have done justice to a Lancôme ad; in fact, she looked a little like Julia Roberts.

"I'm Jessica. You... you must be the police. This is about Emily?" Her eyes were red. She'd obviously been crying.

Kate nodded. "My name is Lieutenant Catherine Gazzara, Chattanooga Police. This is Harry Starke, my associate. We'd like a word in private." She offered her ID.

The girl looked at it. "We can go up to my room," she said. "Lacy is at the farm."

Her room was a spacious apartment on the second floor. It was well-furnished, too, with a large dining table and four chairs, two armchairs, and a couple of sideboards, one of which supported a flat-screen TV. The large, living room window offered a view over the grounds to the east: a large meadow where maybe a couple dozen horses grazed contentedly on the wet grass. Beyond the meadow, dense woodland stretched away into the distance and to... the hidden lake on Wicker Road, where Emily had been found.

"Please, sit down." Jessica sat at the head of the table. Kate took a seat on one side of her, and I sat on the other.

"If you don't mind, Jessica," Kate said gently, "we'd like to get a few personal details." She set the recorder on the table in front of her. "Do you mind?"

Jessica shook her head.

"Good. Let's begin with your full name, home address, and date of birth."

Kate made a note of the answers on her iPad, and then continued. "And when did you first meet Emily?"

"We started school here together, in the fall of 2012. Will you tell me what happened to her? They didn't give any details, the TV news." She was starting to cry again.

Kate shook her head. "I'm sorry, Jessica. We don't have all the details yet."

"She was strangled," I said suddenly. I watched her face. It went white. Kate glared at me from across the table. "We found her in the woods about a mile away. When did you last see her?"

"Saturday night. We went out. We... we...." She sat there, head down, staring at the table.

"She met someone." I waited for her to answer. She didn't.

"Jessica. Emily met someone, at the Sorbonne."

"Erika," she whispered. "She met Erika. They went home together, to Erika's. That was the last time I saw her."

"Erika Padgett? The vet?"

She nodded.

"Jessica," Kate said. "We know Emily was gay. Were they dating?"

"I'm not sure what you mean by dating. They met a few

times. They went out to eat a couple of times, and to the movies once, all over several months. I think it was casual. Not a steady relationship—" *sniff*—"if that's what you mean. And they spent time together at the horse barn, but that was... well, I don't know what it was. Emily spent most of her time studying, or with me." She looked at my face, and then said sharply—too sharply?—"I'm not gay, but I do, did, love her. She was my best friend." And with that, she dropped her head into her hands and burst into tears.

We waited until she got ahold of herself, until she'd wiped her eyes on a paper towel, blown her nose, and looked up again. It was pathetic. She was devastated.

"So," I said gently. "If she wasn't in a relationship with Ms. Padgett, was she dating *anyone*?"

"No." *Sniff.* "I don't think so. Not that I know of."

"What about you, Jessica?"

She looked at me with narrowed eyes. "What do you mean?"

"Were you best friend friends, or were you...?"

"*No.* I told you. I'm not gay. I have a boyfriend." It was said with just a little too much angst. "She was my friend. She had a lot of friends."

"I understand. So, did she go out much?"

"We all did. Mostly in the evenings, but sometimes on weekends. She stayed with her parents on the weekends, and she went to horse shows. They were always overnight things. Other than that...."

"Tell me about your boyfriend, Jessica."

"*What*? Why?"

"Well, you say you're not gay, that you have a boyfriend. It's just routine. I'm just filling in the gaps."

"His—his name is John."

Hmmm. How original.

"And John's last name is?"

"I'm not going to tell you that. It's... well he has nothing to do with anything. He didn't even know Emily."

"Then why won't you tell me his name?"

"I...."

"Jessica," Kate said gently. "We're not accusing you of anything, or John, but we have to know."

"John Parker," she whispered.

"And where does he live?"

"On Valleywood Drive in Middle Valley."

"Phone number?"

Kate made a note of it. "Thanks Jessica."

"So you're sure Emily wasn't in a relationship, then?" Kate asked.

"No, I'm not sure. I just don't know. She had a lot of friends; I told you."

"Okay, Jessica," I said. "Not much more, I promise. Let's talk about Saturday night. You left here at what time?"

"It was at seven thirty. Autumn was designated driver."

"That would be your friend Autumn Leaf?" *Jeez, how does the girl handle that?*

"Yes, there were the four of us: me, Emily, Lacy, and Autumn. We met up with Robin and Nick at the Mellow Mushroom around eight. We had a few drinks there, and then we went to the Big River Grill and had dinner. Then we went to the Sorbonne."

"And Erika was waiting for you?"

"No, she was just... there. By herself. She wasn't waiting for us."

"Could she have been waiting for Emily?"

She thought for a moment, then shook her head. "I don't think so. Emily didn't say anything about that, but she spotted her the minute we walked into the bar. She had a couple of drinks with us, then she went and had several more with Erika. I don't think it was arranged."

"So. They met. They had a few drinks. And then what?"

"Then we left. They were still there. I assumed they left together. And that's it. That was the last time I saw her." Again, she burst into tears.

I waited until she calmed down, then I showed her the photos of the two boys they had been with at the Sorbonne. "Who are they, Jessica?"

"That's Robin Lucas, and that's Nick—Nicholas—Kyper. They're just friends. They run around with us sometimes."

"Okay, just one more thing, Jessica. Then we'll leave you alone. When and where did they first meet?"

"I..." *sniff,* "I don't really know. At the horse barn? Months ago. I don't know."

Kate turned off the recorder and slipped it into her pocket. I got up from the table, grabbed a fistful of paper towels from the roll in the kitchen, and handed them to her. "Here. Dry your eyes. We're going to take a look at her room. Which one is it?"

She wiped her eyes and looked up at me. They were red, bloodshot. I felt a rush of pity for her.

"Next door. But it's locked; you'll need a key. You can have mine."

"I already have one." But then I realized that I didn't. "Nope, I left it home. If you wouldn't mind?"

She rose from the table and went to one of the sideboards, opened a drawer, took out a single key on a leather fob, and handed it to me.

"I won't need it anymore, will I." More tears.

Kate took a pair of latex gloves from her jacket pocket and put them on. I did the same and unlocked the door.

"So what do you think?" Kate asked once we'd gotten inside Emily's room.

"About what?"

"Jessica, of course."

"I think her love for Emily was a little stronger than just friendship. Maybe they had a thing for each other. Maybe they didn't. Maybe Jessica had a thing for her but Emily didn't know it."

"Yeah, I suppose. She sure as hell was upset."

"That or she's one hell of an actress."

"Harry, you're a cynic."

"Well, yeah. I make it a habit to be one. When did you ever meet a murderer that told the truth, or wasn't a good actor? She was lying about the boyfriend. Friend, maybe. Boyfriend, no. She had her phone in her hand before we got out of the door. Give him a call. I bet he won't answer."

"Okay, I will." And she did. And I was right.

"Busy," she said dryly.

"What she said about Emily staying weekends with her family, that wasn't true either. Either Emily lied to her, or Jessica lied to us. Johnston told me he hadn't seen her in at least five weeks."

"So you think she's a suspect?" she asked.

"I didn't say that, but if they were lovers.... You know me. I like to keep an open mind. You do too."

She nodded, sucked her bottom lip into her mouth, then let it go and pursed her lips.

"No comment?" I asked with a grin.

She gave me a wry smile. "No comment."

Chapter Eleven

mily's apartment was the twin of Jessica's. The walls were decorated with large prints of showjumping stars, riders and horses. The view from the window was the same pastoral scene: meadow, horses, and woodland. There were two beds in the bedroom —one with only a bare mattress, the other with a purple bedspread— but it had an awful feeling of emptiness and abandonment. Maybe it was the unoccupied section of the room; maybe it was something else. Whatever it was, our voices seemed to echo off the walls and high ceiling.

The table was bare, the four chairs arranged neatly around it. The kitchenette was tidy, sink empty, food in the refrigerator, countertops bare. The closet was full of clothes, obviously Emily's. I checked the bathroom while Kate sorted through the clothing. The bathroom was almost bare except for several large towels, some shampoo, soap, and other toiletries—nothing of note. The top of Emily's sideboard was also bare, except for the usual family photographs and a glass that contained several colored pencils and an equal number of gel pens, also colored. One by one, I pulled the drawers out—two at the top and three more below, one above the other—and looked through the contents: underwear, sweaters, so on and so forth. I went to the other sideboard and looked through the drawers. All empty.

"Kate, where is she?"

"What? You know where she is."

"No, I mean, where's all the stuff that made her what she was? You know, knickknacks, photos of her with friends, notes, jewelry. There's not a single personal photo other than those of her family. That's not usual. What about her computer? She had to have one. Phone? That's still up here somewhere, but where? We need to find it. Hold on a minute. I'll call her."

I took out my cell and made the call, and we listened: nothing. I disconnected.

"It makes no sense," I said. "Did she have an iPad or Kindle? I'll bet she did. Someone's been here and cleaned up, taken her stuff."

"You may be right, but if so, who?"

I shook my head and, deep in thought, without thinking about what I was doing, I pulled open the top left drawer and sorted through the flimsy pieces, looking but not seeing, trying to make sense of it. I picked up a bra: white lace, wispy. One of the straps was caught on something. I pulled. It wouldn't come. I pulled again. It was stuck. I moved the rest of the pieces aside and saw why. The end of the strap was caught between the wall of the drawer and the plywood bottom.

"Hey. Come and look at this." I took out my phone, held up the bra, and photographed it.

She looked, then looked sideways at me. "False bottom?"

I nodded. After she'd emptied the drawer and pulled it out, she turned it upside down. There was no bra strap sticking out of the bottom.

"Let's take a look at it." I took the drawer from her and set it on the table. The bottom was a tight fit—no gaps anywhere, but there was a small hole at the rear, maybe an inch from the back wall. I tapped the plywood with my knuckles. It sounded hollow. I pulled the bra strap. It didn't move, and neither did the bottom. If I pulled harder it would break; I was sure of it.

"I don't suppose you have a knife or a screwdriver?" I asked Kate.

She smiled. "What do you think?"

I stared down at the interior of the drawer and at the tiny hole, and then I had an idea. I went to the closet and grabbed an empty wire clothes rack. I straightened the hook, and then put the end of it into the bathroom doorjamb and bent it into the shape of an *l*, the arm about a half-inch long. I inserted it into the hole and pulled. It was a very tight fit, but it began to move, slowly at first, the two pieces of wood squeaking one against the another. And then it was free.

"What do we have here?" The space below the false bottom was no deeper than the book that lay inside it, maybe a little more than an inch thick. In fact, it was clear that book had supported the plywood, hence the solid feel when it was *in situ*. Had it not been for the snagged strap, we never would have found it.

I photographed the book, and the prepaid phone that lay beside it, and the neat stack of photographs—they were held together by a short length of red satin ribbon—then lifted the book out. Kate reached for the photos.

The book was roughly eight inches by ten, and obviously homemade. The cover was two pieces of thick white cardboard, three-hole punched. The interior pages were white cartridge paper, also punched. It was all held together by more red ribbon. The front cover was covered in doodles; the pages were a riot of color. Drawings, sketches, notes, doodles; there were even a few photographs glued in. At the back were six pages of lined paper. On them were listed, line-by-line, what appeared to be a random series of letters and numbers. I handed the book to Kate.

"What do you make of it?"

She traded me for the photos and flipped through the pages, all the while shaking her head.

"It seems she was quite an artist. Some of the girls are beautiful. But the doodles, the numbers? I have no idea."

I turned on the phone and went to recent calls. There were none. Either the phone had never been used or it had been wiped.

"We'll take it all with us." I picked up the photos. "I'll put this stuff back together and we'll get out of here. I want to see this Rösche character—and Dr. Jepson."

I slipped the false bottom back into the drawer and pushed it home, the squeak of wood against wood grating on my teeth. With the plywood back in place, there was no way to tell what it was. Someone had gone to a great deal of trouble to construct it. I pushed the drawer back into its slot in the sideboard and then put the underwear back inside it. After one last look around, we were out of there. I locked the door and, once we were back in the car, put the key in a small paper evidence envelope, labeled, dated, and signed it. The same with Emily's book and the photographs.

Mirrors and Aviators were still parked in their cruiser at the side of the building. Aviators had his elbow hanging out of the window and a shit-eating grin on his face.

I started the car, pulled it alongside the cruiser, and rolled down the window.

"Okay," I said to the still-grinning Aviators. "How about you escort us to see your boss?"

"What you find in that room, bub? We saw you carry something out."

"Are you going to take us, or do I have to go back to the office and get directions?"

He didn't answer. Instead he turned and said something I

couldn't hear to Mirrors, who hit the starter, put the car in gear, reversed, then headed away, wheels spinning, showering the side of the Maxima with gravel.

"*Goddamn it.* He'll pay for that." I followed them along a winding road to the north end of the campus, where they parked the car in front of a single-story, block-built structure with a large blue sign that boasted "Campus Police."

The two clowns climbed out of the car and walked to the steps.

"Y'all wait here," Aviators shouted. "I'll see if the captain wants to see you."

"This is bullshit," I said to Kate. "C'mon."

We got out of the car and walked toward the entrance. By the time we reached the bottom of the flight of four steps, they were back. They came down the steps and stood together at the bottom, arms hanging loosely at their sides. *What the hell do they think this is,* High Noon?

I don't like to fight. But sometimes it happens. When it does, I do what it takes to end it as quickly as possible. Eyes, ears, mouth, and nose; throat, groin, fingers, and toes are to me legitimate targets. If the opponent is inexperienced, one solid hit to the throat—the trachea well or carotid artery— liver, solar plexus, or the kidneys is usually all it takes.

"He said he's too busy and for y'all to make an appointment." He was grinning again.

I walked up to Aviators—Kate followed, just behind and to

my right side—and said, "Get the hell out of the way. If you don't, I'll move you."

"Oh yeah?"

He didn't have a chance. Never saw it coming. I whipped my right hand up to his throat and grabbed his neck, my thumb on one side of his windpipe, fingers on the other, and *squeezed*. He choked. His tongue came out. His face first went red then blue as his air and blood flow were cut off. He tried to grab my hand but he couldn't, and he slowly sank to his knees.

I grabbed his Glock from its holster with my left hand, ejected the mag, and tossed the weapon into a nearby ornamental fountain. Unfortunately, I missed. The weapon hit the edge of the concrete and bounced off into the gravel.

In the meantime, Kate had stepped in close to Mirrors and grabbed both of his ears and was twisting them, hard. He too dropped to his knees, howling with pain, but she didn't let go.

"Let him go, Harry. He's about to pass out."

I looked down at Aviators. She was right. His head was tilted back, face toward the sky. His eyes were closed. His hands hung loosely, knuckles dragging the floor.

"Spoilsport." But I did as she said. He fell forward. His face hit the floor. He groaned and rolled over onto his back, his hands at his throat.

"Now you," I said to Kate.

"Get his weapon."

I did, and she turned Mirrors loose too. He fell backward onto his ass. I walked to the fountain, picked up Aviators' Glock, and jacked the slide. Good job. There had been one in the chamber. I ejected the mag in Mirrors' weapon and jacked the round out of its chamber too. Jeez.

We left them there on the ground and walked into the building. Rösche was in the first office we checked, just to the left of the entrance. I slammed the two Glocks down on his desk, so hard that the glass top fractured under the impact and a dozen cracks spider-webbed across it. He didn't even flinch. He just stood up and leaned forward, his hands flat on the desktop.

He was not at all what I'd expected. No fancy uniform, just a pair of tan slacks and a white polo. He did have a holster with what appeared to be another Glock 17 on his belt at his right side, but other than that, he might have been the local golf pro.

He was maybe six feet tall, a couple of inches shorter than me and a good twenty pounds lighter. He had a thin face, with sharp features and thin lips. His hair, mostly dark brown, was streaked with gray. Handsome? Yeah, I suppose you could say that.

"So," he said, calmly. "What did you do to them?"

"Do? Do what to whom?"

He laughed once, and smiled. It wasn't a nice smile. More of a grimace, which turned his face from handsome to...

well, I've caught barracudas that would have been proud to give me that look. We had, in the space of twenty seconds, seen two completely different personalities. But it was soon over. The grimace was replaced by a gentle smile; the golf pro was back.

"Come on, Harry. You know what I meant. What did you do to Lester and Henry?" He turned his head to look at Kate. "Lieutenant Gazzara. It's nice to meet you." He offered her his hand. She ignored it.

"Okay, be that way. How about you?" He offered his hand to me. I also ignored it, more in support of Kate than a need to act tough.

"They're outside. They'll be fine."

"Yes. I'm sure they will be." He sat down, the fake smile set on his face like a mask. His eyes were half closed, narrow slits filled with contempt.

"How did you know who we are?"

There was that laugh again. It was almost a bark. "Sheriff Hands told me you'd be calling—not a fan of yours is he?— and your reputation precedes you. You're quite famous, Harry." He switched his gaze and stared at Kate, ran his tongue lewdly over his lips and said, "As for you, my dear...."

She glared right back at him.

"You're Harry's trusty sidekick, so what's not to know? Oh, and I did get a call from our chancellor. Apparently she wants me to cooperate with you. Who would have thought? After all, you have no standing here, either of you. But, her word is my command, so cooperate I will. Take a seat. What can I do for you?"

It was all said in a deceptively easygoing tone of voice, with an attitude to match. The man was obviously sure of himself, his abilities, and his position, and he was mocking us. I didn't like it worth a damn.

Kate put a hand on my arm, and we did as he said. We sat on two hard wooden chairs in front of the desk. That put us, even me, a good six inches lower than him—by design, I was sure: the damned chair legs had been shortened.

Screw you, Rösche. I've dealt with too many other power-crazy shits just like you to allow you to pull your crap on me.

I got up, pushed the chair out of the way, walked to the side of his desk, and grabbed a chair of normal height and set it down beside Kate.

"Very good, Harry. Very good." He clapped, slowly. His mouth was smiling; his eyes were chips of flint.

"Stop screwing around, Rösche." His eyes narrowed even further. "I'm here—*we're* here, and we have a job to do, and we're going to do it. We have the chancellor's blessing and the necessary permissions and there's nothing you or that pirate Hands can do about it. Now let's get on with it. What the hell do you need with a bunch of heavies like... what did you say their names were? Lester and Henry? They look and act like goddamn mercenaries."

"And I have six more just like them. You know this territory, Starke. It's wild country up here, and there are more than five hundred girls on campus, some of them very high profile. One is the daughter of the vice president, for Christ's sake. They need to be protected."

That was an excuse. I had a pretty strong feeling there was more to it. *But never mind that for now.*

"What do you know about Emily Johnston?" I asked.

"Not a damned thing, other than that she was found dead in the woods a mile from here, which only goes to prove my point about the need for protection up here." There was that mocking smile again.

"We've just been through her room. There's nothing there. Where is it?"

He shrugged. The smile remained set. He didn't answer.

"I was told by one of the students that one of your crew hauled off a couple of boxes of stuff. What happened to it?" It hadn't happened, but he didn't know that, and somebody sure as hell had cleaned out her room. It had to have been either Rösche's people or one of the faculty. My money was on Rösche.

Again, he shrugged. Then he tilted his head, got up, went to a cupboard at the back of the room, and took out a small cardboard box.

"You were bluffing, Harry," Rösche said, "but what the hell. There's nothing here, just school work... and there was only one box, not two." He dumped the box on my lap and returned to his seat.

There wasn't much in it, I saw, just a Dell laptop and an iPad and several standard-looking notebooks.

"Now, if there's nothing else...."

"There is," Kate said, as she placed the photograph of the woman we now knew to be Erika Padgett in front of him. "What can you tell us about her?"

I was watching his eyes when he looked down at it. It wasn't much, but there was a slight twitch of his left eyelid. He was surprised.

He picked the photo up and shrugged. "It's Dr. Padgett. She's a vet. Why do you ask?"

"We think she was the last person to see Emily Johnston alive," Kate said. "Any idea where we might find her?"

He looked at his watch. I hadn't noticed it before. Now I did. It was a gold Breitling Bentley Chronograph, $26 thousand new. I knew. I owned one just like it. *How the hell does a security guard afford a watch like that?*

"It's almost four thirty," he said. "If you cut the crap, you might still have time to catch her. She works at the Jepson Animal Clinic on Taft Highway. Now," he said, rising to his feet. "If you'll excuse me, I have to see to my two people, make sure you didn't break anything." Again the icy smile.

"Oh, and please stop by again, but before you do... call and make an appointment."

I stood and tucked the box under my left arm. Then I adjusted my jacket and the holster to make sure my M&P9 was visible.

Lester and Henry were on their feet and on their way through the front door as we walked out of his office. Aviators, whichever one he was, was clutching his throat with both hands. Mirrors looked downright sheepish, obviously not pleased to have been laid low by a woman, especially one as lovely and deceptively feminine as Kate. I couldn't help but grin at him. What I got back was a cross between a growl and a meow.

I clapped him on the shoulder. "Cheer up. I've seen her take down better men than you."

"Screw you, you son of a bitch."

I nodded and walked down the steps to the car, nodding and smiling to myself. Life was good.

Chapter Twelve

The drive to the Jepson Animal Clinic took less than ten minutes, and we arrived in the parking lot in front of the low, one-story building at just after 4:45.

The reception area was a pleasant surprise: pristine, brightly decorated; it reminded me of one of those walk-in emergency medical clinics that's so popular these days. Two young ladies in brightly colored scrubs sat behind the desk, one of them on the landline, the other sorting paperwork. There wasn't an animal in the place—or should I say patient.

"Hello," Miss Paperwork said. "Would you like to sign in for me, please?" She was wearing a bright blue top with little colored fishes on it.

"Oh, I'm not a—I'm here to see Dr. Padgett."

"I'm afraid Dr. Padgett isn't in today. Can one of the other doctors help? Dr. Jepson is free."

"Yes, please. But before you bother him, maybe you can help us."

She looked at me skeptically, and then at Kate, who stepped forward, badge in hand.

"I'm Lieutenant Catherine Gazzara, Chattanooga Police. This is my colleague, Harry Starke. We're here on official business, so, if you wouldn't mind." She slipped the badge back onto her belt.

But the girl still looked doubtful. "Chattanooga? You're in the wrong city, aren't you?"

Damn. We should have stopped by and checked in with Danny.

"Kate. I need to make a quick call. Do you mind handling this for a moment?"

She didn't, so I stepped outside, already pulling my phone from my pocket and called Raymond "Danny" McDaniel.

"Hey, Danny," I said when he answered. "It's Harry Starke. Have you got a minute?"

Danny was the chief of police of Signal Mountain. I'd known him for years. In fact we'd worked the Chattanooga SWAT team together for a couple years early on in our careers, before he went to Vice and I went to Homicide. He was a friend, yeah, but common decency dictates you check in when you're in someone else's jurisdiction, and I hadn't.

"Wow. Long time no see, Harry. No hello? No how the hell are you?"

"Oh hell, Danny. You know how it is. I always did have a one-track mind."

"Sure. What can I do for you?"

"You heard about Emily Johnston, right?"

"I did. You're not on that, are you?"

"At Johnston's request, yeah, and it's the reason for my call. I've just come from Belle Edmondson where she was a student. I—that is we; I'm working with Kate Gazzara— have a lead that brought us into your patch. I needed to check in with you."

"Sure thing. How is Kate? Haven't seen her in a while either. You two still an item?"

"Er, no. But she's fine. Listen, I hate to ask, but can you come over to the Jepson place? I'd like to run a couple of things by you."

"The animal clinic? Sure. You there now?"

I said that I was.

"Okay. Give me ten."

I went back in just as Kate was beginning an interview with Dr. Jepson in a back room. Kate introduced me, and I sat down beside her, iPad in hand.

Jepson was about fifty-five, a small man of average build. His hair was prematurely gray and receding, and he wore a white lab coat that looked at least a size too big for him. His name—Henry Jepson, DVM PhD—was embroidered in red on the left breast pocket.

"You want to take this, Harry?" Kate asked.

I shook my head. "You go ahead. Danny'll be here in a few minutes."

She briefly explained to Jepson why we there, and then asked him about Erika Padgett.

"I haven't seen her since last Friday evening. She left when the clinic closed for the weekend, and she didn't show up for work this morning. I would have called her, but I've been quite busy...." He was silent for a moment. "It's not like her. I don't think she's missed a day in the five years she's been here."

"Would you mind giving her a call now?" Kate asked.

"Of course." He took a cell phone from his lab coat pocket and hit the speed dial. Even sitting across the room I could hear it go to voicemail.

"Erika. Please give me a call as soon as you get this. I'm worried about you." And he did look worried.

"So," Kate continued. "What can you tell me about her? I'm interested in her private life, away from the clinic."

"Nothing. Nothing at all. She works here five days a week, and she's on call, as are we all. I've never met her outside of the office. She's a bit of a loner. Very nice, of course, attractive, but she seems to prefer her own company."

"How about friends?"

"Again, I'm sorry, but I don't know of any. As I said, she seems to be a bit of a loner."

"How about boyfriends?" I asked.

He looked sharply at me. "Er... no. At least I don't think so."

Oh yeah you do.

"Dr. Jepson," I said. "You say she's worked for you for five years, yet in all that time you've learned nothing about her, about her life outside of your office. I find that a little... implausible?"

His face reddened. "Mr. Starke. I'm not sure I like...."

"Oh, I meant nothing by that, Doctor," I said, watching his eyes. "I wasn't suggesting that you were... *lying.*"

And there it was, that telltale twitch at the corner of his mouth. *What are you hiding, Doctor?*

I decided to let the sleeping dog lie, at least for now. "I wonder if you'd let us have her address," I said, changing the subject.

"Yes, of course." He almost leaped for the door. He returned a few seconds later with Padgett's personnel file and one of her business cards, her address and private phone number written on the back of it. I thumbed the number into my iPhone and hit send. Straight to voicemail.

Kate and I rose to our feet. I offered him my hand as I thanked him and said goodbye, and he took it, and then he shook hands with Kate, and showed us to the door. Danny was just pulling into the parking lot.

"He's hiding something," Kate said, watching Danny park. "I wonder what? I don't see him fooling around in the Sorbonne."

I nodded. "Did you catch the look I got when I asked about her boyfriends? You think he might be fooling around with her?"

"Now that's a thought."

"It sure as hell is."

We watched as Danny climbed out of his cruiser and strode toward us. When he was close enough, he stuck out his hand.

"Harry, you bastard. It's been years. You too, Katie. Why the hell haven't you been to see me?"

"That works both ways, Danny. How are things here on the mountain?"

"Quiet, of course. Just the way I like 'em. You wanna go get a coffee and a sandwich? Hey, I know. You want Mexican? El Metate's good, and it's just down the road."

"No," I said with conviction. "But a coffee would be good. "

"Mickey D's it is then. Follow me."

You have to understand Danny. He's a cop's cop. He's my age, with an affable, outgoing presence that belies his abilities. For almost ten years he led a Chattanooga PD SWAT team. Six feet tall, blond, tanned, slim, he's always immaculately dressed. He has his uniforms tailored in New York, and they fit him perfectly. He wears white shirts and blue ties. The antique Union cavalry Stetson, complete with crossed sabers, is an anomaly that suits both the authority of his station and his character. I always thought he was born 150 years too late.

We took a booth in the McDonald's on Taft Highway and got coffees all around. It had been quite a while since I'd last sampled the delights of "Mickey D's," and I had to admit it, they did serve good coffee.

"What the hell happened, Harry? *Emily?* My God. Johnston must be a mess."

I didn't answer right away. I shook my head. Tried to clear away the specter of Emily's broken corpse lying on Doc Sheddon's table.

"He *is* a mess, Danny, and so is the case. She was brutalized, sexually and physically. She went missing a week ago, last Saturday night, late, but she didn't die until sometime late Thursday or early Friday morning, and she wasn't dumped until late on Saturday, in the woods off Wicker Road."

"Damn. That's Israel Hands' jurisdiction. Good luck with that one."

"Oh he'll play ball. He has to. He has an election coming up."

"So you say. I wouldn't count on it. Who found her?"

"Some woman walking her dog. Danny, how well do you know Dr. Padgett?"

"I know of her. Good looking babe... whoops, sorry Kate. She is a looker, though. And good at her job. Large-animal doctor. Specializes in horses and cows."

"And Jepson?"

"Good vet. Bit of a lady's man, even though he's married. Came here from Florida back in the nineties. Runs a good shop, wealthy, likes a drink, lousy golfer, wife's a bit of a mouse. There's been some talk about his philandering, but, well, you know small-town gossip."

"How about the college, Danny?" Kate asked. "You ever hear of any, I dunno... anomalies? Drugs, sex, anything?"

He shook his head. "It's not like most universities. It's small, and *very* exclusive. Money alone won't get you in. You need status. Most of the students are daughters of billionaires, politicians, Middle Eastern princes and the like. You get a degree from Belle Edmondson, you're set for life."

I nodded. "Okay. Now the biggie. What do you know about a Captain Conrad Rösche, head of security at the college?"

He pursed his lips, leaned back, clasped his hands behind his neck, stared at me for a moment, his chin almost on his chest. Then he switched his gaze to Kate, then back to me.

"Oh shit, you don't think...? Goddamn it, I hope not. He's one crazy bastard, a chameleon. One minute he's an easy-going, country club type; the next he's a raving lunatic who would cut your throat if he thought he could get away with it. Two years ago, maybe a little less, he beat a man almost to death on the golf course over there." He pointed out the window. "I arrested him, but it was on private property and the guy wouldn't press charges. He was scared shitless, and I don't blame him."

"Yeah," I said. "That's about how I'd figured him. Anything else?"

"Oooh yeah. He likes to hurt women, too. I know of several. None of them will talk or file charges, though."

"How about his crew?" Kate asked. "We met a couple of them. They were not your average security guards."

"Good question. But I don't know anything about that. That mob of so-called officers he has over there...." He paused. "I dunno. What the hell he needs them for I have no idea. It's a college for women—girls. His men walk and drive around in twos, like they're on the streets of East LA. They wear body armor, for Christ's sake."

"They ever cause any trouble?" Kate asked.

"No. In fact you'd hardly know they were there."

"So if it's not the women they're protecting," she said, "what else could it be?"

Danny slowly shook his head. "Your guess is as good as mine. They're out of my jurisdiction, and they stay out, so I don't worry too much about them."

"Could it be drugs?"

He shrugged. "Again, you know as much as I do... but I'll bet they're up to something. Well, Rösche, anyway."

"Just one more thing," Kate said. "How about the chancellor? What do you know about her?"

At that he grinned widely. "Now you're talking. She's a class act, though I'm not sure she's all she makes out she is, and I have no real reason to say that. It's just that she... well, she doesn't strike me as being quite kosher. She comes off as... well, I don't know what they call it in England, but upper-class? Aristocratic? But I don't think she actually is. In fact, I have my doubts that she's even English. I've attended several functions where she's been present, and that accent ain't always what it should be. Oh, and when I said Doc Jepson is a bit of a ladies man—she was one of his ladies."

"Oh yeah?" I asked. "How do you know?"

"Harry, you're a member of the country club, right?"

I nodded.

"Me too." He grinned. "We have one here on the mountain, and you know how things work, right? Not just at functions, but any old time when members get together and take on a little more ballast than they should. They get tipsy, right? And when they get tipsy...."

"Yeah, Danny, I get it. So when she drinks, she plays, and Jepson was one of her playthings."

"That's about the size of it, but I think there's more to her than that. I think she plays for both teams. Don't know that for sure, just... well, little things, here and there. Maybe." He looked at his watch. "Sorry, guys. It's been great to see you both, but I need to get back to the office. But hey, if there's anything you need, back-up, me...." He looked at Kate. She smiled. "You name it and it's yours, okay?"

We stood, shook hands, and he left.

"There was a time...." Kate said thoughtfully, as she watched him go. "Oh forget it. He doesn't change, though, does he?"

"Nope." We watched him pull out of the parking lot, and then I glanced at my watch. "Emily's computer and iPad need to be dropped off at your computer lab," I said. "Will you take care of it?"

She nodded, and downed the last of her coffee. "I'll do it on my way home. I wish we could let Tim have it, but.... Maybe you could have him come to us, take a look at it in our lab."

"Yeah. I'll do that. Listen, are you busy this evening?"

"Not especially. Why?"

"You want to come around to my place?" I asked. "We have a lot to discuss, and we need to go through Emily's book. We also need to talk strategy. I'll have dinner for three delivered."

Her eyes narrowed, and she cocked her head to one side. "For three? I take it you're including Amanda."

"Well yes. Is that a problem?"

"For me, no. For her.... Harry, I get the impression when I'm around her that she'd rather I wasn't there."

"Really?"

"Of course you wouldn't have noticed. You're a man. So, maybe I should give it a miss tonight. How about we meet at your office in the morning, early, say about eight thirty?"

"Well... if you say so. I think you've got it wrong, though. Maybe I should talk to her."

"No, I haven't, and you'd better not. That would embarrass the both of us."

I shrugged. "Have it your way. I'll go through the book myself. I don't want to turn it over to Hands just yet. C'mon. Let's get out of here."

Chapter Thirteen

It was right around seven o'clock when I arrived home that evening. The rain had returned and the sky was already turning black. Lookout Mountain was invisible, and I could barely make out the lights on Thrasher Bridge.

I hit the garage door opener and rolled the Maxima inside next to Amanda's Lexus. Somehow I found even the sight of her car reassuring, calming.

She was in the kitchen, cooking something that smelled delightful. She was wearing a white sleeveless dress with a short, flared skirt: gorgeous. I took off my jacket and flung it onto a chair. The holster and M&P9 followed it. I walked into the kitchen, stepped behind her, slipped my arms around her waist, and nuzzled her ear.

"Stop it, Harry. You'll make me burn myself." Reluctantly, I let her go and turned away.

"Hey. I didn't tell you to leave. Here." She handed me a

glass of scotch, Laphroaig over a single cube of ice, and smiled. "I heard the garage door."

I closed my eyes, and savored the smooth, smoky palette of the Quarter Cask malt. There are some things in life that no amount of money can replace. Laphroaig was one of them; Amanda Cole was another.

"So," I said, "how was your day?"

"The usual. Work, research, and I've been talking to contractors about the house."

"Oh? How did that go?"

"It went well. It always does when you have the money to spend on what you want. I also heard from Stacey Breedlove, the realtor. You can close on Friday afternoon, if you want. Can you do that? The quicker you do, the quicker you can get the contactors in there."

"Damn. That was quick. Well... yes, okay. Give her a call and set up a time."

"Harry! For God's sake, quit ordering me around. I'm not your secretary."

"Oh. Sorry. Okay. I guess I'll do it, then." I put on my best 'little boy lost' face and waited. Nothing. "Ah hell, as if I don't have enough on my plate...."

"All right, all right, I'll do it. First thing in the morning. Early or late afternoon?"

"Late. The later the better."

"Harry," Amanda turned off the oven, and turned toward me. "Changing the subject, you remember I told you I'd been doing some research?"

I nodded.

"I have something for you. I've been doing a little digging through our archives. Emily is not the first girl to have disappeared from that school. She's not even the second. There have been two others. Emily makes three."

I stared at her, my mouth full of scotch, then I gulped it down and almost choked as the fiery liquid hit the back of my throat, "No shit," I said, coughing. *That ain't no way to drink good liquor, damn it.*

She nodded. "In both instances the disappearances were investigated by our two friends, Detectives Hart and McLeish. The first, Angela Young, disappeared back in 2011. She was the daughter of Georgia State Representative, Michael Young, from Buckhead, Atlanta. Twenty-one years old. The second, Marcy Grove, was a local girl, also twenty-one. She vanished in 2013. She was the daughter of a Dr. Henry and Mrs. Martha Grove of Lookout Mountain. They live on East Brow Road, not far from your new home. Both girls are still missing."

I laid down my glass. What she'd just told me put a whole new perspective on the case. Three girls don't just disappear from an exclusive college. But.... "Why didn't I hear about this?"

"Probably because it was hushed up. Bad for business. Bad for the school."

"Jeez, I wish I'd known that earlier today.... Why, I wonder, didn't anybody up there mention it?"

"As I said: bad for business."

I thought about it, picked up my glass, stared down at the whiskey, swirled it around, and then laid the glass down again.

"Okay," I said. "We need to talk to the parents, and to Heart and Sole."

"I already have. I followed up with both sets of parents this afternoon. They were surprised to hear from me, and pleased that someone was taking an interest again. Both said they hadn't heard anything from the sheriff's department in over a year. Representative Young was... angry. There's probably a better word for it, but that's what he was. Marcy Grove's mother, not so much. I think she's come to terms with the fact that her daughter's gone and has moved on, or she's been trying to. She sounded... sad, resigned."

There's no describing how I felt. I had no children, but I couldn't help but wonder what it must feel like to get the news. I heaved a sigh, shook my head, grabbed my glass, took a large swallow, and looked at Amanda. Her face was an alabaster bust, beautiful but pensive.

"Then I called Detective Hart," she said. "What a waste of time that was. 'The cases are still ongoing so I can't comment,' was what he said.

"I asked if he was actively working them, 'No comment.'

He's an ass. Look, I haven't even scratched the surface. We have our archives, but that's all. Can you spare Tim to do a little digging for me?"

"I'll spare him to do a lot of digging. Listen, I know you. I know that once you set your mind to something you get kinda reckless. That's not what I want."

I looked at her. She was smiling. "Oh, Harry. You do care."

"There's no need for sarcasm. Of course I care. Anyway, if you think I'm going to let you loose to run among the wolves up at Belle Edmondson, you can forget it. I'll do the field work; you get the exclusive, if there is one."

"Hah. So you say. Not going to happen, my big bulky friend. What qualifies you as an investigative journalist? Solving a murder is one thing; being able to build a story that will grab the public by the shorts is quite another. I'll do my own story, thank you."

"Amanda...."

The look on her face stopped me dead. It could have curdled milk. I just closed my eyes and shook my head. There was no point in arguing with her. I'd done it before and I'd lost every time.

"Fine," I said. "Here's how it's going to be. I'll assign Bob to work with you. No, you *do not argue*. He'll provide protection for you, and muscle when you need it." I shook my head. "Damn. I wish Kate was here. We need to go through Emily's stuff. I asked her, but she said no."

"Why was that?"

I was about to tell her the truth when I remembered what Kate had said about not telling her, so I didn't.

"She said she'd rather meet at the office in the morning." *Not exactly a lie, but what the hell.* She still had that look on her face, so I changed the subject. "Look, let's eat. Then you and I can take a look at it, but first, I need a shower and a change of clothes. You want to join me?"

"Hah. You should be so lucky," she said, and five minutes later I was. Life was good.

When we finally got to it the food, homemade broccoli and cheese casserole, was cold, but what the hell. She nuked it for sixty seconds and it, along with a bottle of 2013 Egon Müller Riesling, was delicious.

Jeez, I love this woman!

The meal was a quickie, and when we were done I dumped the two plates in the dishwasher, the casserole leftovers in the fridge, and refilled our glasses. Then I went to my office and made a half-dozen copies of Amanda's paperwork. Those I set aside for morning, and returned to the living room, where Amanda was seated on the sofa in front of the picture window looking out over the river. That surprised me, because she was seated in exactly the same spot where she'd almost lost her life less than six months earlier, when the ill-fated Mrs. Hartwell had opened fire with an AR15 from across the river. Neither of us felt comfortable there anymore, hence the pending move to Lookout Mountain.

"Hey, you all right?"

She looked up at me. "Yes. Why?"

"Nothing. You seem a little quiet. That's all."

She lowered her head and again stared out of the window. "I have a lot on my mind. I was trying to think it through; what my theme would be for the story, but there are too many threads.... I don't know."

"It will come," I said. "Play it by ear, for now. You'll see. Listen. I have something I need to look at. Emily Johnston's journal. At least, that's what I think it is. We found it in under a false bottom in her dresser drawer. Come to the table and take a look with me."

She rose to her feet. "How are you two getting along, working together again?"

I looked at her. The unasked question was in her eyes. I put my hands on her hips, pulled her close, kissed the tip of her nose, slid my arms around her waist, and kissed her gently.

"It's fine. Very professional. I told you: it's over. Has been for a long time."

"Yes, well, she's very beautiful, and you... well, you know."

"No, I don't know. Yes, she is, beautiful, but you, you are more than that... and... well, there's no one else, hasn't been since we broke up."

"Since she dumped you, you mean." She said it playfully, but I couldn't help but wonder.

"Okay, so she dumped me, but it's still true: there's no one but you. There never will be."

She put her arms around my neck and whispered in my ear, "Thank you."

She leaned back, put her hands to the back of my neck, and kissed me—it said all I needed to hear—and then she pushed me gently away.

"So let's look at it then."

I handed her a pair of latex gloves and pulled on a pair myself, and we sat down together at the dining room table.

We looked at the front first. The outside had only doodles on it. It reminded me of a large tattoo—the name, Emily, was cleverly incorporated into the design. I turned it over. The back cover was a little different from the front. It was a riot of colored patterns, at the center of which was a single word: Kalliste.

I set it back down on the table and opened it, flipped through the pages. Inside were a total of thirty heavy cartridge-paper leaves that might have been cut from a sketchbook. On the first was a photograph of Emily and two other girls, one of whom I recognized as Jessica Henderson. The other—I looked at the photos on my iPhone—appeared to be Autumn Leaf. The tag line below the photo proclaimed that it had been taken on Panama City Beach in 2015.

The rest of the pages, at least the next twenty or so, were more of the same: drawings—hand-drawn portraits of young women in various stages of undress—sketches, notes, doodles, and a few more photographs, all headshots of young women, some of them with Greek-sounding names attached. The doodles were mostly intricate designs with words woven into the swirls: Kalliste, again, and a half-dozen others. It was typical of the sort of thing school kids get up to when they're bored. Did any of it mean anything? God only knew. I certainly didn't.

"Any ideas?" I asked.

"I had one just like it. Well, not handmade, but you know what I mean."

I did, but I had feeling this journal was a little different. Hell, it had to be. She'd gone to great lengths to hide it, and that alone made it special.

"Any of these weird words mean anything to you?"

She shook her head, "Kalliste looks Greekish. The others... well that one might be Jessica. I'd say they're just doodles."

"Yes, but that one, Kalliste, is written several times; it must mean something, right?"

"I suppose...."

"I'll have Tim check it out tomorrow morning." I flipped through the pages. "Now here's something."

I was looking at the six pages at the back of the book. The first four pages were filled with lists. Each entry was preceded by a set of initials, the first of which was E. P., followed by a long list of dates and times.

There were more than sixty of them.

"What do you make of them?" I asked.

"Contacts probably. None of the dates are later than the day she disappeared, so maybe they're a record of some sort. Appointments, maybe?"

"Hmmm, maybe. Something else for Tim to look into. He's going to be a busy boy."

She put her hand to her mouth and yawned. I looked at my watch. It was just after eleven.

"Let's wrap this up for tonight. What's your work schedule like?"

"I have to be at the station by nine in the morning. Why?"

"I think maybe you should join us in my office tomorrow morning, early. Can you get someone to cover for you?"

She made a call and made the arrangements.

"So, let's have just one more little drink and then go to bed, yes?"

Sleep didn't come easily that night. I lay beside Amanda and listened to her breathing. Normally it would put me to sleep, but not that night.

I lay on my back, hands behind my head, and stared up into the dark reaches of the cathedral ceiling. The bogeymen were back: the tricks the mind plays when you stare up into the gloom. Inky shadows, vast gooey black shapes that undulated and morphed into fantastic creatures. They'd haunted me often when I was kid, when I'd scream for my mother. Just bad dreams, she'd tell me. The hell they were. Now they only came when my mind was in a whirl, when I was stressed.

I let my thoughts wander as I tried to assess the few facts and pieces of information I had. They were few indeed, but they churned in my mind and spawned a hundred questions without answers.

I last looked at the bedside clock at 1:33, dropped my head back onto the pillow, and closed my eyes. Only a second later, Amanda was waking me up. It was six thirty, and the bedroom was filled with the heavenly aroma of Kona coffee.

I sat up and grabbed the cup from her hand. She sat down beside me on the bed, her own cup cradled in both hands. She could have come straight from Rivendell. The tousled hair and the flimsy, pale blue chemise reminded me of the beautiful elf princess, Arwen.

"So." She looked at me over the rim of the cup. "You had a rough night."

"You noticed, huh?"

"Yes, I was awake half the night with you. You know you talk in your sleep, right?"

"Er... no! Did I say anything I shouldn't?"

"You told me you love me."

"You sure it was you I was talking to?"

"You ass, Harry Starke." She put down the cup. Took mine from my hand, put it down too, and climbed on top of me. And suddenly, I felt much better.

We showered, dressed, and I made breakfast... well, I put the bread into the toaster, and I made more coffee.

"So, what are your plans for today, after we get through at the office?" I asked, buttering a piece of burnt toast I should have tossed into the garbage. *Someone's been screwing around with that toaster.*

"I'm going to talk to my executive producer. I want to do an in-depth investigation of the disappearances of those two girls. Maybe I can get into places and minds that you can't."

"Hmmm. That might work. Do you think he'll go for it?"

"I think so. He's given me a pretty free hand in the past, and if anything comes of it... well, it's money in the bank for the company."

I thought about it for a minute, then said, "You're planning on going up there, right?"

"Well, yeah. How else am I going to interview people?"

"I don't like it. It could be dangerous. There are some really rough people working that property. We ran into some of them yesterday. It wasn't pretty."

"I'll take a cameraman with me when I go up there."

"Hmmm. Nope! I still don't like it. As I said last night, Bob goes with you."

"Oh, Harry. Don't be silly. I can look after myself. I'm a journalist. No one will bother me."

I've heard that before, and I don't buy it. Rösche and his guerrillas will eat you alive.

"I'm not going to argue with you. Bob goes with you. So what's your plan?"

"Damn it, Harry.... Okay, Bob goes too. I'll tell them I'm doing a local interest piece about the history of the place. It is, after all, one of the nation's historic places. That way, maybe I can get a look around the place, casually work in some questions about the missing girls, and Emily."

I downed the last of my coffee, checked the kitchen clock.

"It's ten minutes to eight. We need to go."

I got up, put my cup and plate into the sink, and together we headed out the door. We took both cars.

Chapter Fourteen

It was just after a quarter past eight and the sun was shining when I walked into the outer office. Kate had not yet arrived, but most of my staff had beaten me there. Only Tim was missing. The outer door opened again, and Amanda walked in, followed by Tim and Kate.

"Jacque." She looked up at me from her desk. "I need you, Bob, and Tim in the conference room. Grab some coffee and let's get to it."

"Good morning, everyone," I said when we were all seated. "I invited Amanda to join us because she's planning on doing an investigative story about Belle Edmondson College, and that's going to involve you, Bob. There are some nasty types up there. She's going to need protection. You're it. We'll talk about it later, okay?"

Bob grinned at Amanda. She glared at me, but she didn't object.

"First thing is, it now looks like we may be dealing with

three murders. Amanda has done some research into Belle Edmondson, and Emily is the third girl to go missing over the last five years. Here are copies of her research."

I handed a copy to each of them.

"Kate," I said. "What do you think?"

"I think I need time to go through this before we jump to conclusions."

I nodded. "That we do. Tim, that's what I want you to do first. I want to know everything there is to know about Angela Young and Marcy Grove—their friends, parents, interests, habits, and especially places they visited on nights and weekends, the works. I also want you to check into the investigations conducted by the sheriff's department. And I want background checks done on Detectives Hart and McLeish. Can you do that?"

He just grinned at me.

Stupid question. If he can't, nobody can.

"I've also listed several more people I need you to check on, including Emily's friends—you already have the list—and don't forget the two males, Robin Lucas and Nicholas Kyper. Finally—and these are important—Captain Conrad Rösche, Chancellor Victoria Mason-Jones, and Dr. Henry Jepson, veterinary surgeon. I also want you to pull Emily's phone records for the past twelve months...."

I thought for a second. "And see if you can locate her phone —Padgett's too. I have a feeling that's a lost cause, but we have to try. Okay, that's it for now, but I'm sure there'll be more. Get to work on those background checks as soon as you can. I want it all. I want to know what they ate for breakfast this morning, which side of the bed they sleep on, how often they take a leak, everything."

I paused, trying to get my head around it all, then continued. "Amanda spoke to the parents of the two missing girls yesterday. So, Bob, I want you to follow up on that. You'll need to interview them in person. But before you begin... well, we'll talk about that in a minute."

I turned again to Tim. "Hands please, Tim." I waited while he donned a pair of latex gloves. "We went through Emily's journal last night," I said as I handed it to him. "As you'll see, there are a lot of weird-looking numbers listed at the back of the book. I need you to figure out what they are. I think they're coded phone numbers; you'll figure that out. There's a lot of other strange stuff in it that needs clarification, including a large number of references to something, or someone, called Kalliste. We need to know who or what it is. Can you run it for me, now, please?"

He nodded and left to go to his oracle. He was back less than five minutes later, took his seat, and placed an open laptop on the table in front him.

"There are several references to Kalliste. She has her origins in Greek mythology. She's a sea nymph, a daughter of Triton, the sea god, and the island of Kalliste, modern-day Santorini, in the Aegean Sea, was named after her. Triton, so the story goes, presented her to the Argonaut Euphemos as a clod of earth. When the clod was washed overboard during the voyage it became the island of Kalliste. That, I suspect, is not what you're looking for. The name is indeed Greek. It means 'the most beautiful.' Now, here's the interesting part: I found a website named Kalliste. It wasn't easy. It's well-hidden which, for a commercial site, is more than unusual. Here. Take a look." He spun the laptop so that it faced me.

At first I thought I was looking at a website belonging to a high-end clothing store. The landing page showed a number of full-length images of what I thought were sophisticated models showing off expensive clothing.

"So?" I asked, looking at him quizzically.

"Click on one of the models."

I clicked on who was wearing a floor-length, white, sleeveless gown and was taken to another page featuring the same model wearing a sophisticated business suit. I clicked again and was taken to another page, and then another, six in all. With each change of page came a change of clothing, each new outfit a little more revealing than the previous one. On the final page she was wearing a bikini. The pose was classic: right knee cocked inward, hands on hips, head lowered.

I looked at him, "So? It's a high-end store."

"It's high end all right. Each girl has a similar set of pages, a kind of mini-website all her own. They can blog, add photos, and send messages. Now, click on the little gold disc in the upper right corner of the last page."

It was small. So small I hadn't noticed it. It was a tiny gold disc with a stylized figure of a woman on it. It looked like a goddess of some sort. I clicked. The page dissolved slowly and gave way to a video, one of those short, trailer-type movies. It featured the woman in the images. The bikini had been replaced by a pale blue negligee. She lying on her stomach on a large, expensively covered bed. Facing the camera, she was propped up on her elbows, her hands clasped together in front of her.

"Hello," she said. Her voice was low, husky. "My name is Hestia, virgin goddess of the hearth, home, and chastity; daughter of Rhea and Cronus and... mistress of the art of...." At that point, she lowered her chin and looked up at the camera through half-closed eyes. She said no more, but there was no mistaking her message. "Ask for me by name. Ladies only, please. Thank you."

"Wow," I said, leaning back in my chair, staring at the now-frozen image on the screen. "What is that about, do you think?"

"It's a lesbian dating site," Jacque said. "Either that, or she's a hooker catering to women."

I clicked the "Home" button and was taken back to the landing page. There were several pages featuring perhaps a couple of dozen women in all. I clicked on another one and was again presented with several pages of the model in various stages of dress, all tasteful, all sophisticated. I picked another, navigated through to the last page, and clicked the gold disc. This one called herself Artemis, and she claimed to be the virgin goddess of the hunt, daughter of Zeus and

Leto, and twin sister of Apollo. She was beautiful. Her message was the same as Hestia's.

"So how do we contact her?" I asked.

"At the bottom left corner," Tim said. "There's a tiny green button. It's not labeled, but it will take you to a contact form."

I spotted the button, clicked it, and was taken to a six-line form with a comment box. I looked at Tim. He shrugged.

"You want me to do it?" he asked.

I swung the laptop around to face him.

"Go ahead."

"Who shall I be?"

"Oh for Christ's sake, Tim. Make something up."

"Oh, I don't think so. You don't think they won't check? If it was me running this thing, I'd do a background check like none you can imagine."

"Here," Jacque said. "Let me do it. They can check all they want. I am what I am. They'll get all the right answers."

The form asked for first and last name, phone number, address, e-mail, age, and gender.

"No. Wait, Jacque," I said. "A background check on you would bring up your employment. We don't want that. Tim. We need to use one of the aliases. Then if they run a check, it will come back clean. And you," I said to Jacque, "I'm not sure you should do this."

"And why not? I have you and the rest of the crew to protect me, do I not?"

I nodded, reluctantly, and looked at Bob. He winked.

"Do it."

She filled in the details Tim provided, including the number of a throwaway cell phone, and then in the comment box wrote, "I would like to contact Artemis." She looked at me, then Bob, then hit send. She was immediately rewarded with a statement that read, "Your request has been received. Thank you, Jennifer. Artemis will contact you within forty-eight hours."

"Here... Jennifer?" I said. "Let me have it." She turned the laptop toward me and I began flipping through the landing pages. Four pages in, I spotted her. "Oh shit. Here we go." I turned the computer to face Kate.

"Oh. My. God. It's *Emily*!"

It certainly was.

I clicked the image and was taken to her landing page. She was standing, facing the camera, with her left hand on her hip, her right hanging loosely by her side; her feet slightly apart. She wore a white, form-fitting jersey wool dress. By page seven she was sitting facing a mirror in only a white chemise. I clicked on the button to start the video. She turned her head to face the camera. The message was exactly the same as before, word-for-word, but her name was Adrestia, goddess of the equilibrium between good and evil, daughter of Ares and Aphrodite. *Jeez.*

"Jacque. Do your stuff, please."

She filled in the form, hit send and was again rewarded with a thank you and a promise of contact within forty-eight hours. Somehow, I didn't think that was going to happen.

"Jacque. If you get a response, how will you handle it?"

"I'll try to get myself a date. I can do it. I can talk the talk. I've been gay all my life."

"Okay. That's good. If it's a call to the burner, which I'm sure it will be, take notes. We need every word. Better yet, Tim, set her up with Google Voice and then she can record the damned call. Yes?"

"A better option would be Call Recorder Pro. I'll set her up with that one."

"Good. Jacque, if money is involved, pay whatever they ask. Tim, she'll need a credit card to go with the alias."

"You got it. It's already part of the package."

"Okay, good. Jacque, Kalliste is your baby. Work with Tim and see what you can find. Make a date if you can, but *do not* go in alone. You can use Heather as backup. Understood?"

"Yes, sir, and thank you."

Thank me? What for? And then I realized that this was the

first time in the almost ten years she'd worked for me that I'd let her be part of an investigation.

"You're welcome, Jacque, but for God's sake be careful."

Jacque's my personal assistant, but more than that, I like the kid. She has attitude, and can cut you down to size in just a couple words, but people always underestimate her. Including me. I was already worried.

I nodded at her, and then I turned to Bob.

"Okay, Bob, I want you to work with Amanda. You'll help her with her investigation in any way she might need, and in any way you think necessary. The two of you should make a good team."

He grinned at me, then at Amanda. She was still glaring at me.

"So, the first thing you do is spend some time together planning what you need to do; you can use my office. Bob, you are her protection, and you'll provide muscle if and when she needs it. And you might as well know now: they have a security team up there, and they ain't your regular rent-a-cops. They're tough, and their boss, Conrad Rösche, is even tougher. Danny McDaniel says he's crazy. I'm holding you personally responsible for her safety. She goes nowhere near that school, or anywhere else, on her own. You got that Bob, Amanda?"

"You got it, boss."

"Harry—"

"No. It's my way or no way. I mean it, Amanda."

"Oh for God's sake." She was exasperated, but I knew she would do as she was asked, though somewhat truculently.

She gathered her things, turned to Bob and said, "Okay, Iron Man. Let's go." And together they left the room to go to my office. Bob grinned at me as he headed out the door.

"I want regular updates," I told him, "and don't let her out of your sight."

"As if. I love her almost as much as you do," he said as he closed the door behind him.

I winced. The room was full of people, including Kate. Time to go. "Tim," I said, "I'll leave you to it. I'll check in with you later.

"Kate, I think the first thing we need to do is talk to Erika Padgett. Have you tried calling her?"

"Twice," Kate said. "Last night and then again this morning, but she's not answering. The calls are going straight to voicemail. Hey. You were a bit hard on Amanda, don't you think?"

"Maybe. Let's go."

Untitled

Chapter15

I knew where she lived, more or less, but I punched Erika Padgett's address into the car's GPS system anyway. We were maybe fifteen minutes away, depending on traffic. Which turned out to be heavy. It took us almost thirty minutes. The address was an end-unit condo that backed up against the river.

I pulled into the driveway and we sat for a moment, getting our bearings. Heritage Landing is a gated community of high-end dwellings. I say high end. You could probably find something really nice for around $350,000. The one we found ourselves outside, however, was probably double that.

Kate thumbed the bell, and we waited. She thumbed it again, and we waited some more. Nothing.

"Doesn't look like she's home." I walked to the garage, stood on tiptoe, and looked in through the window. The white Mercedes was inside. I walked back to the front door.

"Let's take a look around back," I said, and Kate followed as I stepped carefully around the side of the building.

But the windows all had blinds, even the sliding glass patio door.

"What do you think?" I asked. "Want to call her again?"

She did. No answer. "Let's see if the next-door neighbor's at home," she said.

She was. A woman in her mid-thirties, she was helpful enough, and friendly, especially when Kate showed her ID, but could tell us only that she hadn't seen Erika leave for work that morning, which was unusual.

"How unusual? Kate asked.

"It never happens. She's always working. She's a vet, you know."

"When was the last time you saw her?"

"Last night. She came home from work about six thirty, and left again about an hour later."

"Did she drive, or did someone pick her up?"

"Oh, she drove. She doesn't have many visitors."

"Did you see her come back?"

"No, but I know when she came home. I always know when she comes home. I have a dog, Harris, he's a Jack Russell.

Sleeps on the back of the couch so that he can look out of the window. He sees and hears everything, and barks. He woke me up at eleven fifty-five. Then I heard the garage door open and close. They adjoin. They're so *noisy*."

"Well, thank, you... Mrs.?" Kate asked.

"Collins. Lindsey Collins, and it's miss," she said, casting a somewhat coy, sideways glance at me.

"Thank you, Miss Collins," Kate said. "We'll take another look around. Here's my card. If you can think of anything that might be helpful, please give me a call."

We returned to the front door and Kate thumbed the bell again, and we waited. Nothing.

"I don't like it," I said. "The car's here. We know she came home last night. She's not answering her phone. I think there's cause for concern, don't you?"

"You're not suggesting we break in, are you?"

"Yep! That's exactly what I'm suggesting," I said, trying the doorknob. It was locked.

I looked at her.

She shrugged and rolled her eyes. "Go for it."

I took out my picks, and in less than a minute I had the door open. There was an awful smell about the place, and it was quiet. So quiet I could hear a clock ticking somewhere. Kate followed me into the small foyer and then into the living room—both of which were empty. Everything appeared to be in its place, all clean and tidy. The same with the bath-room: spic and span. Next, a small bedroom: nothing. Finally, we were at the half-open door of what had to be the master bedroom. Again, all looked neat and tidy. Except... there was a pile of clothes on the bed, which didn't look as if it had been slept in. Some were neatly folded, some were still on racks. And the stench was stronger. I walked into the room, past the adjoining bathroom door, and then around the foot of the bed.

"Oh shit!"

"What?" Kate pushed me aside to look.

The two folding closet doors were wide open. The woman was naked, suspended by her neck from the rail inside. Her legs were spread, stretched straight out. Her hands were resting in her lap. Her bottom was barely off the floor. There was a large blue dildo lying on the carpet between her legs. And... she'd lost control of her bowels when she died, it looked like, which accounted for the terrible stink.

We both backed carefully out of the room and out onto the front porch.

"Call it in, now," I said.

She did. And then she called Doc Sheddon.

A nearby cruiser was the first to arrive, followed less than a minute later by another. Kate had the two officers secure the scene and start a visitor log. Detective Sergeant Lonnie Guest arrived a few minutes later. At first I didn't even recognize him. He must have lost at least a hundred pounds since I'd last seen him.

"Hey LT. Hiya, Harry. Long time no see. Whadda we have?"

"Lonnie," Kate said. "I'm off the clock, so officially this is yours, but that doesn't mean I'm out. You hear? Do you understand what I'm saying?"

"Yeah. I understand: it's mine, but it's yours, right?" he said with a grin.

"You got it brother. We've got what looks like an accidental death, but I want a CSI team down here ASAP, so get that organized."

"But, Kate, if it's accidental...."

"I said it *looks* like it was accidental. Get the team."

He looked puzzled, but nodded and made the call.

"Now we wait," she said to me. Then: "Are you okay?"

"Hell no I'm not okay," I replied. "When is finding a body ever okay?" I shook my head, turned to Lonnie and said, "And what the hell happened to you? You look like a damned stick insect."

He grinned at me. "Didn't Kate tell you? I had a lap band put in. I lost eighty-eight pounds in six months."

"You got to be kidding me," I said. "How the hell did you manage that?"

"Oh give it up, Harry," Kate grabbed my arm. "Here's the ME."

Sheddon was indeed just easing himself out of his black SUV. "Hey, Kate, Harry, Lonnie. Wow. Lookin' good my man."

Lonnie grinned at him.

"So what do we have? I thought you two were working the Johnston case."

"The Johnston case?"

"Forget it, Lonnie," Kate said, but I cringed nonetheless.

"You didn't hear that," she said. "You understand? I'll explain later."

He looked perplexed, but clamped his mouth shut. *Smart man, Lonnie. A lot smarter than I always gave him credit for.*

"What we have," Kate said, "is what appears to be an accident."

"An accident? If that's what it is, why am I here? Jeez, Kate, I don't get much time off."

"I said it *appears* to be an accident."

"Ah. Let's suit up and go take a look, then. There's gear enough for all in the back of my car."

Five minutes later, dressed from head to toe in Tyvek and wearing latex gloves, the four of us stood together in a semi-circle around the remains of Erika Padgett.

"Whew. She's a bit ripe," Sheddon said.

"Autoerotic asphyxiation?" Lonnie asked.

Sheddon shook his head, stared down at her. "I don't think so. Someone has gone to a great deal of trouble to set it up to look like it, but.... See? Look here. The cord used to strangle —or, hang her, is trending upward, but the ligature mark is lower, and almost perfectly horizontal around the neck, and it ends here... and here." He pointed. "The knot is at the right side, at the back of her ear, as you can see, but there's no bruise. Had she self-inflicted, the ligature marks would be angled from under the chin upward toward the ear, and the knot would have dug into the soft flesh here. Nope. This is a homicide. She was strangled, probably with the cord, and then suspended. Oh, and whoever did it was maybe a little taller than her, because the ligature marks are horizontal."

He leaned in close, squinted through his glasses, and touched the corner of her mouth with the tip of his latex-gloved finger.

"She was gagged, too, probably with duct tape. There's adhesive residue around her mouth."

"PMI?" I asked.

"Not long. Six to nine hours, I should think. Rigor is not too far along. I can't get to the rectum to take her temperature, but...." He slid a hand under her armpit. "Yes, she's still warm, and lividity is not yet complete. So, between midnight and three in the morning. I'll be able to give you a more accurate time when I've done the post mortem."

"That tallies with what the neighbor said. We know she was alive just before midnight, because she heard her."

Sheddon nodded thoughtfully, but he didn't answer. He just went on about his business, clucking like an old duck.

"Kate," I took her by the arm and led her out into the kitchen. "We need to look around before CSI takes over." Then I had a thought.

I went back into the bedroom, "Doc. You say there's adhesive around her mouth. What about prints? If she was manhandled into position, we might get lucky."

"Fingerprints on her flesh? It's possible, though highly improbable." He looked down at her. "We can't do it here. They'll need a tent, and there's no room. Hmmm. If we're going to do it, we need to move quickly. Any prints there might be will be gone within twenty-four hours. We can't mess with her hands and feet. I'll have to bag those, and the bags will have to stay on throughout the process. I'll have the techs process the scene and the body and we'll whiz her away to the lab. In the meantime, Kate, I suggest you get Willis organized. He's the best latent-print man I know. Have him meet us at the lab in, say, an hour. Now, get out of my way and let me get on with it."

Kate pulled out her phone. I said to Sheddon, "Doc, I need to take a quick look around the room and the rest of the house before you turn the techs loose. I'll stay out of your way, okay?"

He nodded, absently, and turned back to the body.

"Lonnie: keep everyone out until we get through, please. Let's do this."

Kate finished her call quickly, and then we got to work. We touched nothing we didn't have to. I opened the dresser drawers and carefully lifted items of clothing to see what might be hidden beneath. What few items there were on the dresser and nightstands and on the vanity in the bathroom I photographed with my iPhone. The medicine cabinet was almost bare, just a few vitamins and one prescription container of Belsomra, a sleep med. Only one thing stood out: there was an almost full cup of hot chocolate—now cold—and a Kindle on the nightstand beside the bed.

Okay, I thought. *I'm going to get naked, strangle myself to achieve an orgasm, so I need hot chocolate and a book? I don't think so, but what the hell do I know? Hello... what's this?*

"Kate. Look at this."

Under the Kindle, which almost completely covered it, I could see what appeared to be a slim black leather book. It was either a journal or an appointment book. I photographed the Kindle, and then lifted it carefully, by its edges, and placed it on the bed. I picked up the book and opened it. It was one of those weekly planners, and there were literally hundreds of dates and appointments noted in it. I photographed it, placed it in a paper evidence bag, had Kate sign the bag, and then set it aside: it was going with us back to the police department. The Kindle was password-protected, so that too would have to wait. I bagged it and set it aside.

"Kate," I said, as we re-entered the living room. "I don't see a computer, iPad, or her phone."

I took out my own phone and punched in the number Dr. Jepson had given us. I held it to my ear; it was ringing. I walked around the apartment, listening. Nothing. It rang four times, and then the call went to voicemail.

"Find anything?" Doc Sheldon leaned his back against the doorjamb.

I shut the phone down and pocketed it. "Just a datebook, and a cup of hot chocolate by the bed. Nothing else."

"Well I found these in her hair." He held up a small paper evidence bag.

"What are they?" Kate asked.

"Hairs. Small, white, non-human, I think, similar to those we found on Emily. If so, we have a physical connection."

"When will you know?"

"A couple of days, or so.... Okay," he said after a short pause. "I'm done here. Can I let the boys in? We need to get her photographed and out of here if we're going to try for prints."

"Yes, I think we're done, too," Kate said. "Harry?"

"Yep. What time is it? I need a beer."

"I couldn't eat a thing, but there's the Brewhaus on Frazier. It's close."

"That's fine. I couldn't eat either. Let's go get a quick beer and then head on up to the school and talk to Her Majesty."

"Okay. I'll call and let her know we're coming."

"The hell you will. I want to catch her with her pants down."

"Not literally, I hope."

I grinned at her. "Doc, we'll see you later. Kate, you drive. I want to talk to Willis, let him know what we need."

The Brewhaus on Frazier is a popular spot on the North side, a German-American bar-cum-restaurant that specializes in bratwurst and schnitzel; the beer's good too. The only problem is the lack of parking, but we arrived just before eleven, right at opening time, so I was reasonably sure we wouldn't have to wait.

Kate went inside to grab a table and hopefully order drinks while I sat in the car and made a couple of calls, the most important of which was to Mike Willis, head of CSI operations in Chattanooga.

Willis is a strange little man, very strange, but there's no one I'd rather have working a crime scene for me, because the man is a genius. He's been in charge of his department for as long as I can remember, long before I became a cop more than nineteen years ago. He kind of reminds me of the White Rabbit in Wonderland: he's always in a hurry.

"Hey, Harry, my man. How the hell are yah?" The greeting was typical of him, and the tone genuine.

"I'm good, Mike. You?"

"Yeah, yeah, good, but busy. What can I do for you?"

"They're taking a body into Doc Sheddon's dead end. She's naked, and she's been abused, tied up, tortured. We need her body checked for prints. Can you do it?"

"How long has she been dead?"

"The doc says six to nine hours."

"Okay. The window of opportunity is closing, so I'll get right on it. They haven't handled the body, have they?"

"No more than necessary. They cut her down and lifted her onto the gurney. Draped her with a cloth. No plastic."

"I'll do what I can, Harry. No promises. Talk to you later."

Chapter Fifteen

ifteen minutes and one beer each later, we were back in the car and heading north on Cherokee Boulevard towards Signal Mountain Road.

"Okay, Kate," I said as I swung the car around one tight bend after another. "I didn't take to Jones. But now I'm really wondering what she's hiding. How could she not tell us about those two other missing girls?" It wasn't a question I expected an answer to, and I didn't get one. "And now we have another dead body, and it too is connected to the college. Loosely I admit, but... well, that's *four*. It can't be a coincidence."

"There's also the Kallisty connection. What do you make of that?"

"Right now I'm not even thinking about it, and it's Kalliste, not Kallisty. We do need to dig into it, but first I want to know what the hell Jones is up to."

"Okay, Kalli*ste*. What the hell does it matter? I want to

know who the hell is running it, because if our girl is a part of it, and we know she is, then it's probably connected to her death. There's some really bad people cruising dating websites like that one. And speaking of cruising, I can't believe you let Jacque make those calls. She's a clerk, not a cop."

"I wouldn't let her hear you call her a clerk if I were you. She's very sensitive about her job description. Anyway, she can handle herself. I know. I taught her. Look, let's find out what Jones is up to, and then we'll take a look at the website, okay?"

She nodded. I looked sideways at her as I slung the car around the final tight bend, past Balmoral Drive, and on up the rise into the town of Signal Mountain. She looked stoically back at me, but eventually nodded. I smiled. It was good to be working with her again. We'd had a long and enjoyable partnership together, until... well. Until I screwed it up.

We drove through the college gates and on up the drive to the administration building.

There was no room to park out front, so I took a spot in an open area just to the right. I had barely stopped rolling when one of the security cruisers drove up alongside.

They must have damned cameras everywhere, I thought.

We put on our visitor badges and got out of the car; Mirrors and Aviators did too. I had yet to figure out which one was Lester and which was Henry, but it didn't really matter. I wasn't planning to get to know them socially.

"Back again, huh?" Mirrors asked.

I was already headed for the steps. "Duh."

"I asked you a question, asshole."

I hesitated, and was about to turn, but Kate grabbed my arm and urged me on up the steps.

"We'll be waitin' for you," I heard Aviators shout, and I grinned.

"We need to see Ms. Mason-Jones," Kate told the clerk at the desk.

"Do you have an appointment?"

Kate flashed her badge.

"Oh, I see. Well, if you'll wait here for a moment, I'll see if she can see you."

She came out from behind the desk and started down the corridor towards the chancellor's office. Kate followed her; I followed Kate.

The clerk realized we were on her heels, turned, seemed about to say something, changed her mind, shook her head and continued walking. She pushed open the door to Jones' outer office and walked in; we followed. She continued on to Jones' office door, knocked, waited, then opened the door and walked inside. We followed.

"I'm sorry, Chancellor. These people insisted on seeing you. I asked them to wait, but...."

"It's all right, Mandy. I'll take care of it. Thank you." Oh, she looked pissed.

"Lieutenant Gazzara, Mr. Starke. In the future, I'd appreciate it if you'd make an appointment instead of barging in unannounced. Now. Please be quick. What can I do for you?"

No sit down? Screw you, lady.

I sat down uninvited. Kate also sat. She took the digital recorder from her pocket, turned it on, and set it down on the desk.

"Ms. Mason-Jones," Kate looked her in the eye. "When we were here the other day, you didn't mention that two other girls from the college had gone missing. Why not?"

She leaned forward, placed her elbows on her desk, and clasped her hands together. "I didn't think it was relevant. And besides, this is a very exclusive facility and I can't afford to have any bad publicity."

"Not relevant." Kate looked at her as if she thought the woman was stupid. "One of your students is brutally murdered, and you didn't think that two more missing girls, probably also murdered, was relevant. What *goddamn planet did you come from*, lady?"

Wow, Kate. You go girl.

I could tell that Mason-Jones was stunned, as Kate had intended she be.

"I don't like your—"

"I don't give two flying—I don't care what you like. We now have at least one, probably three dead girls, and you don't seem to give a shit. Tell me, when did you last follow up on the investigation of the missing girls?"

"I.... It's been a while," she said quietly.

Kate nodded. "Detectives Hart and McLeish, correct?"

"That's correct."

"When did you last talk to either of them?"

She shrugged. "As I said, it's been a while."

"A while? A month? Two? A year? How long?"

She didn't answer. She just stared stoically at Kate.

"I thought so. It's been so long you can't remember. You know what I think?"

Mason-Jones didn't answer.

"I think you had it covered up," Kate said. "I think those two county buffoons are in your pocket, and probably Hands too."

I couldn't help but grin at that one. Hands in your pocket. Classic.

"Well, no more. I am now senior investigating officer on the murder of Dr. Erika Padgett. Her body was found within the Chattanooga city limits and, as they all seem to be connected, you can bet your hoity-toity ass I'll be looking hard at the other three cases, too, and at Belle

Edmondson college. Now, is there anything you want to tell me?"

"Erika has been murdered?" She said it quietly, then seemed to realize what it was she was being told, and her eyes widened, and her mouth dropped open. Whether or not it was a genuine reaction, I couldn't tell. The woman was good, very good.

"Oh my God," Jones said, her hand to her mouth. "When... I was only talking to her on Friday. She's dead?"

I reached into my pocket, took out my iPhone, and made like I was checking a text. I pulled up Emily's phone number, hit send, and listened to see if it rang anywhere in Jones' office. It rang four times and then went to voicemail. I tried Erika's number. It also rang four times before going to voicemail. They weren't in the office, unless they'd been switched to silent mode. I hadn't really expected anything, but it was worth a try.

"Tell me about the two girls," Kate said.

It didn't work. Jones blinked rapidly a couple of time, took a deep breath, and shrugged, just a slight movement of her shoulders.

"I didn't know them. Oh, I'd met them both, of course, but only in passing. I had no reason to. Their grades were good. They were diligent in their studies. No complaints from their professors. They were... well, not outstanding, but decent."

"Do you remember when they went missing?"

"Of course. How could I forget?"

"Tell me."

"Tell you what? I wasn't here. Well, I was, but it was all handled by Edna Morgan. They were reported missing to her, and through her to me. A report was made to the sheriff's department. Those two detectives conducted interviews with the girls' friends, searched their rooms, and then they left, presumably to look for them."

"And you've heard nothing from them in more than a year, and you didn't bother to follow up with them, check on the status of the investigation? I'm not sure I understand your thinking, Ms. Mason-Jones. Two young women disappear from your school and you act like it's no big deal. Do you not have a responsibility to their parents to at least try to find out what happened to them?"

"What was I supposed to do? We called the police. We reported them missing. I don't see what else I could have done."

Kate nodded, stared at her, eyes narrowed. "Let's talk about Dr. Padgett. Where were you last night between midnight and three o'clock this morning?"

"Oh you can't be serious. I'm a suspect? That's ridiculous."

"Where were you, Ms. Mason-Jones?"

There was an almost imperceptible pause. "I was home, of course. Where else would I be at that time of night?"

Did she hesitate?

"Can anyone corroborate that?"

"Well, no. Of course not. I live alone."

"So what did you do while you were at home, alone?" There was an edge to Kate's voice.

"I ate dinner, watched a little TV, Fox News, and then I went to bed."

"What time would that have been?"

"I don't know. Around ten-thirty, I suppose."

Kate stared hard at her, then made a note in her iPad, switching her gaze back and forth from Jones to the tablet as she did so. It was quite an act, and it was having an effect.

"Look," Jones said. "I can't prove it, but I was home all evening. I made several phone calls to friends. I can give you a list...."

"What time was the last call you made?" Kate asked.

I sat back in my chair and watched the chancellor squirm. She was having trouble maintaining eye contact, and it was easy to see that she was trying hard, but you have to know Kate to understand what was going on. Kate was testing her. I'd seen her do it many times before. She was unbeatable in a staring contest, and could spot a lie like no one I'd ever known.

"I don't know, late. Well, after ten. I told you, I went to bed early."

Kate nodded, dropped her eyes to the tablet, and resumed the tapping.

"Okay," Jones said. She almost leapt to her feet. "I don't have time for this foolishness. I have appointments, so I must ask you to leave, now."

We rose to our feet. Kate had the tablet on the palm of her left hand and continued tapping as she turned and walked out of the office. I grinned at Jones, thanked her, said good-bye, and then followed Kate out into the corridor.

"Let me see those notes," I said as I caught up with her, and grabbed the pad out of her hand. I laughed as I looked at the jumble of letters. "I knew what you were up to."

"I'm sure you did, but the question is, did she?" She paused. "Give me a minute." She left me holding the pad and returned to Jones' office. She was gone for only a few minutes before she returned with a wide smile on her face.

"Just doing my Colombo thing," she said, grabbing the iPad out of my hand. "I told her I'd need to talk to her again. She didn't look very pleased. Can't imagine why." She smirked.

"So what do you think?" she asked as we got back into the car. "Is she a suspect?"

"Of course she is. Everyone is, plus, she's rattled. She says she has no alibi, but did you catch that hesitation when you asked her where she was last night?"

"Yes, but I don't think it meant anything. She was just getting her ducks in a row."

"Maybe, maybe not. She didn't mention the two missing girls when we questioned her previously. Why not? It's not natural. Anyone with even a modicum of empathy's reaction would be, 'Oh no. Not another,' but she didn't even look bothered that Emily was missing. 'Utterly devastated,' my ass. And that accent. But all that could just have been out of arrogance—it's all just a little bit beneath her and her station in life—or she just doesn't care. I *was* bothered by that performance when you told her about Padgett. It was an act. I'm sure of it."

"What about her cell phone?"

"What about it?"

"Well we have her number, so Tim can track her, right?"

"He can, and I'll have him do it, but unless it actually places her at the crime scene, it won't do us a whole lot of good. And even if it does, it would be circumstantial. Tracking her phone can only tell us where the phone was, not her, but you knew that."

She nodded and sighed. "True, but we have little else to go on, and you never know, we might just get lucky."

They were waiting for us when we exited the building, leaning against the cruiser: sunglasses on, arms folded, legs crossed at the ankles.

Talk about the Dukes of Hazard. Cletus Hogg would have been proud of them. They must have been practicing that pose.

Neither said a word as Kate and I separated and walked to our respective sides of the Maxima, but they followed us all the way with their eyes, hidden behind their dark glasses. No smiles: mouths clamped shut, lips compressed.

I closed the car door, punched the starter, reversed, put the car in gear, hit the gas, and fishtailed out of the lot. I watched in the rearview mirror as they jumped into the cruiser and gave chase. They followed us as far the gate.

"What now?" Kate asked.

"Damned if I know. I think we need to go back to the office and see if I can make some sense of what little we have. Maybe Tim will have something for us. You up for that?"

"Sure. We have plenty of time."

Chapter Sixteen

The office was quiet. Jacque was the only one at her desk. Bob and the rest of the crew were nowhere to be seen.

"Any messages?" I asked. Jacque shook her head. "Nothing from Bob?" Again, she shook her head.

"Okay. This place reminds me of Doc Sheddon's morgue. Where is everyone?"

"Tim is in back doing whatever it is he does. Bob has gone off somewhere with Amanda. Heather is—"

"Okay, okay. I get it. Give Tim a buzz please, and have him join us in my office."

I went to the break room to make coffee. *Damn. No dark roast.*

"Hey, Jacque. We're out of coffee." No answer. I was about to say it again when she appeared in the doorway, one hand on her hip, a box of K-cups in the other.

"Thank you, darling," I said with my best grin.

She shook her head in disgust. "All you had to do was look." She was putting on the accent, pretending to be mad at me. It didn't work. It never did. I knew her too well.

"Kate, you want coffee?"

"Black, two sugars, please."

"Hey Tim," I said as he poked his head around the corner. "Grab your stuff and a coffee and let's get started. Oh, actually, before you do, see if you can track this phone. It belongs to the chancellor. I want to know where it was last night between seven and three o'clock this morning. And this one. It belongs to Erika Padgett. She's dead." He nodded, the news about Padgett flying right over his head.

We went to my office and I dumped myself down in the leather monstrosity that was my office chair and gratefully allowed the upholstery to enfold me. Kate took one of the guest chairs in front of the desk, and we waited. Tim arrived five minutes later and took the other chair.

He cleared his throat, and began. "She—that is, her phone— was at the Integra Hills complex all night until seven this morning. I checked the tenant records. She has an apartment on Integra Hills Lane."

"Damn," I said. "Not conclusive, but.... And the other one?"

"Give me a minute."

For several minutes we sat there, sipping on our coffees as Tim paged through his laptop with his spare hand.

Finally: "Okay, Tim. What do you have?"

I cringed as he set his cup down on the polished surface of my desk.

"I pulled Emily's phone records, but they're extensive and I haven't had time to analyze them yet. Can you give me twenty-four hours?"

"I can, but I don't want to. Quick as you can, Tim. It's important."

"Okay. You asked me to try to find her phone, and this other one, Erika Padgett's. The good news is, they are both still active—but you knew that, right? Okay, okay. I was able to triangulate Emily's. It's within a three-quarter-mile radius of where her body was found. It must be in the woods somewhere. The killer must have thrown it away."

"Good work, Tim."

"There's more. You also asked me to try to find Erika Padgett's phone. Well," he said, with some excitement, "it, too, is still transmitting, and... it's somewhere in the same area as Emily Johnston's. It's also in the woods up there somewhere."

"Whoa? Both of them, together?"

He nodded.

"Jeez," I said. "That's a kick in the ass if ever I had one."

I turned to Kate. "We have to find those phones. How the hell we're going to do it, I have no idea. That's some wild country up there, heavily forested. I don't have the manpower to search an area that big, and I sure as hell don't want to turn it over to Heart and Sole. Do you think...."

"Chief Johnston? I'll ask him, but if it's in those deep woods, unless we can get a better fix, I don't think it's likely we'll find them. I'll go call him. Tim, can you narrow it down any?"

"No, that's the best I could do. I'd start at the crime scene and work outwards from there. Sorry."

She nodded, and left to make the call. She was back in about ten seconds. "He's sending a team up there at first light. He can only spare a couple dozen uniforms. Lonnie will lead them."

"Good. That's something. Carry on, Tim."

"I still don't have much on Angela Young and Marcy Grove. They had no online presence that I could find, either of them, other than their Facebook pages, but that stopped when they disappeared. What little there was on Facebook was all mundane stuff, photos of friends, parents, pets, vacations, all the usual stuff. Nothing that grabbed my attention. Same with their friends, mostly girls. So that was a dead end. Then I wondered if they knew each other. The answer, as far as I can tell, is no. As to their social lives... I couldn't get a handle on that. No data. Sorry."

"Boyfriends?"

"No. At least, I don't think so." He paused, sipped his coffee.

"Are you okay, Tim?" I asked.

He squinted quizzically at me. "Yeah, why?"

"You're very quiet. It's not like you."

"No, I'm good. Been keeping late hours is all. Talking to friends in England online."

"How about these girls' parents?"

He shook his head, "Clean. Squeaky clean. And wealthy, very wealthy. You probably know Dr. Grove. He's a member of your club."

I thought about that. I was sure I didn't know any Groves, but that was easy to check. A quick call to August, my father, would do it. "Okay, go on."

"Angela Young, as we know, disappeared on September 27, 2011; Marcy Grove on November 20, 2013. They were reported missing when their parents called the school. After several calls that were not returned they were finally put in contact with one of the vice presidents, a Mrs. Edna Morgan. According to Miss Amanda's research, it seems the calls finally triggered an in-house investigation that confirmed the girls had been gone for several days—in Grove's case, *six* days. Morgan called in the local police and filed a missing persons report. Enter Detectives Hart and McLeish. Okay, so far so good. Um. The rest is off the record."

He reached for his cup and drained the last of his coffee.

"Off the record?" Kate asked.

Tim looked at me, eyebrows raised in question. I nodded. He cleared his throat, and continued.

"I... er..." he lowered his voice to a whisper, "I hacked the sheriff's departmental computer."

"You did *what?*" Kate almost shouted, and Tim jumped.

"I hacked their system. It was easy. I've done it before. I have access to their entire system. The passwords they're using are a joke. Did you know that Sheriff Hands has a dog he calls Captain Flint?"

"Okay, Tim. That's enough," I said, frowning at Kate, who glared back at me. "What did you find?"

"About these two cases? Next to nothing. They're both classified as cold. There are files for each girl with names, dates, and so on, just primary information. And there are records of several visits to the campus at Belle Edmondson, ostensibly to conduct interviews, but what few interviews are recorded are cursory. They lack any kind of detail, and were limited to two or three friends, mostly roommates. In short," he looked first at me, then at Kate, "there was never an earnest investigation into either girl's disappearance."

I sat back in my chair and stared at him. I looked at Kate. She rolled her eyes and shook her head.

"Let me see those files," I said, reaching across my desk.

He handed me the laptop, and I skimmed through the few pages that made up the files. Tim was right. There had been no investigation. They had just gone through the motions and shelved the cases, allowed them to go cold.

"Son of a bitch," I said handing the laptop back. "What the hell is going on?"

"There's no telling," Kate said. "I think perhaps we should go talk to those two members of Hamilton County's finest."

"I agree," I said. "When we're finished here, we'll head over there. In the meantime, why don't you ask Johnston to request the files? We're not supposed to know what's in them, so if we go and pick them up, that will let Tim off the hook. It will also give us an excuse to talk to Hart and McLeish."

She nodded, took out her phone, and called the chief. She explained what we wanted and why, nodded several times as she listened to him.

"That will work. Thanks, Chief. Let me know how it goes." She disconnected.

"He said he'll make the call right now. He'll let us know."

"Okay," I said. "What's next, Tim?"

"The two guys. Robin Lucas and Nicholas Kyper. I ran backgrounds on them both. They're clean. Just a couple of local guys. Not even a parking ticket between them. You want their details, or should I hang onto them?"

"Just keep them handy. We may need to talk to them, but they're not a priority."

"How do you do that, Tim?" Kate asked. "How can you run backgrounds on people without their IDs, their Socials...?"

He grinned at her, "Sorry, Lieutenant Gazzara. It's better that you don't know."

"Better for me, or for you?"

"Both!"

"Okay," I said, shutting down what could become a very sensitive situation. "Let's get on with it."

Tim nodded. "Dr. Henry Jepson. He's clean too—"

"No he isn't," I said. "He has a reputation as a womanizer. I need you to dig a little deeper. We're looking for complaints. Something we can confront him with, and possible witnesses. If he's been molesting women, maybe he's taken things to the next level. Okay?"

He nodded. "Will do. Now, the chancellor, Victoria Mason-Jones. She seems to be everything you would expect in an academic of her standing. She's forty-eight years old, educated at Cambridge, has a PhD in English Language along with a Master's in Business Administration. She emigrated to the U.S. in 1992 when she was twenty-four. She's an over-achiever and has been an administrator all her professional life, beginning as an assistant principal at a small private school in Florida where she taught English. She's been chancellor at Belle Edmondson since the summer of 2007, nine years. She has good credit. Owns her own home. Takes two vacations a year. And that's about it."

"That's about what I expected," I said. "But there's something about the woman I'm not getting. Kate?"

"Other than the funny accent, and that she didn't tell us about the two missing women? Nope. She seems okay to me. I've met a few like her. She's a well-educated professional woman, Harry. What do you expect?"

I didn't have a good answer, because I didn't know what it was that was bugging me. So I simply shook my head and gave Tim the nod to continue.

"So that brings me to the inimitable Captain Conrad Rösche." He paused, clicked his mouse a couple of times, and then leaned back in his chair and looked at us. "This is one nasty son of a bitch, Mr. Starke. He's fifty-two years old, ex-military, Special Forces. He did two tours in Afghanistan and was well into his third when he was investigated for war crimes. No charges were brought, but he resigned his captain's commission soon after, so...."

"What war crimes?" Kate asked.

"Murder. Apparently three Taliban prisoners escaped, and it was said that he either gunned them down himself or ordered his men to do it. It was suggested that he allowed them to escape so that he could kill them. All three were armed with M16s, but no ever could find out where they got them. Anyway, no one talked and nothing was ever proved. So, if he did it, which is the general consensus, he got away with it." He paused again, then continued.

"And there's more. A fourteen-year-old Afghan girl reported him to a medical corpsman. Accused him of raping her. She was found two days later in a gully with her throat cut. He had a rock-solid alibi for that one, and that investigation ended with no charges being brought against him. He left the military in 2005." He hadn't even finished speaking before he was standing up and heading for the door. "Excuse me. I'll be back."

I watched him leave, then turned to Kate. "Sorry, what was that?"

"I said, what do you think?"

"I think we already knew what he was."

"Sorry about that," Tim said a few moments later, coming in and sitting down again. "I um... needed a drink of water. Sorry. Now. Where was I?"

"Rösche had just left the military."

"Oh yes. From there he went into private practice, and by that I mean he hired himself out to the highest bidder, which was Destrex Security, a very tough outfit. Destrex was hired to run security at Belle Edmondson in September of 2007, which is when he arrived there. His finances are murky, to say the least. His credit is excellent. He has one bank account that I can find, with a balance of just $18,730. That, I think, is total BS. I'd say most of his assets are located in offshore accounts. He lives alone in a rented apartment. One more thing. Since he's been at Belle Edmondson, he's been clean, and by that I mean there have been no complaints against him or his operatives. He runs a tight ship."

It was at that moment that Kate's phone rang. She answered it, listened for a moment, then said, "Good. Harry and I will head on over there in a few minutes. Thanks, Chief. I'll keep you up to speed."

She disconnected, looked at me, her eyebrows raised in question. I nodded.

"Okay, Tim," I said. "Good work. I need to wrap this up for now, but I need you run a background check on Erika Padgett—yes, I know she's dead, but her past isn't, and she's a priority, so please get right on it...."

He started to rise to his feet.

"Tim, for God's sake sit down and let me finish. I want to know everything there is to know about the Kalliste website too. I want to know who owns and runs it. I want to know who the girls really are, everything about them. Can you hack the thing? Get at the files?"

He looked at Kate, then back at me. "Of course not. That would be illegal."

We all smiled at that one, even Kate.

"As soon as you can, please, Tim. Now you can go." And he did.

I waited until he'd closed the door, and then turned to Kate. "Before we leave we need to strategize a little. There are a lot of questions that need answers. You want to take notes?"

She opened her iPad and raised an expectant eyebrow.

"Before we get started," I said, "you must have some thoughts, ideas...."

She sat quietly for a moment, her forehead creased in concentration, but eventually she shook her head. "It's too soon, Harry. The list of suspects is almost nonexistent. Who do we have? Just her friends, all of whom seem harmless, Conrad Rösche... and maybe... nah, that's too fantastic."

"You're thinking the chancellor, right?"

"Yeah, but, no. No way."

The thought had crossed my mind too, but she was right. The idea was probably a non-starter. Or was it?

"You said friends...."

"Well. We always figure the prime suspect is likely to be someone close to the victim: husband, boyfriend, girlfriend. Jessica, maybe. They were close."

"It's a thought, I suppose. I don't know why, but I'm liking Rösche, mainly because I can't think of anyone else. How about Jepson? He's a player. We can't rule him out, not yet anyway. So we have maybe four persons of interest, sort of, not counting the sheriff's department. They are Victoria Mason-Jones, Jessica Henderson, Conrad Rösche, and Dr. Jepson. Damn, Kate. There must be more than that. I don't feel good about any of 'em."

"How about alibis?" she asked. "Since we don't yet know what happened to Emily, and when, any alibis we got would be good only for Erika. But if we think the two are linked, an alibi for Erika's murder would eliminate that suspect from Emily's, right?"

"Only if we can prove the two deaths were linked."

"That's what I said, Harry, damn it." She was as frustrated as I was.

I shook my head. "I know, I know. It's just…. Look, let's ask ourselves the questions and see where they take us."

"Go for it," she said.

"One: Where the hell was Emily between the early morning hours of October second when she left the Sorbonne until she was dumped around ten o'clock on the evening of October eighth? She was alive until sometime on the seventh. We know that. So where was she?

"Two: Where did Emily and Erika go that night after they left the Sorbonne?

"Three: We know they knew each other before the night at the Sorbonne, but how and where did they meet? At the school or online?

"Four: Unless Erika had a place other than her home, she could not have hidden Emily and that probably means she didn't kill her either. So the question is, who abducted Emily and how?

"Five: Why was Erika killed? Was it because of her connection to Emily, or something else? And where did she go the night she was killed? We know from the neighbor that she didn't get home until almost midnight. Where was she?

"Six: Why was Emily on the Kalliste website? Was it for money? Was it for fun? Was she coerced?

"Seven: What about the other two missing girls? Are their deaths connected? If so, how? And yes, we have to assume they're both dead.

"Eight: Why were those two cases not properly investigated? Does the sheriff, and his acolytes, have anything to hide?

"Nine: Conrad Rösche is a killer, a rapist, and an ass. I'd say that makes him suspect number one, right?"

Kate shrugged, and continued typing.

"Number ten: How about Emily's friends? Are they somehow involved, especially Jessica?

"And then there's Jepson? I don't see how he could be involved, but you and I both know that nothing is ever as it seems." I thought for a minute. There were too many questions, and we had answers to none of them.

"Kate, I think we need to meet one of the Kalliste girls. What do you think?"

She looked sideways at me. "I think we should. I also think we have more than enough to work on for now."

"More than enough," I agreed. "And I think we should begin with Rösche and the sheriff's people."

Chapter Seventeen

The Hamilton County Sheriff's Department on Market Street was less than five minutes away from my offices. We could have walked, though we didn't. Detective Anthony Hart met us at the front door.

"Well, well. If it ain't Lieutenant Gazzara," he said. "And her lapdog, Harry friggin' Starke. You ain't welcome here, buddy. Here, take these and go." He handed two thin files to Kate and turned to leave.

"Whoa," I said. "That's not going to cut it, Tony. We need to talk to you and your buddy, McNasty."

He stopped, turned slowly to face us. "Screw you, Starke. I don't have to talk to you."

"That's so true," Kate said, taking a pair of handcuffs from her jacket pocket. "You certainly do not, but you'd better, because if you don't, I'm going to haul your ass over to Amnicola. Now. What's it going to be?"

"Now I ain't sure you have the legal right to do that, but," he said, obviously trying to save face, "I have a couple of minutes. What is it you want?"

"Just to talk. We have a few questions," Kate said, "for you and Detective McLeish."

"Yeah, well. I'm here. Alex ain't. So come on back. I'll give you five minutes."

He took us to a small conference room, where he sat down on one side of the table and we sat on the other.

"Okay, so let's get on with it. I don't have all day."

"Harry," Kate said. "You want to take it?"

"Shee-it!" Hart said under his breath.

She handed me the two files. I made a pretense of looking through them; I already knew what was in them. I flipped through the first and then handed it off to Kate. I scanned the second file, and then looked at Hart.

"What the hell?" I said. He didn't answer.

He sat there, arms folded, grinning, rocking gently on the back legs of his chair.

"You can't be serious. Is this all you have?"

"That's it," he said.

I flipped through the file again, making a show of reading the first couple of pages.

"This file documents what is supposed to be an investigation into the disappearance of Angela Young on September 27, 2011. There's almost nothing in it, for Christ's sake."

He continued to rock and grin, but said nothing.

"Kate?" I said.

She nodded. "This one's the same." Her voice had a hard edge to it.

"You want to explain?" I asked him.

"Nah. That's department stuff. Those cases are ongoing and I ain't at liberty to discuss them."

"Is Hands here?"

The smile left his face. "Yeah. Why?"

"Maybe he can explain this incompetence."

"No need to involve him. I'll tell you what I can," he said. His eyes were narrowed, and he looked as if he wanted to shoot someone.

"You just said you couldn't," Kate said.

The grin was back, and the rocking began again, "Well, Lieutenant. In the interests of interjurisdictional cooperation and good will...."

Good will, my ass. You're scared the sheriff will bust you.

"So why," Kate asked, "are these investigations so... so... let's say superficial?"

"I dunno what you mean. We went through the motions,

interviewed a number of contacts and potential witnesses and we came up with nothing. Those two ladies vanished off the face of the earth. We opened the files once in a while, asked a few more questions, but there weren't nothin' new, ever. They just went cold. Hell, you both know how it is in this part of the world. People disappear all the time. Sometimes we find a body months or years later, but most times we don't. It's the way of things around here."

I was dumbfounded by his attitude, by his lack of feeling. Something like this would tear at my guts until I figured it out. I sat and stared at him, slowly shaking my head.

"What?" he said, an offended look on his face. "You'll couldn't have done any better. Weren't nothin' to go on. Still ain't."

"So you interviewed Rösche, the chancellor, Michelle Scott, all three both times, and the roommates, friends, and the parents. That's all?"

"Yeah, that's all."

"You interviewed Scott both times. Why was that?"

"She knew the girls, worked with them. They was into that 'questrian shit an' all."

"Both of them?"

"Yeah, both of 'em. They spent most of their spare time at the horse barn, doin' whatever, screwin', I shouldn't wonder."

"You're a piece of crap, Hart," I said, as I got up from the table. "How the hell you keep your job beats me. There were *no investigations*." I waved the file in his face. "*None*. You went through the motions all right, and that's all you did."

"Screw you Starke."

"You ready, Kate? Or do you have something more you want ask this piece of garbage?"

She shook her head and rose to her feet. We left Hart sitting there, grinning and rocking.

"Just one more thing," I said to him, just before I left. "You recovered her car, Emily Johnston's car. What did you find?"

"Not a thing, Harry. It was as clean as the proverbial whistle."

"Well," I said, when we got outside. "That was an eye opener. What do you think?"

"I think he wouldn't last five minutes in my department. Harry, we have a real problem here. We have Padgett's death, which is officially my case now, but the other three cases are out of my hands. I'm not sure where I fit into them, if at all."

"That's what you have me for. I don't have to fit in. All I need is Johnston's request for my aid, which I have, and you to back me up. That's it. I can go where I please and do as I see fit."

"Maybe, but I get the feeling it's not going to be that easy. You're right about one thing though. There was no investigation into those two missing girls, and there's not a whole lot we can do for them now after so long, except maybe bring their folks a little justice. But I do have a feeling they're connected to the other two deaths. I also have a feeling that website is a part of it all."

"Oh yeah, that's a given. And one more thing: we also need to interview Michelle Scott. All four dead women were involved with her and her department. That can't be a coincidence."

I checked the time. It was already after five.

"Look," I said. "I need a few minutes at the office before Jacque locks up shop."

I drove the couple of blocks to my offices. The sky was blue and dotted here and there with fluffy white clouds. It looked like it was going to be a beautiful evening, and my thoughts turned to what I was going to do for dinner. I needn't have bothered. No sooner had Kate left and I'd dropped into my chair than there was a knock on the door. It opened, and Jacque stuck her head in.

"Hey, boss. You got a minute?"

I looked at my watch. It was almost five thirty.

"For you, always."

She came into the room looking every inch the professional woman she was. Her dark gray skirt was accentuated by a loose-fitting white blouse, and her long black hair was tied back in a ponytail.

"I heard back from Artemis," she said, sitting down on one of the guest chairs in front of my desk.

"Er... you've lost... oh, okay, the woman on Kalliste. How did it go?"

"It went well. I actually heard from her yesterday. She called. We talked for a few minutes. Mostly she asked me questions, about my sexuality and how I reached her. I dodged that one. At least I think I did. I told her I couldn't break a confidence since my friend was married. She seemed to buy it. She asked if I understood that she was an escort, and expensive. She also told me that she was available for business dates, parties, or just a quiet dinner." Jacque smiled. I wasn't sure why until she said, "She made a point of telling me that sex was not an option. I'm not sure I believed her. Maybe she was being guarded, in case the call was being recorded. I don't know. Then she asked me to e-mail a photo, said she would look at it and then call me back. I'm pretty sure she, or someone, ran a check on me."

"And she did, right? Call you back?"

"She did. Just a few minutes ago," she grinned at me. "I have a date."

I put my hands behind my head, rocked my chair back, and stared at her, slowly shaking my head.

"What?" she asked. "It's what you wanted."

"I don't know, Jacque. It could be dangerous. You had a narrow escape last time. That hit and run nearly killed you. I don't want to put you at risk again."

"Well, aren't you one to talk. I can look after myself, especially where a woman is concerned. And besides, I like the look of her."

And that bothered me even more.

"That's just it," I said, letting my chair tilt back to its proper position. "This Artemis, she's going to have a minder. You've already arranged to meet her, right?" I leaned on my desk, arms folded, and looked sternly at her. It made not a bit of difference. She just crossed her legs, folded her arms, tilted her head to one side, and looked me squarely in the eyes.

"For tomorrow night. Very public. Dinner at Porters. She said I should book a room there. I already did. Oh, and I'm going to need some money. She charges $250 an hour, so let's say $2,000."

That was about what I'd expected, but... "Why did she want you to book a room?"

"I don't know, and I didn't ask."

She was right about the location being public, at least. Porters is one of Chattanooga's nicest restaurants. It's located in the Read House Hotel downtown.

"Whew... I dunno, Jacque."

"Oh come on, Harry. What can go wrong?"

Okay, so that's only the second time I can remember that you've called me by my first name.

I smiled at her. "Jacque, you have no idea. Okay. Here's what we'll do...."

Jacque left some ten minutes later, but I stayed to make a couple of calls. Once that was done I did a quick search on Google, got the answer I was looking for, gathered up my iPad and phone, and headed out the door.

I was already in my car with the motor running when my cell phone rang. It was Amanda.

Chapter Eighteen

"Harry! Oh my God. I'm so glad you answered. Bob—he got shot while we were up there; he's in the hospital."

Shot? The pit of my stomach hit the back of my throat. I felt like I'd been hit by a Mac truck.

"*What?* How the hell did he get shot? Christ! Don't answer that. I'll—God, I'll be there in a few minutes. Where are you, Erlanger?"

"The emergency room, yes."

Shot? He's been friggin shot? What the f...? My mind couldn't grasp it.

I'd been to the ER at Erlanger before—several times in fact, and three of them on my own account—so when I got there I knew exactly where to go.

There was a uniformed sheriff's deputy seated outside his

door. They'd just finished prepping him for the OR when I arrived. He was on top of the bed, and he didn't look good. His face was the color of old newspapers and he looked like he'd swallowed an onion. His chest was bare, and there was a large dressing covering most of his right side. Amanda was seated beside the bed, looking unusually disheveled. Her hair was a mess, the blouse under her jacket was torn to the waist, and her mascara had run. She'd been crying. She was holding his hand.

"Christ. Look at the two of you."

They both looked at me. Bob's eyes were bleary and he was obviously in a great deal of pain.

"Can you speak?"

He nodded.

"Where were you shot, and what with?" I asked.

He pointed with his finger. "Right here."

I could barely hear him.

"Glock 17," he said, "9 mm. Don't think it was a hollow point. Christ, Harry. I feel like I've been kicked by a horse. It hurts like hell."

I sat there, just staring at him, not knowing what to say or even think. This was serious shit.

"What the hell happened?"

Bob tried hard to grin at me, but it didn't quite work. "You should see the other guy," he whispered.

"The silly fool took you at your word and tried to protect me," Amanda said. "One of those damned security guards— there were four of them—grabbed the mike from me and tore my blouse. Bob grabbed him. Next thing I knew, one of the other guards pulled a gun and shot him."

"What the.... And?"

"I went down," Bob whispered. "Jerked the Sig as I fell and nailed the bastard. He ain't dead but he should be, would be if I hadn't been rolling around on my back. Got him in the upper right arm. I was aiming for his chest. Son of a bitch."

"You shouldn't talk, Bob," Amanda said. "It's okay, Harry. We have it all. The camera was rolling. It was self-defense. The other man is in a room just down the hall. He'll live, but his arm... oh my God. What a mess. The bullet hit the bone pretty high up. He'll probably lose it."

No shit. Bob's weapon is a .45 loaded with hollow points. The guy was damned lucky it was only his arm.

"Transport's here," a voice behind me said. I turned around to face the nurse and nodded.

"Can I have another quick word?" I asked.

"Very quick, and then we have to get him to OR."

"Okay, buddy," I gripped Bob's hand. He almost broke my fingers as he gripped them—a good sign—and grinned up at me.

"Get outta here, Harry." He could barely speak, and his voice sounded bubbly, as if his chest were full of liquid, which it probably was. "I'll be back in the office tomorrow morning, bright and early." He was trying to make a joke, but it wasn't funny and we both knew it.

"Sure you will, but I'll be right here when you get out of surgery."

He nodded, closed his eyes, and let go of my hand. It flopped down on the bed beside him.

"You'll let me know when you're done?" I asked the nurse.

"Of course. There's a waiting area just down the hall. I'll come and get you."

There were only two other people in the waiting area. We found a couple seats in the corner and sat down.

"Would you like some coffee?" I asked.

Amanda shook her head.

"Me neither," I said, more to myself than to her. "So, you want to tell me about it while we wait?"

"About what happened up there?"

I nodded. "Start at the beginning, before this happened." I nodded in the direction of Bob's room. I was only half interested in the answer. My mind was somewhere deep in the bowels of the hospital, with Bob. I'd asked only to try to take her mind off what was happening to him.

"It didn't go well. I'd talked the project over with my producer and we decided I would take the direct approach.

We'd done several pieces on the college before, but the missing girls? That hadn't been covered since Marcy Grove disappeared in 2013...." Her mind was wandering. I knew what she was going through.

"I don't know why we hadn't done a follow up... at least one... I would have thought...." Again, she stopped talking and stared down at the floor. I let her have a minute.

"I'd planned to interview the chancellor," she said eventually. "Mason-Jones, and some of her staff. It was really weird, Harry. No one would talk to me. It was as if they'd been warned off. I did manage to catch Edna Morgan in her office—she runs Student Affairs. She sure as hell wasn't pleased to see me.... And she didn't say much, either, just that all three women, including Emily Johnston, had been reported missing and that she'd filed reports with the sheriff's department. Harry, she was nervous the whole time I was with her. She kept looking at her office door, as if she were expecting someone to walk in on us. The interview lasted all of three minutes. You can watch it, if you like. I'm not sure if she knew anything more than what she told me."

"I'll take a look at it. Not today, though. Jeez, I can't believe this...." It was hard to concentrate. I kept thinking of Bob. "I dunno. Maybe we can learn something from her body language. Then what?"

"Well, I went to the chancellor's office and met with her secretary. She let the chancellor know we were there, and why, but she wouldn't talk to us without an appointment. So we went looking for Emily's friends. I wanted to talk to

Jessica Henderson in particular, to get some human-interest stuff. We sure got plenty of that...." She looked down the hall toward Bob's room.

"We rolled onto the lot outside her block.... Jessica's." She swallowed. "And... Harry, it was as if they were expecting us. We were flanked by two security vehicles almost immediately."

"Jones," I said. "She probably called them."

Amanda nodded. "Probably. Anyway we got out of the car, all three of us. Charlie, he's my photojournalist, had his camera rolling. The men in the cars—four men in blue uniforms—got out of their vehicles. One of them approached us with his hand up, palm out towards Charlie's camera. I stepped between them and told him why we were there and what I intended to do. He told me we were trespassing and that we were to leave. I recall asking him if he'd heard that Emily Johnston had been murdered.... And then I extended the mike toward him expecting an answer. Or not." She paused again, and took a deep breath.

"Harry... he just grabbed the mike with one hand and the collar of my blouse and jacket with the other and began to drag me toward his cruiser. I heard my blouse tearing and that... that was when Bob stepped in. He jumped forward and punched the man in the side of his neck. He let go of me, dropped to his knees. Bob... God, Bob turned toward me, pushed me to one side, and went for his gun, but he was just a little too late. One of the men on the other side of our car fired his gun, and Harry... I felt the wind of the bullet as it went by me. It hit Bob and... oh my God. I was so close to him I heard it hit him. It—it was sickening. I'll never forget it." There were tears in her eyes.

I put my arm around her shoulders and pulled her to me. She put her head on my chest, and I held her for a moment, until finally she pushed me away.

"Bob was kind of thrown backward by the impact, and he went down. He only got off the one shot before he hit the ground, at the guy who'd fired at him. Jesus, Harry. I heard the bone crack when the bullet hit him.... I've never seen anyone shot, and then two all at once, and so close—but Charlie got it all. He was far enough away that he got them both. The guard had his gun aimed at Bob before he even went for his. Oh my God, Harry. Talk about the OK friggin' Corral. The man's arm was shattered. It was hanging like a broken tree branch. Blood everywhere, pumping out of—"

Tears were rolling freely down her cheeks now, and I pulled her to me again. I knew what she was going through. Being that close to someone when they get shot is bad enough. When it's someone you know....

"And then?" I asked.

"One of the other men. One of the security guards—he was a big man, wearing mirrored sunglasses—started shouting and waving his arms around. I couldn't hear what he was yelling, but he must have stopped what was happening, pushed the other two away, and then he made several phone calls. I tried to help Bob, but he's so damned big I couldn't move him. He just lay there on his back, telling me he was okay, the stupid ass. Only a minute later, some guy in a blue uniform with captain's bars arrived and began shouting orders."

"And Charlie got all this?"

"Oh yeah. Charlie's a pro. He'd have kept rolling no matter what, even if it had been me that had been shot. He got everything. Anyway, the police arrived first, and then an ambulance from Signal Mountain, and then another right after it, and I rode here with Bob. And... well, here we are."

"Sheesh," I said. "I could do with a drink. Why the hell don't they serve alcohol in hospitals? They'd make a damned fortune."

"One more thing, Harry. The man in charge, the captain, he demanded Charlie give him the memory card from his camera."

"Son of a bitch. He didn't give it to him, did he?"

"He gave him the card that was in the camera. But it didn't have much on it. He'd swapped them out. I have the one with footage on it."

She reached inside her jacket, took something from the pocket, and handed it to me. It was a Sony XQD memory card.

"How the hell did you manage that?"

"I didn't. Charlie did. I told you he's a pro. This was, as they say, not his first rodeo. He's very proactive, is Charlie. I need that, by the way," she said, taking the card back. "Don't worry. It's date and time stamped. I'll make copies and lock this one away in the company safe."

We sat quietly for a moment, and then she asked me, "What will happen now, Harry?"

"They'll fix him up. Don't worry."

"That's not what I meant. What about the police? Will he be charged?"

"If you have the goods, if Charlie did in fact get it as you said he did, no. Well, not Bob. He was in fear of his life, and yours—and Charlie's, for that matter. It was a justified shooting. The other guy? I'd have to see the footage, but from what you've told me, I'd say there will be some charges. You can't go around shooting people for no good reason, even if you were trespassing, and I'm not sure that you were."

And so we sat there, waiting, making small talk. Amanda was in a hell of a state, worried sick that Bob was going to die. I tried to tell her otherwise, but jeez, I wasn't even sure myself. The man is a robot, but a 9 mm to the chest....

I wasn't watching the clock, but it must have been at least another hour before the nurse finally appeared, accompanied by a young doctor.

"He did fine," the doctor said.

Whew. I felt as if a great weight had been lifted from me.

"He has a broken rib and his lung is collapsed. He has a tube in his chest, in the space between his chest wall and his lung. It's attached to a suction device that will evacuate air and any residual blood or bodily fluids from the chest cavity, and will help to keep the lung inflated. Once the lung heals and can stay inflated on its own, we'll take the tube out, probably in a couple of days or so. In the meantime, he needs rest. He's awake, but barely, and you can see him, but only for a moment."

"Will he be okay?"

I didn't like the way he looked away as he answered. "He's big and strong and he made it through surgery. But recovery will take time."

I thanked him and turned to Amanda. She shook her head. "I can't. You go. I'll wait here."

I hesitated, then nodded, told her I'd be but a minute, and walked down the hall to his room. The door was closed. I knocked lightly, but there was no answer, so I just went inside. Damn it if he wasn't asleep. The right side of his chest was covered by a large dressing, and I could see the tube. The green, yellow, and blue lines on the monitor were moving steadily from one side to the other; their rhythm was steady, as was his breathing. I stepped to the side of the bed and gripped his hand.

"Hang in there, buddy," I said quietly. There was no response.

My mood was pretty damned dark as I walked back down the hall to where I'd left Amanda. Her mood apparently wasn't much better, because she was sitting just as I'd left her: feet apart, knees together, elbows on her knees, hands clasped. Staring at the floor.

"C'mon," I said, touching her arm. "Let's get out of here."

"How is he?"

"Perky as a Pekingese," I lied.

"You should call Kate. She'll want to know."

As it happened, I didn't need to, because just as I was pulling my phone out, she walked into the waiting area.

"How is he?" she asked.

"Amanda, can you give me a minute? Maybe bring the car around?" She nodded, so I told her where it was and handed her the keys.

I waited until she was out of earshot, then looked at Kate and shook my head. "Not good. He has a broken rib and a collapsed lung. I was just about to call you. How did you know?"

"Jacque. Amanda called her. What the hell happened?"

I filled her in as best I could. She listened without interrupting until I'd finished.

"Can I see him?"

"Best not. I just looked in on him. He's out cold. The doctor said he needs rest. Tomorrow, maybe."

She nodded. "Better get her home." She twitched her head back toward the hospital entrance. Amanda had just walked back in. "She looks like shit."

Kate was right. Amanda did, in fact, look like shit. I don't think I'd ever seen her look so distressed.

"I guess we couldn't have timed it better," a voice said behind me. "Got all three of 'em together in one big bunch. We was just about to come after you, Ms. Cole. Y'all saved me the bother."

I didn't even have to turn around. I'd have recognized that whiny voice anywhere.

"What do you want, Hart?" I asked. He and his partner, McLeish, sauntered down the corridor, hands in their pockets, shit-eating grins on both of their faces.

He sniggered. "I need to talk to—I want to say the lovely Ms. Cole—but she ain't looking too hot right now."

"For a dumbass, you've got a smart mouth, Hart. Keep a civil tongue in your mouth or I'll rip it out of your head."

"Tsk, tsk, Harry. A little sensitive tonight, ain'tcha?"

"Now, Ms. Cole. Let's go find somewhere quiet where can talk." He put his hand to her elbow. She jerked it away as if she'd been scalded.

"Can't it wait until tomorrow?" Kate asked. "She had a rough day."

"*She's* had a rough day? What about that boy down the hall who'll probably lose his arm? She's witness to a double shooting."

"You didn't mention Bob Ryan," Kate said. Her eyes were like two chips of flint. "He could die, and if he does, that *boy down the hall* will be facing a murder charge. And if he doesn't die, your *boy* will be facing an *attempted* murder charge."

"Oh, now, now, LT. We don't know any such thing. Way I heered it, Ryan's the one that fired the first shot."

"You piece of shit!" Amanda just about exploded. "I was there, with a *cameraman*. We got it all. Your *boy* fired the first shot. Bob was already down when he fired back. Your *boy* is going to jail, with or without his arm. And you can get the hell out of here, because I'm not talking to you, *ever*."

Hart looked at her, his face grim. He'd not been expecting that news. *He's been talking Rösche. Rösche doesn't know it was recorded, and there's no way he can access that Sony memory card without the proper equipment.*

"Tough luck, Hart." I said. "You on the air tonight, Amanda?"

"No, but Jerry is. 'Channel 7 reporter witnesses double shooting.' That's news. The whole damn county will have seen it by eleven thirty."

"You can't do that," Hart said.

Now, why would you say that?

"The hell I can't," Amanda snapped. "I'm a journalist."

He stepped forward. "I think you'd better come with me."

"One more step, Hart," I said, "and I'll break your damned arm."

"You wouldn't. That would be an assault on a police officer."

"Try me."

I thought for a second that he would, but he didn't. He took a step back, turned, and together the two of them walked away.

"This ain't over, Starke," he said over his shoulder. "I'll be in touch."

"Whew," I said. "That was close."

"Harry," Kate said. "You're going to have to quit that shit. You cannot threaten or assault law enforcement officers and expect to get away with it. Good job he didn't want to get hurt. You pull that stunt on me and I'll take you up on it."

I grinned at her. "So you say."

"Get her out of here, before they change their minds and come back for her. I'll be at your office at eight in the morning. That good?"

"Yes. But listen, can you spare a few minutes to watch our backs right now? I'll take Amanda to the station and wait while she gets done what she needs to get done. I have a feeling we blindsided them and Rösche with the news we have the shooting on camera, and who knows how important that is to them."

She agreed, and we went out into early evening traffic. I headed toward Channel 7; Kate followed at a discreet distance. The trip was, thankfully, uneventful.

Jerry Robinson, Channel 7's evening news anchor, was waiting in the newsroom when we arrived. He took the memory card, made several copies of it, and returned the original, along with one of the copies, to Amanda. She locked it in the company's safe.

We were too late to get the memory card to the newsroom in time for six o'clock, but they and every other news outlet in Chattanooga already had the outline of what had happened. All of them but Channel 7 had it wrong.

We were shown a recording of Rösche being interviewed by one of the other stations, and he went to great lengths to lay the blame on Bob. Channel 7, however, had interviewed Charlie, Amanda's cameraman. They ran this story as a teaser:

CHANNEL 7 ANCHOR AMANDA COLE WAS INVOLVED IN a double shooting earlier today at the Belle Edmondson College for Women on Signal Mountain. Amanda is unhurt, but is still at the hospital with the two victims. Tune in to Channel 7 at eleven for the full story and Amanda's coverage.

I took Amanda to her apartment in Hixson, where she grabbed a few things, and then we went on to my place. I don't think she said two words the rest of the evening. She was dead on her feet, and I wondered if she might be going into shock—a bit late, but it happens—but there was no going to bed. We both wanted to see Channel 7's coverage of the shooting.

Jerry Robinson had edited the footage down to less than sixty seconds, and the result was graphic. Jerry warned his viewers that it was.

It was all there, just as Amanda had related it to me, from the grab at her clothing to Bob's retaliatory punch, to the two gunshots. Jerry played the gunfight sequence first in real time and then again in slow motion. I watched, spellbound, as the guard pulled his weapon and aimed at what appeared to me to be Amanda's back. I watched as Bob flung her sideways with his left hand and pulled his Sig with his right. He barely had it out of the holster when the bullet slammed into him. The impact threw him backward and sideways and, as he went down, he fired. The guard's right arm, just below the shoulder, exploded in a mist of blood and pulverized flesh and bone.

"Oh my God," Amanda whispered. "Poor Bob. I didn't realize—I didn't see this. It's horrible."

We were on the sofa watching it. I put my arm around her. I didn't know what to say. I was shaken to the bone.

"Well, I guess that settles the question of whether it was self-defense or not." I turned off the TV, stood up, took her hand, and gently pulled her to her feet.

"C'mon. Let's get some sleep. By the way, I think it would be a good idea if you came to the office with me in the morning. What do you say? Can you fix it?"

She said that she could, and she did.

Later, once we were lying together in bed, she suddenly rolled onto her side to face me, her hands together under her cheek like a little girl. "Harry, you've been shot before, haven't you?"

"Uh-huh. You know I was. Last year, when we investigated the Tom Sattler thing."

"I know that, but that wasn't much, was it? Just a flesh wound."

"Flesh wound? It went right through my upper arm."

"Yes, but it wasn't that bad."

"Bad enough when you're on the receiving end."

"I'm not belittling it, but I mean... *shot*, like Bob was. Harry, his lung is collapsed. He has a tube in his chest. He might— he might die."

"Bob, die? Not a chance. He's too damn ornery, and too tough. He'll be fine, up on his feet in a couple days. You wait and see." I said it, but I wasn't as confident as I tried to sound. Gunshot wounds to the chest are bad at best; at worst, the bullet can bounce around in there, do all kinds of crazy things. But I wasn't kidding about Bob. He's one of the toughest men I know. If anyone could handle it, he could.

"He'll be fine," I said. "He'll be fine."

Chapter Nineteen

The first thing I did when I awoke the next morning was call the hospital. I wasn't worried about them not giving me information. Bob had no family that I knew of, and he had me listed as his next of kin.

I learned that he'd had a comfortable night, but wasn't yet out of danger; he would be in the ICU for at least another forty-eight hours. I asked to speak to him, but was told that he was resting, and that I could go in to see him later.

Then I turned on the TV. It was chaos. Every station in town was running Jerry Robinson's edited version of the shooting. I don't think there had ever been anything quite like before. Even the nationals had it. I flipped over to Fox and Friends and watched Heather Nauert run it. Bob was being lauded everywhere as a hero that had saved Amanda's life.

Jeez, this ain't gonna go down well, and it ain't going away anytime soon either.

When she came out of the bathroom, dressed and ready to leave, she was still pale but looked a whole lot better than she had the night before. She was dressed conservatively in black pants, a white blouse, and a lightweight burgundy blazer.

"How's Bob?" she asked.

"He had a good night. He's resting. We'll go and see him later. Right now, though, we need to go."

Charlie, Amanda's camera guy, had taken her car back to the station, so we went by to pick it up. I waited while Amanda went inside to talk to her boss, and then she followed me to my offices. We parked in my lot and I closed the electronic gates, something I hadn't bothered to do for several months.

It was a little after eight when we walked into the outer office that morning. Jacque had not told anyone there about what had happened to Bob. The news hit everyone hard.

Heather, my second lead, was devastated. Tim? I thought he was going to throw up. His face lost all its color, and he hurried away. A second or two later, I heard the restroom door lock, and it stayed locked for a long time.

Me? In the cold light of day? There aren't words to explain how I felt. The man had saved my life twice in the past three years. I thought of him as a brother, and I leaned on him, probably more than I should have. He had always been there for me, and now he wasn't, and I felt hollow, like someone had torn my guts out.

The worst thing about it was that people around me were getting hurt again. Mike, my intern a couple years ago, had gotten beaten up. Jacque had been the victim of an attempted murder. And now Bob.

Who the hell will be next?

It wasn't something I wanted to dwell on, and I had better and more urgent things to attend to anyway. It was time to get a handle on exactly what we were up against.

We were now a man short, which meant that, with the regular daily workload, I was in trouble. Heather would have to take on Bob's role as Amanda's protection, at least when—and if—visits to the college were planned. I could pull in Ronnie Hall from my white-collar division. He wasn't a field investigator, but he'd been with me for almost ten years and had learned a lot. Besides, he was all I had. Leslie and Margo, the only other members of my staff, were secretaries.

I went to the Keurig and made myself a cup of Dark Italian roast, and then had Jacque gather the principals in our small conference room.

We'd just gotten seated when Kate arrived. She was a few minutes late, but as always she looked stunning. Today, however, something was missing. Her face was pale and serious, and her voice when she told everyone hello had lost its crispness. She was almost as close to Bob as me, and it showed.

"Right," I said quietly. "Now that everyone's here... let's try to figure out where we are. Heather, did Tim bring you up-to-date on what we know so far, and what Bob was doing?"

Heather Stillwell is a deceptively, and purposely, nondescript-looking woman. She's almost forty-one, and dresses well, but her clothes are often unremarkable and chosen to hide a very remarkable body. She's a little over five foot eight, with short brown hair, an oval-shaped face, and brown eyes. She has a black belt in Krav Maga, works out for an hour every morning, teaches self-defense in her spare time, and is an expert shot with just about every weapon known to man, from a revolver to a bow and arrow. Having once been a special agent for the Georgia Bureau of Investigation, she is also something of a mystery. To this day, I have no idea why she left that somewhat exalted position to work for me, but I'm glad she did.

"He did," she replied. That was another thing; she was always very conservative with her conversation, never using three words when two would do.

"How about you, Ronnie?" I asked.

He nodded.

"Before we get started," Kate interrupted, "would you mind telling me how Bob is? I called, but no one would talk to me."

"He had a good night. He's comfortable, but they expect him to be in the ICU for at least a couple of days more. We're going to see him at noon. You want to come with us?"

She nodded.

Then there was a knock on the door.

Jeez, what now?

The door opened, and Lonnie Guest stuck his head in. "Is it okay?" he asked.

"I asked Lonnie to join us," Kate said. "I thought with Bob.... Well, I thought we could use an extra hand... and maybe muscle, too. I fixed it with the chief. It wasn't a problem. He's my partner, and we're investigating Erika Padgett's murder, so it was a no-brainer."

I looked up at Lonnie. The usual shit-eating grin was absent. For the first time since I'd known him back at the academy, his face was serious.

I nodded. "Come on in and sit down, Lonnie. Glad to have you. You'll have to catch up as you go, I'm afraid."

"No probs. How's Bob?" he asked as he sat down beside Amanda.

I took a moment to fill him in and was just about to begin when my cell phone rang.

Chief Johnston? What the hell?

"Hey, Chief. What's up?"

"What's up?" he growled. "What the hell is going on, Harry? I just caught the news on Channel 7, and I just got done talking with Israel Hands. If Bob could walk, he'd arrest him."

"That would be a waste of time. It was self-defense cut-and-dried, as you well know if you've watched the news. He's just posturing. Doesn't like the interference. Listen, Wes. I hate to cut you off, but I have a lot going on here right now."

"Yeah, well. How's the investigation into Emily going? You still on it?"

"You know I am, now—"

"Okay, okay. I'll let you go, but first... how's Bob? Is he going to make it?"

"Yeah, Wes. He's going to make it." I listened for a moment longer, then hung up, slumped back in my chair, and looked at each one of them in turn.

"Everyone ready?"

They all nodded.

"Okay," I sighed. "Look, I know you're all in a state of shock; I am too, but we have to get over it. We have a job to do, a crime—several crimes—to solve. Bob's tough. Very tough. He'll be fine." *Hell, I hope so,* I thought. "So, with that said, we need to get done here quickly. I need to be at the hospital by noon, and I want to go to Belle Edmondson afterward."

I looked at Amanda. She looked at me and slowly shook her head. This wasn't going to go well.

"Heather," I said. "As you know, Bob was working with Amanda on her project when...." Amanda opened her mouth, presumably to protest. I gave her a look that would have killed a cat stone dead, and she closed it again, her lips clamped tightly together.

"His job," I continued, "was not only to help with her investigation, but also to protect her. I want you to take over that duty."

"Damn it, Harry," Amanda said.

"It's okay, Amanda," Heather said. "I know you don't know me as well as you do Bob, but we'll get along. I'm not bad at what I do."

"I know that, Heather. I just *do not* want anyone else getting hurt because of me."

"Bob didn't get hurt because of you," I said, quietly. "He got hurt doing the job he loves; the job he was being paid to do. Heather will do the same." She didn't answer, so I moved on.

"Ronnie," I said, handing him the copies of the two files we'd obtained from the sheriff's department. "I had Bob down to follow up with the parents of the two girls who went missing earlier. Those are the files that Hart and McLeish put together, for what they're worth, which is not a whole hell of a lot. I'd like you to take that on. There's no need to get heavily involved. They're not going to remember much after all this time, but you never know. The Groves are local, Lookout Mountain, so you can visit them in person. The Youngs live in Atlanta. You can do that by phone, initially. If you think they're worth a visit, do it. Unfortunately, those files are all we have, but maybe you'll find something useful in them."

He flipped through them and nodded.

"Moving right along," I said. "Tim. Did we find anything in Erika Padgett's datebook?"

"Er, no.... Well, not a whole lot. It is what it is. Most of the entries were for visits to farms, whatever. She was a busy vet. There are one or two personal entries, and Emily's name comes up a half-dozen times, usually on weekends. But Emily's is the only name listed like that. They must have seen quite a lot of each other," he mused.

"I'm sure they did," Jacque said dryly. The sarcasm went right over Tim's head.

"We need to know where she was that night, Tim. Between seven and midnight. Can you track her phone?"

"Yes, that shouldn't be a problem. Do you want it right away?"

"In a bit. Before you do that, take a look at the Kalliste site. See if Padgett has a listing. If she does, it will throw a whole different light on things. You can do that now, please."

He nodded, and began tapping away on his laptop. It didn't take him long.

"Nope," he said. "She's not here."

"Okay," I said. "I'm not sure if that's good or bad; good I suppose. It probably means she's either not connected to it, unless she was one of Emily's clients, which she might well have been, or she was killed for some other reason, and that makes me wonder if we're looking for two killers."

"Oh that's a stretch," Kate said. "Too much of a coincidence, and neither one of us believes in those. And what motive could someone have for killing a vet?"

"Well," I replied. "One at least springs readily to mind. Jealousy. The BDSM community is a strange world. If she, Erika, had a steady girlfriend or boyfriend. and she began seeing someone else, Emily, for instance...."

"I don't buy it," Kate interrupted. "My experience with BDSM is that they have only one thing on their minds, and that's finding a new way to get themselves off. And she was vet, for God's sake. Come on, Harry. A vet! It makes no sense that a well-known professional woman would get mixed up in that world. That she was gay, maybe, okay, I'll buy that, and that she might have been one of Emily's clients, yes, I can buy that too. But...."

"Whether she was into it or not, it's how she died. Someone did it to her, and I'm betting it was a woman. Remember the strap marks on Emily's thighs? Those were not faked. The girl had spent hours in a sling.

"Now," I said, and looked again at Tim. "You asked for twenty-four hours to analyze Emily's phone records. What did you come up with?"

He riffled through the pile of paperwork and then handed me a thick sheaf of printed papers. There were hundreds of phone numbers on it. Some he'd highlighted in yellow and written names alongside. They were all female names.

Some numbers were repeated many times, and those he hadn't highlighted at all. But there were several more—I counted eleven—that were highlighted in green; there were no names attached to them.

I looked at him. He looked back, smiling, the overhead lights reflected in the lenses of his oversized glasses.

"Well?" I asked.

"Oh... yes. Sorry. The numbers highlighted in yellow are one-offs... well, no more than two or three calls to each, and they are all listings for young ladies located in just about every state in the union. I know. I called a few of them.

"Those not highlighted at all are family or friends. No big deal, except for the one highlighted in blue. That one is Erika Padgett's number. As you can see, they called each other quite often. The last time on the afternoon of the evening when Emily left the Sorbonne with her." He paused, looked around significantly, then continued.

"The numbers highlighted in green are different. As you can see, they were all called fairly regularly right up until she disappeared, which you would expect, right? But they're all burner phones, disposable, and not a one is still in service. Who they belonged to, I have no idea, and they will help you not at all. They're just something to think about, to muddy the waters."

He was right.

"Is there nothing there we can use?" I asked.

"Sure. She was, and still is, on Kalliste. Her name there was Adrestia, right? So the numbers highlighted in yellow are obviously her... what—customers? Clients?"

It made sense. "You say you called some of them. What did you say to them?"

"I just told them I had a wrong number and apologized. They all sounded nice, the few that I called."

I looked at Kate, eyebrows raised.

"You think we should call them?" she asked.

"Well, if they were indeed clients, maybe we could learn something." I handed her the records.

She flipped through them. "Whew. There's a hell of a lot of them. It will take at least a couple days to get through them all." She sighed. "I'll get someone at the office on it. Maybe we'll get lucky. We're looking for someone who might be willing to admit they make dates with lesbian hookers, and then talk to the police about it."

"It's worth a shot," I said.

"Good luck with that," she murmured, then looked at me. I shook my head. She shrugged.

"All righty then. Let's keep moving. Tim, what about Emily's journal?"

"There are six really interesting pages at the back of the book," he began. "The first four, as far as I can tell, contain nothing more than a list of... clients, I guess. Just initials and dates. There are sixty-three sets of initials. Each set has a number of dates in sequence, one after the other, spread out over a period of two years. Some have just a couple, some as many as eight or nine. There's no way to know for sure what they mean, but I think it might be a list of her appointments. I haven't done it yet, but we might be able to tie the dates to her phone records. If so, then we would have some specifics."

"Kate?" I asked.

"Yes, I'll handle it. I'll need a copy, please, Tim."

He nodded. "Sure thing. You can have mine. I have another." He handed it to her.

"The last two pages, however," he continued, "are different. They appear to contain a series of coded entries. At first glance, to the casual observer, what we have is very confusing. Here, take a look."

He sorted through his pile again and finally pulled out several sheets of paper and handed one to each of us. On them were eight samples.

Hulndsdgjhw - NDIzNTU1OTMzNg==

Vkhlodzlofra - NDIzNTU1OTE2Mw==

Ukrqgdehqqhww - NDIzNTU1MjE3Ng==

Plfkhoohvfrww - NDIzNTU1Nzc3Mw==

Mhvvlfd - NDIzNTU1MTkyNA==

Odfbpfploodq - NDIzNTU1ODQoMQ==

Dxwxpqohdi - NDIzNTU1MTEwMw==

Pduldqqhvlggrqv - NDIzNTU1Mzk4Mg==

"THERE ARE MORE, OF COURSE. THIRTY-SEVEN IN ALL. I just listed these eight to give you an idea. They are also much more interesting than the rest, although I'm still working on them."

No one was listening by then, though. They were still staring at the baffling series of upper- and lowercase letters.

"To you guys," he said, puffing himself up, "they make no sense. To *me*, however...."

He caught the look I was giving him.

"They're simple enough," he said quickly. "The first string on each line is a simple Caesar or shifted-alphabet code. It took only a few minutes to figure them out. The second string I'm also quite familiar with. Each is phone number encoded using Base 64."

"And you decoded them, right?" I asked impatiently. *Slow down, Harry. Give the geek his five minutes of fame.*

"Of course."

"Damn it, Tim. Tell us."

"She must have encoding software on her computer," he said. "The catch is, all of the phones are burners, disposable, untraceable. The names are easy, just a Caesar code. With a little time you probably could have worked it out yourself. The alphabet is shifted by a factor of only three. In other words, *a* becomes *d, b* becomes *e,* and so on. It couldn't be any simpler. If she didn't use an encoder, she could easily have done it by hand. Anyone can. All you do is write the alphabet on two strips of paper. Line them up so the top strip's *a* matches the bottom strip's *d*—or another letter of your choosing—and then you can encode, or decode. Okay, okay. I don't know any other way to say it. It's what I do."

I sighed, shook my head, and then nodded for him to continue.

"It's a little different for the phone numbers. The codes were generated by Base 64 software on her computer." He looked at me, then held up his hands. "Okay. I'm done."

I looked at the list he'd given me.

The first name was Erika Padgett, 423-555-9336.

It was followed by Sheila Wilcox, Rhonda Bennett, Michelle Scott, and... Jessica, all complete with phone numbers. *Now that* is *interesting. Why would Jessica have a burner? Hmmm.*

I looked at Jacque. "Do you have your Jennifer phone with you?"

She dove into the bag she used to transport her entire life from one place to another and, after a little digging, came up with the phone and waved it at me. "Who would you like me to call this time?"

I handed her the list. "Try Erika Padgett first, and put it on speaker."

She did. It rang four times. "The number you have reached is no longer in service. Please hang up and try your call again."

I nodded. I wasn't surprised. "Okay, let's give Jessica a try."

She tapped in the number; the phone at the other end began to ring. After the fourth ring: "The number you have reached is no longer in service. Please hang up and try your call again."

Now that... is a puzzle.

I looked at my watch. It was almost eleven thirty; time to go.

"That's it, folks. We need to get out of here. It's time to go see Bob. Heather, Ronnie, Tim, you know what to do. Amanda, Kate—let's go. Everyone, we'll meet back here this afternoon."

Chapter Twenty

We ate lunch at the Public House on Warehouse Row. It was a pretty day. None of us were very hungry after the ordeal at the hospital, but we also hadn't eaten anything at all that day, and the coffee—I think I'd had six cups by then—was beginning to fry my brain. Finally, after some ten minutes playing with the menu, all three of us settled for clam chowder and a house salad and... more coffee. No, I had the coffee. The ladies both had iced tea.

"I need to go back to Channel 7," Amanda said as we left the restaurant. "I need to talk to my producer. And, Harry, I'm not happy about this thing with Heather." She looked at Kate, then at me. "I'm just not comfortable with it. Hell, I don't even know her. Well, hardly."

"Okay," I said. "So tell me. When are you planning to go back to Belle Edmondson?" I saw Kate smile out of the corner of my eye.

"Who said I was going back up there?"

"You think I don't know you after all this time?" I shook my head. "Well I do, and here's how I think it's going to go. You've decided to look into Rösche and his private army—"

She looked away.

"Aha. I knew it. I know just how you think, and it ain't going to happen, Amanda. That son of a bitch is too much for you, even with Heather along. You can continue with your story about the college, but you leave Rösche to me and Kate."

By now we were outside the restaurant and standing in front of my car. Amanda's face was white.

"Just who the hell do you think you are, Harry Starke, to tell me how to do my job. I'll do *exactly* as I please, and no one, not even you, will tell me different."

I'd stepped over the line, and I knew it. I looked at Kate. She shrugged, turned, and walked away. I waited until she was out of earshot.

"You're right," I said quietly. "That was unforgivable, and I'm sorry. Please forgive me."

I thought she was going to burst into tears, but she didn't. She just nodded and said, "It's okay. I know what you meant, and why, and I appreciate it. I really do." She stood on tiptoe and touched her lips to mine. "Now, please take me to my car."

"I will, but will you promise me you won't go digging into Rösche's affairs?"

She sighed, shook her head, looked me in the eye, and nodded.

"Say it," I said.

"*Okay....* I promise."

"And you'll work with Heather?"

"Oh for God's sake, Harry. Yes, I'll work with Heather."

I couldn't help it. I was so relieved, I grabbed her and gave her a bear hug.

"Thank you," I whispered in her ear.

"Either get a room, you two, or let's get back to work." Kate gave us both a weird look as she opened the car door and got inside.

I drove back to my offices, where Amanda had parked her car.

"What are you doing this evening?" I asked her.

"Dinner with you, I hope. Can we go to the club?"

"Dinner is good, but the club? No. Jacque has a date, remember? And I need to be there. It will be too late when I get done. How about something quick and easy when I get home?"

"You are talking about food, right?" she asked with a sly smile.

"Get outta here. I'll call you later." And she left.

Kate and I walked into the outer office from the parking lot, and were met with what felt like a sea of anxious faces. I told them how Bob was, what little I knew, and then looked longingly at the Keurig....

Nah, better not.

"Tim, my office, now."

He followed us in, laptop cradled in the crook of his arm.

"So, were you able to find out where Padgett was?" I asked as we took our seats.

"She left her home at 6:37," he said, tapping at the keyboard. "From there, she went to the Integra Hills complex in Ooltewah. That's where Victoria Mason-Jones lives, as you know. Padgett was there all evening. She left at eleven thirty and arrived home just before midnight."

I looked at Kate. She shrugged.

"Okay, Tim. That's all for now. Good work. Thanks."

He closed the door behind him. I sat back in my chair and stared up at the chandelier. Kate said nothing.

"So Padgett was screwing Jones *and* Emily..." I mused. "Hmmm, I wonder." I leaned forward and fired up my laptop. "Give me two seconds," I told Kate. "I want to take another look at something,"

I opened up the Kalliste website and, starting with the first model, I began to browse. I had an idea of what I was looking for, and it didn't take me long to find something.

They were all there, unrecognizable unless you knew what you were looking for: Lacy was Calliope, Autumn was Nemesis, Marianne was Persephone, and then there was Cassandra and one I hadn't expected, Hera.

"Oh yeah. Jackpot," I said it so quietly I almost whispered. *"That's* what I'm talkin' about."

"What?"

I opened my desk drawer and grabbed the key ring.

"Here. Take a look at this." I tossed it to her.

"Okay...." She looked up at me.

"It's Jessica's key to Emily's room."

"I know that. So?"

"Take a look at the fob," I said.

"Why?"

"Just take a look."

"Oh.... But who is it?"

"Look at the metal disc. Familiar? It should be. You've seen one like it before. In fact, you've seen several, on the Kalliste website. The little gold discs that you click on to get to the videos. It's a twin to one of them.

"The model—this particular one—calls herself Cassandra. Cassandra is another of those damned Greek goddesses. I looked her up. She was the daughter of King Priam and a princess of Troy. Cassandra, so legend has it, had dark brown curly hair and brown eyes and was both beautiful and clever. That remind you of anyone?"

She shrugged. "Not that I can think of."

"Okay. C'mere. Take a look."

She got up from her seat and came around the desk, leaned over my shoulder, and looked.

"She looks... familiar, but...."

"It's the hair. It's a wig, I think, and the clothing. Here," I said, shoving the mouse toward her.

She clicked through the half-dozen images of the model and then, finally, she clicked on the gold disc. The image on the screen dissolved. Cassandra was the quintessential Greek goddess. She was wearing a thigh-length white toga. It was trimmed in gold. She was stunning. She was also Jessica Henderson.

Kate looked up at me. "No way."

"Oh yes way. How I missed it before, I don't know. Maybe it's the hair. It's much longer here, and she has bangs that almost cover her eyes. But the voice gives it away."

"Oh my God. Do you think...."

"That she killed Emily? Dunno. I knew there was something that first time we interviewed her. I thought maybe she was in love with Emily. This, I wasn't expecting. Now. Hit the 'Home' button and find Hera."

"Hera? Who the hell is she?"

"You'll see. Go on. Click it. That one there."

She was standing facing the camera, wearing a gold mid-thigh-length toga. Her feet were apart, in line with her shoulders. Her arms hung down and outward, placing her hands about twelve inches away from her hips. In her right hand, she held a short-sword; in her left, a dagger.

It took Kate a minute to recognize the queen of the gods, but when she did, she exploded.

"No friggin' *way*. Are kidding me? Get outta here!" Her eyes were wide, her mouth open wide, and she was shaking her head. "*Victoria friggin' Mason-Jones?*"

"Ain't that a hoot? Queen of the gods, no less. I love it."

"Well screw me stupid," Kate whispered. "She has so much to lose. Why would she risk exposing herself on a dating website? Not even a dating website—an escort website."

"Several reasons, needs being the most obvious. Money? I doubt it. But let's suppose she runs, or even owns the site. She'd be in control, safe. At least she'd think so."

"Could she be being coerced, do you think?"

"It's possible, but I doubt it. My choice would be needs. The type of women that hire these girls have needs quite different from those of a man, and they're usually much more understanding, more sympathetic in their attitudes toward the girls. Jones strikes me as a dominant personality. She also struck me as highly sexual."

"Oh yeah. You'd know all about that."

"Oh, come on. And don't look at me like that. Yes, I've been around, and I know a cougar when I see one. It's obvious that she's just that, but with... special needs."

She looked skeptically at me. "And?"

"So we now know that we have at least a half dozen people at the college, probably more, who are involved with Kalliste on some level or another. We also know Emily was one of the goddesses, which begs the question: what about the other two missing women? Were they involved too? They aren't on the site now, obviously, so there's only one way we'll ever get the answers we need, and that's to find someone who knows, and ask them."

Kate nodded. "Jessica might know something. She was close to Emily, and she started school there in 2012. Grove went missing in 2013. There's only one other person who's been around long enough to have known them both, and that's Victoria Mason-Jones. She's been at Belle Edmondson since 2007. The first girl, Angela Young, disappeared in 2011. And Marcy Grove in... November 2013. Jessica has been at Belle for almost fifteen months, and maybe some of the others have too."

"So we talk to her, and we confront Hera," I said.

"Sounds like a plan."

"When do you want to do it?"

"Today. This afternoon. You up for it?"

"What the hell do you think, Harry?"

"Good. I want to check one more thing, and then we'll head on up the mountain. I want to take another look at the security footage from the Sorbonne."

I pulled up the file and ran the footage forward at one-and-a-half speed, then back again, starting and stopping it. Two things stood out: Emily was being watched by Jessica, and Jessica didn't look happy. Oh, she was smiling, laughing, and appeared to be having a good time, but she kept glancing over her shoulder at Emily, and when she did, the smile dropped away and her eyes narrowed. It was a serious, almost angry look.

I ran the footage all the way through, until Emily and Erika left the bar. I counted twenty-three times Jessica turned to look at them.

"Why was she watching her so closely?" I asked Kate.

"You think there was something going on between them, Jessica and Emily, or Jessica and Erika?"

"I think... maybe Jessica had a thing for Emily, or Erika. If so, and if she was about to get dumped, we have a motive. Jealousy."

"I dunno, Harry."

"There's something else," I said. "Look here." I pointed to a spot on the screen. "There was someone else watching them. A woman, for sure, but who it is, I can't tell."

She was seated at a table in the far corner of the room. She showed up on only one camera. She had long, dark hair and was wearing a ball cap that, due to the high angle of view, covered most of her face. What it didn't cover, it cast a shadow over. No enhancement was going to produce a recognizable image; even I knew that. But there was something familiar about her. I had the feeling that I'd seen her before. I stared at her, moved to the next image, and the next, and the next, all the way to the end. Nope. I wasn't getting her.

I picked up the phone and buzzed Tim.

"Hey buddy," I said when he came in. "Come and take a look at this."

"That's the footage from the Sorbonne."

"Yeah, but look at her. I think I already know the answer to this—"

"You're right," he said. "It's not going to happen. I'll give it a shot, but there's not much I can do with it."

"Good man, Tim. Quick as you can. You have the footage on your machine, right?"

He nodded. "I'll get right on it."

He left, and I continued to run the footage back and forth, looking for... something, anything, but I got nothing more. *Bummer.*

I sat there thinking as I watched the scene in the Sorbonne unfold for the umpteenth time. If there was anything else there, it was beyond me.

I tilted my chair back as far as it would go, put my feet up on the desk, closed my eyes, and let my mind wander.

Emily was gay, I thought. *They were both on the website. That meant that Jessica was, at the very least, a switch hitter, bi, or even gay. If she had a thing for Emily.... Hmmm. Jealousy is a wicked master. She could have done for both of them. Jessica said she has a boyfriend. We need to talk to him. If it's not a romantic relationship, if she's a lesbian.... But if she did kill Emily, where did she keep her those five days? Not on campus, that's for sure, unless.... Nah.*

"Harry!" I came back to earth with a jolt. Kate had gone back to her seat and was staring at me.

"Sorry. I was away with the birds. I was thinking. Trying to...."

"We need to get out of here," she said. "We need to go talk to Jessica and Mason-Jones."

"You're right," I said, getting to my feet. "And Rösche—"

"Oh no. Oh hell no. You're not going anywhere near that crew."

"I've got to. For several reasons, the first of which is, I want to know what that son of a bitch is doing running a private army up there. The second is, I want to know why he wanted the chip from Charlie's camera."

"That's easy. He wanted to recreate the truth to suit himself."

"You think? Maybe. I guess. We'll see."

I went to my closet. "Here," I said, tossing the Point Blank vest to her. "Put that on."

I got no argument from her; it was a slightly more comfortable model than her own. She stripped off her jacket and slipped into the body armor. It fit her perfectly. I took my own vest from the hanger and put it on, then I went to my desk, opened the drawer, and grabbed my collapsible steel baton. I slid it into my pants pocket, then took the M&P9 from its holster, jacked the slide, and chambered a round. Finally, I donned a lightweight black golf jacket. I was ready.

"Let's go."

I checked with Tim on the way out to see if he'd been able to do anything with the image from the security footage. But when he saw me coming, he simply shook his head and shrugged.

So who the hell is it?

Chapter Twenty-One

The ride up Signal Mountain Road was strangely quiet. Usually Kate and I spent our windshield time together discussing points, but not this time. Bob loomed large in both our minds, and neither one of us was able to bring up the possible outcome of his injury. That he might die was unthinkable.

About halfway up the mountain, on the sharp bend by the flying saucer house, we passed a white Lexus SUV. I was concentrating on the bend too closely to see who was driving, and it was going too fast for me to get a good look at it anyway, but I could have sworn it was Amanda's car. But then, there are a lot of Lexus SUVs on the roads these days. The road straightened as we eased into the small community.

We drove through the big iron gates and onto Belle Edmondson property. The long drive meandered away in front of us, the school buildings hidden by large stands of old-growth trees. We saw no one until we reached the parking lot outside Jessica's dorm building, and then only a lone student laden down with a backpack that sagged and banged against her backside as she walked, head down, ears plugged with buds, towards... well, that was anyone's guess.

"No reception committee," I said as I put the car in park and turned off the engine. "They know we're here though; that's a fact. I see at least ten CCTV cameras."

Kate didn't answer. The look on her face as she got out of the car and walked into the building was one of steely resolve.

"Wait." I placed a hand on her arm. "You or me?"

She tilted her head. "You... I think. But be easy on her. Put her at ease, gain her confidence, present her with what we know."

"Sounds like a plan," I said. "Let's do it."

I knocked gently on Jessica's door. There was a long, heavy scraping noise, like someone moving a table, and the door opened.

"Oh no," she said. "More questions?"

She opened the door, and we went in. She seated herself on one side of the table; we took the two chairs on the other.

"So."

"So, Jessica," I said. "You're gay, right?" I heard Kate's sharp intake of breath, and inwardly smiled. *Put her at ease, my ass.*

The color drained from the girl's face. "*What?* What are you talking about? I'm not gay. I have a boyfriend."

"John Parker? No, I don't think so. He a friend, yes, but you're not romantically involved with him. You were in love with Emily."

"I'm not a lesbian," she whispered, her eyes beginning to fill with tears.

I leaned forward, placed the iPad in front of her, brought up her Kalliste page, and said, "Of course you are, Cassandra," and then I leaned back and watched her. The look on her face was priceless.

"What? But... how... that's not what it...." And then she burst into tears. "Oh my God, oh my God, oh my God."

We said nothing. We waited. She sat motionless, staring at the screen and listening to herself saying, "Hello. I am Cassandra, princess of Troy, daughter of King Priam and Queen Hecuba and mistress of the art of... well, you'll see. Please, ask for me by name. Ladies only, please. Thank you." The voice was lighthearted, playful, and undeniably Jessica's.

I picked up the iPad and closed the cover. She looked first at me, wide eyes filled with tears, then at Kate. The proverbial deer caught in the headlights.

"So," I said, "would you like to talk about it?"

She rose unsteadily to her feet. "Not only no, but hell no. Not without a lawyer."

"Sit down, Jessica," Kate said gently. "You're not in any trouble. At least, not yet. We know all about the Kalliste website, what's been going on here, what you, Emily, and the others were up to, and we don't care. We want to know what happened to Emily and Erika Padgett, and we think you can help us."

Jessica slowly sat down again. "But I don't know what happened to Emily, or the vet woman. They left the Sorbonne together and that's the last I saw of either of them."

"Do you want to find out what happened to her?" I asked gently.

"Of course."

"Then tell us what you know about Kalliste."

She shrugged. "What's to tell? It is what it is. It's not illegal... oh God. If ever my parents find out, they'll kill me."

"How does it work?" I asked. "Who runs the thing? How do they recruit the girls?"

"They use hidden cameras. Other than what I do, I don't know how it works either. It's not bad, though. In fact, it's fun. I get to meet people, visit nice places, nice vacations, dates, and I get paid well."

"Hidden cameras? What do you mean?"

She glanced up at the smoke detector on the ceiling above our heads, and I knew exactly what she meant. I jumped to my feet and shoved the chair back.

"Oh don't worry," she said, sheepishly, tearfully, "it's not on. Not now. I disconnected it. They... they... watched us, Emily and me. In bed together. We were... well, lovers, for a long time, ever since we first met. I loved her... so much. And now...." The tears were flowing freely again.

"We'd been together for two weeks?" She said it like a question, but it wasn't. "Then one day—it was on a Friday afternoon—she came to my room. Emily was here. We were in bed. She told us who she was through the door and we quickly dressed and I let her in."

"They? She? Who's she?"

"The chancellor, Ms. Mason-Jones."

Why wasn't I surprised?

"Go on, Jessica," Kate said.

"She did the iPad thing. Just like you did. She told us our behavior was unacceptable, and that she had no alternative but to report us to our parents and expel us from the college, unless...."

"Unless you did as she asked, right?"

She nodded, picked up a tissue to wipe her nose, then just stared at the table.

"And then?" I asked.

"And then she went into the whole Kalliste thing. She made it sound like fun, and it is—was, until Emily.... She set everything up. Photo and video sessions, the website, telephones, everything. All we had to do was take the calls and pass the contacts on to her. She would let us know a day or two later if we were to proceed and make a date. I became Cassandra and Emily was Adrestia. It was... exciting, and we had some wonderful times, made a little money too. And then Emily found Erika. Well, Erika found Emily."

"And how did that happen?" Kate asked.

"They met initially at the horse barn. I saw how Erika was around her, but she never... at least I don't think she did. Anyway, one day Emily came to me and said, 'You'll never guess. I just had a call, through Kalliste. It was Erika. She wants a date.' Emily was so pleased."

"How did Erika find her on the website?" I asked.

"I don't know, and I didn't ask. All I know is they began seeing each other, a lot, and outside of Kalliste. I told her not to do it. That they would be angry with her, but she wouldn't listen. It was as if... as if she was in love with Erika."

"But you were in love with Emily?" Kate asked.

She nodded. "I was so very much in love with her."

"Did you kill them, Jessica?" I asked quietly.

"What? No... no... no. Oh how could you?" And she burst into tears again.

"It's all right," Kate said.

The hell it is. We have a clear motive now: jealousy.

"Jessica." Kate took the digital recorder from her pocket and placed it on the table in front of her. "I have everything you've told us on this recorder. This was not your fault. Nor was it Emily's. You both were coerced into Kalliste and prostitution—"

"Prostitution?" she interrupted. "It wasn't...." And then she realized that was exactly what it was.

Kate nodded. "And that's not all. We have every reason to believe that everything you did with your clients was recorded and possibly used to blackmail them." She paused for a moment.

Jessica looked at her. "Oh my God," she whispered. "Oh my God. My parents...."

There was no point making promises we couldn't keep. Her parents were going to be told, and that was all there was to it. My biggest concerns were the deaths of the two women, Erika Padgett and Emily. Jessica had the motive. Did she also have the means and opportunity? I needed to find out, but that would need to come later.

"Jessica. I need you to make a formal statement," Kate said. "And I'm going to ask you some questions. You will answer them, and then make your statement. Do you understand?"

"Are you going to take me to jail?"

"No. You're as much a victim as your clients, but I will need you to give evidence. Now. Do you agree?"

She nodded, and Kate changed the SD card in the recorder,

cautioned her, and then took her statement. I excused myself to call Heather. I had her drop everything and come over as quickly as possible. I also made a call to Jessica's parents. I put them on speaker phone and explained the situation to them as best I could, making sure they understood that their daughter was the victim, and then I told them we were bringing her home, and that they were to be kind and sympathetic to her. Whether or not that had any effect, I didn't know. One thing I did know was that we couldn't leave the girl alone by herself.

I reentered the room and listened as she finished. It was all done in less than thirty minutes, but I still had a few questions, and Heather still had not arrived.

"One more thing, Jessica," I said. "You remember Marcy Grove, right? She disappeared back in 2013. You were a member of Kalliste back then. Was Marcy?"

She nodded.

"And your phone, the burner. You got rid of it. Why?"

"When Emily... when she... when I found out she was dead, I threw it away. I wanted out, but they wouldn't let me. They gave me another one." She went to her dresser and took a prepaid cell from the drawer. I made a note of the number and gave it back to her.

"If they call, Jessica, it's very important that you don't let them know that you've talked to us, that we know. You must act as if nothing has happened. Then call me or Lieutenant Gazzara. Do you understand?"

She nodded, staring miserably down at the phone.

There was a knock at the door. It was Heather. Jessica looked at her questioningly as she came in.

"Jessica," I said, "this is Heather. She works for me. She's going to take you home."

Her chin dropped, her mouth opened; she tried to speak but couldn't.

"It's okay. I've spoken to your mother and father. They understand. They're going to look after you until this thing is done. Heather will stay with you until she's sure you're okay."

Jessica looked at Heather, and something passed between them. She nodded, and I looked at Kate. She nodded too.

I put a hand on Heather's arm. "Look after her."

"Well," Kate said as we exited the building. "Now we know."

I nodded. "Trafficking," I said thoughtfully, "and we know all about that, don't we? Unfortunately, we only have her word for it, and she's a liar, a prostitute, and a murder suspect. She'll blame anyone and everyone. I think I believe her, but we need to reach out to the clients. We need some of them to come forward and give evidence. Tomorrow, though. Today, let's go talk to the queen of the gods."

Chapter Twenty-Two

W e found her in her office. She wasn't pleased to see us. The black business suit had been replaced by a light gray one. The ruby ear studs had been replaced by thin gold hoops. She was gorgeous, there was no doubt about that, but she was a far cry from the goddess she depicted on the website.

"This is too much," she said, rising to her feet as we entered her office. "I've just got rid of that woman from Channel 7, now you barge in here without an appointment. I have no time to talk to you. Please leave at once. If you don't, I will have security escort you off the premises."

Hmmm. So it was *Amanda we passed on the highway.*

I smiled at her and sat down on one of the two high-back chairs in front of her desk; Kate took the other one.

"Nah," I said amiably. "I don't think you will. For one thing, neither the lieutenant nor I are the pushovers your thugs

took Bob Ryan and Amanda Cole for. And I think you'd
rather hear what we know from us, rather than Channel 7."

She sat down again, closed her eyes, and massaged the
bridge of her nose. When she looked up at me her face was
a grim mask.

"So what *do* you want?" she asked.

I opened my iPad, went to the Kalliste website, flipped
through the screens until I found the one for Hera, and then
I handed it to her.

"I want you to tell me all about this."

Shock and awe is a military doctrine, and I quote, "based on
the use of overwhelming power and spectacular displays of
force to paralyze the enemy's perception of the battlefield
and destroy its will to fight." It's also a term the use of which
was absolutely appropriate here. The look on Mason-Jones'
face was one of total disbelief. Her eyes widened, she stared
at the screen for a moment, then slammed the leather cover
shut and clasped the iPad to her chest.

She began to stammer, the words disconnected, unrelated,
making no sense. I reached out across the desk for the iPad;
she clutched it to her even more tightly.

"Come on," I said. Give it to me."

She shook her head, "You... you... you can't."

"Oh but I can, and I will. Now hand it over."

Reluctantly, she did so, and with its departure she seemed

to gather strength, pull herself together. She took a long, slow, deep breath, and then said, "I have nothing to say, and now I must ask you to leave."

I nodded. I wasn't surprised, but I wasn't ready to give up, not yet.

"I think you should reconsider that," I said. "There are at least half a dozen of your students on that website. And those are the ones we know of. One of them, Emily Johnston, is dead. Murdered. Two more are missing, presumed dead. Erika Padgett, a close friend of Johnston's, is also dead. We believe all four deaths are connected to this website which, so we believe, you run. We believe that because we know you and Captain Rösche coerce your students into participating in acts of lesbian prostitution—by definition, that's human trafficking—a felony punishable by up to twenty years in prison. This is serious shit, Ms. Mason-Jones. I think you'd better talk."

Her face was white, but she replied calmly. "Once again, I must ask you both to leave my office immediately. From now on you will communicate with me through my lawyers unless you intend to arrest me, which, unless I'm mistaken, you do not have the authority to do."

She stared at Kate. Kate stared back, unmoving.

"I thought not," she said. "Now. I insist that you leave my office."

It was obvious we would get nothing more from her, so I rose to my feet. So did Kate.

"Big mistake, Vicky," I said. She didn't bat an eyelash. She just sat there staring at us. And so we left.

"What do you think?" Kate asked, as we walked out of the admin building and down the front steps.

"She's tough," I said, "but not tough enough. We'll get her. For now, though, all we have is Jessica's word about what's going on. It's not enough. She could just be trying to cover her ass. Coercion is one thing, if that's what's going on here. Freewill participation in a lesbian dating website is quite another. Hell, it all could be quite innocent. They have to meet somewhere, somehow, don't they?"

She gave me one of those looks, part disbelief, part amusement, "Yeah," she said, dryly. "I suppose they do."

We walked in silence to the car.

"What now?" she asked as she opened the door. "You want to talk to the horse woman, Michelle Scott?"

"No point. At least right now. We know how Emily and Erika met. It wasn't at the horse barn. I don't think Michelle had anything to do with it."

"I agree," she said as she checked the Glock 26 on her hip. "So. Let's go step on a roach." I had to smile at that one, but then I saw the look on her face. She wasn't smiling. Other than the two spots of pink high on her cheekbones, her face was pale, and her lips were set in a thin, tight line.

Chapter Twenty-Three

I pulled the Maxima to a stop outside the campus police office. They were outside on the front porch, and obviously waiting for us. They looked like a couple of orangutans.

We got out of the car. Mirrors took a step forward; so did I. That put us almost nose-to-nose. I jerked the M&P9 out from under my arm and jammed the barrel into his nostrils. He yelped, took an involuntary step backward, and grabbed his now bleeding nose with both hands.

"Goddammit!" he yelled through his fingers. "What did you do that for?"

"I did it to get you the hell out of my way, and that goes for you too, Lenny or Squiggy or whatever the hell your name is," I said to his partner. "Either one of you so much as twitches a finger in the direction of those Glocks and I'll blow your friggin' hand off. Now, lead the hell on. We're going to see your boss."

Their boss was behind his desk. He was in uniform, leaning back in his chair, seemingly perfectly at ease. That's what he would have had us believe, but there was just a hint of fear on his thin face as Kate, Glock 26 in hand, and I herded his two monkeys in in front of us.

"Come on in, Harry, Lieutenant." He smiled, but there was no humor in it. "The chancellor said you might drop by. Sit down. Take a load off." He looked with disgust at his two minions. "You two," he said, "can go, but stay close. Oh, and be sure to let the others know where I am."

The instructions were a clear order to fetch help. I wasn't having it.

"You two stay the hell where you are," I said. "In fact, why don't you just sit down over there where I can see you, like good little boys?" I twitched the M&P9 in the direction of two chairs set against the wall at the right side of his desk.

They looked at him. He nodded, and they sat, both looking exceedingly uncomfortable. We remained standing. I was just about to speak, but Kate beat me to it.

"What the hell are you running here, Rösche?" she asked. "This is a high-end college for women. Why do you need a small army of armed mercenaries? And who the hell trained them to attack a female reporter and gun down a man without provocation?"

It was a question he'd been expecting. I could see that, but it was also one he wasn't going to answer, at least not will-ingly. I could see that too.

He grinned. He had all the charm of a cornered rat.

"Oh I don't think it was unprovoked. Your *reporter* was trespassing, and the man, your *employee*, Harry, attacked one of my men. Pretty cut-and-dried case of us doing our job, protecting the vulnerable young ladies we have here, wouldn't you say?"

"Have you seen the news today?" she asked.

"Of course. So?"

"So your men, both of them, are screwed. They're going to jail, you stupid son of a bitch. It's all on camera. And if Ryan dies, your man's going down for murder; attempted murder if he doesn't die."

He shrugged. "Our lawyers have different ideas. They were trespassing and they disobeyed clear instructions to leave. Ryan attacked one of my men as he attempted to eject them from the property and incapacitated him. Ronson was simply doing his job when he drew his weapon in response. I'd say you'll be receiving his suit for personal injury quite shortly; Ryan was, after all, acting on your behalf. Is that not correct? And on private property too."

I couldn't believe what I was hearing. The man was serious. He really thought he was going to get away with it.

I opened my mouth to speak, but Kate put her free hand on my arm. "I'll ask you again, Rösche," she said quietly. "Why the army?"

"Army? You mean my eight security guards? Not really an army now, are they?"

"Let's move on," Kate said. Her face was as set and cold as stone. "What do you know about Kalliste?"

It wasn't much, but it was there: the tiniest twitch at the corner of his mouth, and his eyes unlocked from hers, switched from her to me and then back again.

"Kalliste? What's that?" And there it was, the tell. He knew it was a what and not a who.

I grinned at him and waited to see if Kate had caught it too. She had.

"How did you know?" she asked.

"Know? Know what?"

"That Kalliste is not a woman's name?"

"I didn't." He now looked decidedly uncomfortable. "I just thought—"

She stepped around the desk and jammed the muzzle of her Glock into his crotch, hard. There was nowhere for him to go; his back was already against the back of the chair.

"Tell me, you son of a bitch, or I'll blow your baby bag to hell and back."

He gasped, trying to wriggle out from under the gun, but she simply shoved the Glock harder into his tender parts. His face had gone white and his hands were clamped to the arms of his chair. I watched Mirrors and Aviators, ready if they were to make a move. They didn't. They watched, shocked, as their boss squirmed under the increasing pressure of the Glock.

He was scared shitless, and who wouldn't be? Nobody likes to have a firearm pointed at them, much less have one shoved into their genitals. Accidents happen all the time. I smiled inwardly. I could see what he couldn't: Kate's finger was not on the trigger.

"Do your worst, bitch," he snarled through his teeth. "I was trained by the best. You'll get nothing from me."

She glared down at him, shook her head, gave the Glock another sharp shove, twisted it, and stepped back. He slumped down in the chair and grasped his injured package in both hands.

"So let me tell you what we know, asshole." She sat on the edge of his desk, the Glock in her hand, resting on her thigh and pointing at his crotch, which he was gently massaging.

"We have a witness. We know that you and the queen—the chancellor—are blackmailing students into prostitution. That, you son of a bitch, is human trafficking, and it'll get you twenty years."

"Screw you," he snarled. "Get the hell out of my office, and off the property."

"He's right, Harry. He'll give us nothing we don't already know. Let's get out of here. Oh yeah," she said, glaring at Rösche, "and keep your damned dogs clear of us."

"I've got a job to do, bitch. As long as you're on the property, my people will be watching you."

She turned in the doorway, face emotionless, "You'd better pray that Bob Ryan makes it. If he doesn't, I'm coming after you."

Back in the car, she sat quietly staring out the windshield. What was going through her mind, I didn't know. I knew one thing though: I'd just seen a side of Kate I'd never seen before, and it wasn't pretty. I let her be as I swung the car out of the lot and away toward Signal Mountain. It wasn't until we were almost in Red Bank that she finally broke her silence.

"So, what do you think?" she asked.

"About Rösche?"

She nodded.

"I think Jones is the brains. He just works for her. He's the guy that gets the goods on the women, the video footage they use to coerce them, and probably runs protection for the girls, too. I also think his *cajones* will have turned black by morning."

She nodded again, but made no further attempt at conversation.

It was almost six thirty when we rolled through the gate, into the parking lot behind my office. The rest of the crew was already there, waiting, anticipating. Tonight, Jacque was going on a date.

I had just one thing left to do before we headed out; I called Amanda.

She picked up on the third ring. "Harry. I was just going to call you. I went up to the school this afternoon. It was a disaster. No one would talk to me. She, that Mason-Jones woman, had those pigs escort us off the property."

"Oh jeez, Amanda. I thought you promised not to go back up there."

"I did not. I promised not to confront Rösche. You said nothing about Mason-Jones or Jessica Henderson."

"You talked to Jessica. She didn't say so."

"No. I didn't get the chance. I met with Jones. As soon as I walked into her office, she called Rösche. You're right about him. He's a pig. Anyway. We weren't there but a few minutes. He insisted we leave and not come back. He and one of his men followed us to the gate. Harry, I can hear you smiling. It's not funny. I have a story to produce."

You can hear me smiling? Oh that's too much.

The weird thing was, I was indeed smiling.

"I wasn't," I said. "Well, only a little. Listen. You'll get your story. I promise. Just be patient. This thing is unfolding fast. I don't yet know quite where it's going, but it's going to be big, and—"

She interrupted me. She rattled off a list of questions without taking a breath. Now I really was smiling.

"No, Amanda. Not now. I don't have it all together, and no you can't go dropping hints on the air. You'll screw things up if you do. Please, just bear with me."

She wasn't happy, but she agreed to wait, and I promised to give her what details I could when I got home.

Chapter Twenty-Four

J acque had made a dinner reservation for eight thirty, and they had arranged to meet in the lobby of the Read House at eight. Jacque had also booked a king suite in the hotel and checked in at six that evening. By eight o'clock, Tim and his girlfriend, Samantha, were seated at their table in the restaurant, waiting. Heather was in the lobby seated at a table outside Starbucks.

Kate and I were in the company van, which was parked in the multi-story next to the hotel. I usually have Tim run the electronics, but with Bob still in hospital and Tim in the restaurant, I had to do it myself.

Everyone inside the hotel, including Jacque, was equipped with a watch that could record both video and sound. These were connected to the van's electronics by WiFi. I had one myself—it was the only one I ever wore, because, well, you never know.

At eight o'clock, Jacque came down from her room and

arrived in the lobby a couple of minutes early. Heather spotted her first. She looked stunning in a white cocktail dress. The white of the dress and matching clutch accentuated the coffee color of her skin. She found a seat and sat down to wait, but not for long. At precisely eight o'clock, Artemis entered the lobby from the street.

She looked around, spotted Jacque, and walked toward her. Jacque rose to meet her.

Artemis was a true goddess. She was maybe five foot nine, the honey-colored ringlets a stark contrast to the long-sleeved black pencil dress.

Jacque extended her hand, "Artemis?" I adjusted the sound a little. The watch was working perfectly.

"And you must be Jennifer." The voice was low, quiet. I adjusted the sound again. *Damn. I wish Tim was doing this.*

"Would you like a drink before dinner?" Artemis asked, still holding Jacque's hand.

"Yes. I think that would be nice." I smiled. She was putting on the West Indian accent, and it suited her perfectly.

Heather followed them into the bar. They took a table, and the waiter was on them almost before they'd gotten settled. They ordered martinis. Heather seated herself at a table close by, where she could face and record them.

"So, tell me about yourself," Artemis said.

"Oh, I think you already know all there is to know. Is that not correct?"

"It is, but I'd rather hear it from you."

I crossed my fingers, but I needn't have bothered. Jacque was good. Far better than I could have imagined. She ran out the background of the persona Tim had provided in a relaxed and conversational way that, if I hadn't known better, I would have believed myself.

"So what do you do for a living?"

"Why, nothing, of course. I told you, my father is a very wealthy man. Now, you know all about me. I'd like to hear about you."

Artemis stared at her for a moment and then smiled.

"My real name is Wendy. I... I'm self-employed. Look, let's get to know each other a little before we, well. Let's get to know each other. Did you bring the money?"

"I did, but I'd like to keep it for later, if you don't mind."

"That's not the way it works," she said, gently. "Money up front is the arrangement. You knew that."

"Yes, I did. But as you said, we don't know each other, now do we. So...."

Artemis rose to her feet. "I think not."

"Damn," I said to Kate. "She's blown it."

"I don't think so. Watch."

Jacque smiled sweetly up at her. "Are you leaving then, and so soon? That's too bad. I was so looking forward to tonight.

The money's safe, in here." She patted her clutch. "There's no need for you to leave."

Wendy, or whatever her name was, paused, looked down at her, nodded, and sat down again.

They went into the dining room at eight thirty, ordered, and chatted quietly together as they ate. Between Tim and Jacque, we got most of it, and that wasn't much. Every time Jacque brought up a sensitive point, Wendy deftly parried and changed the subject.

By ten o'clock they had finished their meal. Tim and Samantha, not being able to stretch things out without it becoming obvious, had already left, and both were now inside the van with Kate and me. Tim, thank God, had taken over the electronics.

Jacque charged the meal to her room and together they headed for the elevator. The ride up was a weird experience, at least for us. Jacque's arm was at her side and the image moved back and forth as she moved it. It made my head swim. At one point, they must have kissed, because she put her hand on the woman's shoulder and we were treated to an intimate view of the inside of her ear.

"Very pretty," Tim murmured.

"If you'll excuse me for just a moment," Wendy said. "I need to use the bathroom."

She closed the bathroom door, and Jacque looked at the WiFi spy camera on the sideboard next to the TV—it was disguised as an air freshener—and winked, and then she walked over to the window and stared out over the city nightline. The camera provided a 180-degree view of the room. She stood with her back to it, feet slightly apart, arms folded.

Wendy emerged a few minutes later, looking refreshed and more than a little wary.

"So," she said as Jacque turned toward her. "First things first."

Jacque nodded. She retrieved her clutch from the bed and took out a small stack of hundred-dollar bills, handed them over, then placed the clutch on the sideboard next to the camera.

Wendy counted the money carefully and, satisfied, placed it inside her own clutch.

"So."

"So," Jacque replied with a shy smile.

Wendy stepped forward, slipped her arms around Jacque's waist, and pulled her gently to her. Jacque put her hands to Wendy's neck and kissed her. It was a long, gentle and—so I thought—heartfelt kiss.

Finally, Jacque pushed her gently away.

"Give me just a minute, please?" she whispered, so low we could barely hear her.

She moved away. Then she took off the watch, slipped it

into the clutch and closed it and, unobtrusively, turned the spy camera to face the wall.

"What the hell?" I asked, as the screen went blank. All was now quiet inside the room. The spy camera was not equipped with sound, video only, and the watch was inside the clutch.

Kate laughed, and looked over at me. "It looks like our girl intends to enjoy herself."

Me? Oh I was pissed.

They didn't surface until almost eight thirty the following morning; that according to Jacque, because we had left just before midnight.

Chapter Twenty-Five

"What the hell did you think you were doing?" I asked as she walked in through the office door. It was almost ten o'clock.

"Your office, please, Mr. Starke," she said, as she glared round at Tim and Heather. They were both smiling.

I followed her in. She stepped behind me and slammed the door, then turned to face me. "Don't you *ever* do that to me again."

"What? Do what?"

"In front of the staff. You know what."

I was so angry I didn't trust myself to answer her, so I didn't.

"What did I tink I was doing?" There was that accent again. "I was doin' me damn job. The job you asked me to do. That's what I was doin'."

"But you turned off the sound, and the camera."

"What did you expect, a bloody peep show? Shame on you, Harry Starke."

"I... I.... Oh come on Jacque. I didn't expect you to... well... you know!"

"No I don't know, damn it. Tink about it, mon. I'd just handed her two tousand dollars. We both knew what that was for, so what the hell would she have thought if I'd not gone tru with it? Besides, *I liked the bloody woman.*" She almost shouted that last into my face. "In fact, I wanted her. She was beautiful, and gentle, and she treated me with love and respect, *and I bloody well enjoyed it!*"

Okay. I got it. But I sure as hell didn't know what to do with it. I just stood there and stared at her. I'd always known she was gay, but somehow I'd never really put it together, not until then.

I turned away, gesturing for her to sit down, and I retreated to the safety of my own chair behind my desk.

We sat. We looked at each other. We sat some more, and we looked some more. Finally we both spoke, at the same time.

"Hush!" she said. "It's all right." She paused, then sighed. "Actually, I should say thank you. For one of the best nights of my life."

Again, I was flummoxed. I just shook my head, shrugged, opened my mouth, and then closed it again.

"She's been with Kalliste for three years," she said.

I blinked at her.

"Don't look so damned goofy," she said. "I told you I was doing my job. I talked to her, right? Three years. During that time she's met with only a handful of women. She doesn't do it for a living. In fact, she's a vice president at one of the local banks. She does it to fulfill a need. The money? 70 percent goes to Kalliste. She has no contact with the owners of the website other than by private e-mail within the system."

"How come she told you all this?"

"Oh please. She's not the only one that's good at what she does." She said it with a sly smile.

"Jeez, Jacque. Did she say anything about the owners, how she gives them the money, anything?"

"No, she didn't, and I didn't ask. I didn't want to spook her. But don't worry. I'll find out. If not next time, then... well, whenever."

"There's going to be a next time?"

"That there is."

"And how the hell much is that going to cost?"

"Not a thing. We hit it off. We made a date for tomorrow night. She's... she's... well, I think I'm in love. And, Harry, please don't spoil it for me. I'm 99 percent certain she's clean."

I shook my head, exasperated. "Jeez, Jacque. What am I going to do with you? Go on, get out of here. Just keep me up to speed, okay?"

I stared at the closed door for a long time after Jacque had closed it behind her. I was worried about her. Yeah, I know, I know, she's a big girl, but we're close, always have been, and I love her like a sister. I hoped like hell she wasn't getting in over her head.

I went to the break room for more coffee, returned, and flopped down in the chair again. I wasn't really thinking about anything in particular, just staring at the ceiling, taking a quiet moment and drinking some good coffee.

Emily's journal was on my desk. Idly, I picked it up and began to flip through the pages, not really looking for anything, just browsing the photos. She'd been a happy girl back in the day, and had obviously enjoyed some happy times. The girls, the Kalliste girls, Calliope, Persephone, Nemesis, and Apate. Beautiful, all of them, and more so now that I knew who they all were, except... Apate? No, I didn't know her. I continued browsing. Apate... hmmm... Apate.

I flipped through the book and found her again. I opened my iPad and went to the Kalliste website. She was the last model on page three of the catalog images.

Apate, so said Wikipedia, was the goddess of deceit. Her mother was Nyx, the primordial goddess of night, her father Erebos, the god of darkness. Wow. I paged through the site to the end, clicked on the gold disc. She was dressed in a black, satin toga. Her shoulders were bare, as were her thighs. Her long black hair was interwoven with gold thread. She was lovely, and her message? The same as her companion goddesses—ladies only.

I closed the iPad and picked up the journal. I searched, but could find no connection between Emily and Apate. So why was the photo there? I could think of only one reason. More code: the name. Apate; she was the personification of deceit. Deceit... deception... the photo.

It's the only one taped into the book.

All the other photographs were glued in place, and it looked to me like Apate's might have been removed and replaced. More than once.

Okay, so let's see.

Carefully, I lifted one corner of the adhesive tape. It came away quite easily. I lifted the photo clear of the page, and there it was. I grabbed my iPhone and photographed the page several times. I took images of the photo with the tape still adhered to it, and to the single piece of paper still *in situ* behind it. Secrets; deceit; Apate.

I took a pair of tweezers from my desk drawer and lifted the piece of paper from the page. It was folded twice. I laid it on my desk, slipped on a pair of latex gloves, and opened it to find more numbers and codes, just like those Tim had already deciphered. This time, though, there were only four listings.

I ran a copy of it, placed it back in the book, and replaced the photo and tape. Then I went to Tim and gave the copy to him.

He came to my office a few minutes later.

"Well, she must really have wanted to keep these contacts safe, and she tried hard, bless her," he said, handing me the piece of paper. "They're private iPhone numbers. The names and numbers were encoded twice. By that I mean she encoded them once then she encoded the code, and then she took it a step further and reversed it; she wrote the codes down backwards. Here you go."

Knowing what I did, the first name on the list didn't really surprise me: Victoria Mason-Jones. Numbers two, three, and four, however, hit me like I'd been kicked in the crotch by a horse: Conrad Rösche, Sheriff Hands, and Anthony Hart.

No, she couldn't have been. She was gay, for Christ's sake.

But there was no getting around it. She was either screwing them, or she was up to something else. What that could be I had no idea, unless.... Blackmail, maybe?

"Tim did you—"

"Check her cell phone records?"

Damn, the boy is even beginning to think like me.

"Yep. They don't show that she made any calls to those four numbers, but if she followed the same pattern as the other girls, she would have been using a burner. If that's the case, we'll never know."

He was right. I needed to talk to them, all three of them, but I had no jurisdiction over Hands or Hart, or even Rösche, and neither did Kate. I needed some heavy backup.

I leaned back in my chair and stared up at the ceiling. What I needed now was a heavy hitter. I had friends in the FBI, but as far as I knew, this wasn't a federal crime, so that was out. Kidnapping? Emily had been missing for five days before she was killed, so that would apply, but she hadn't been taken across state lines, so still no FBI. State, though, the Tennessee Bureau of Investigation. Yep, that would work.

I flipped the lock screen on my iPhone and called Michael Condon.

"Deputy Director Condon. How may I help you?"

"Hello, Michael. It's Harry Starke. I know it's been a while."

"Well, well. Harry Starke. You're right. It has been a while. You must want something, and if you're coming to me for it, it must be big."

"It is, Michael. I have a situation. I don't have standing here, and my contact at the Chattanooga PD doesn't have jurisdiction. I'm looking into the death of Emily Johnston. She was found out in the county."

"Yeah, I heard about that. Terrible. How is Kate, by the way?"

"She's fine. I'm investigating at Johnston's request. She's been detached and is working with me. Can you help?"

"Hamilton County, or... well, what?"

"Hamilton, Signal Mountain."

"That would be...." I heard his keyboard clicking. "Sheriff Israel Hands' jurisdiction. Why not go to him?"

"It's Hands and his deputy I wanted to question," I told him, and then went on to explain the situation.

"No shit, Harry. The damned sheriff? I don't know. You're something else, my friend. I don't know if what you have—just a couple of names in a dead girl's journal—is probable cause. But... well, I never did like that son of a bitch."

I could almost hear the wheels turning inside his head.

"Okay, here's what we'll do. You'll need to have Chief Johnston make a formal request for aid directly to me. When he does that, I'll assign an agent to work with Kate, and you. You should know this though, Harry: we, that is you, can investigate him, but Hands is under no obligation to talk or answer questions. If he chooses to, fine. If not... there's nothing anyone can do, outside of the governor's office. Hands is top dog in Hamilton County."

"Good enough. Can you stay by your desk for a few minutes? I'll have Johnston call you right away." I could almost see him shaking his head in exasperation.

"Sure, Harry. I have all the time in the world."

"Now, now, Michael. Sarcasm doesn't become you. Call me back when you're done with Johnston, okay?"

"Sure."

I called the chief's private cellphone, explained what I needed and why. And oh boy was he pissed when he learned that his daughter had been involved, one way or another, with the sheriff and at least one of his deputies. I managed to calm him down a little, and he assured me he'd make the call right away. It was maybe thirty minutes before Condon called me back. I'd almost given up on him when my iPhone began its dance across my desk.

"Hey, Michael," I answered. "Everything okay?"

"I don't know about that. I did manage to sort things out with Wes Johnston. He wanted to go and take Hands apart. I managed to stop that, I think. I hope. If he goes off half-cocked he's likely to end up in the county jail, and so are you, my friend. Do you have any idea how shaky the ground you're walking on is? Friends in high places you might have, but they won't do you any good when you take on the sheriff; he's just about untouchable unless there's hard evidence that he's committed a crime."

"Yeah, I know all that. I know the risks, but we have probable cause. Not that he's actually committed a crime, but that he might be involved in something... well, that he might be abusing his power in some way."

"Okay. Christ, okay. Here's what I've done: I've just gotten off the phone with our Knoxville office. Kate will be contacted shorty by Special Agent Gordon Caster. Yeah yeah, I know, you're leading the investigation, but this has to go through Kate as a sworn officer. You know that. He knows the routine; he'll take the lead with Hands. Harry, this is a very sensitive situation. There's no telling how Hands will react."

"Fine, but will Caster cooperate?"

He was silent for a second, then said, "Christ, Harry, you're something else. No, he will not cooperate. You and Kate will do the cooperating. When Johnston made the request, he effectively turned the investigation over to us. This thing has to be done right."

I didn't answer. I was pissed, and I didn't want say something I'd regret.

"Harry?"

"I heard you Michael."

"Now don't get your panties in a wad. I gave Caster instructions to get in and get out, ask your questions, and then leave you to it, unless...."

Oh hell. Here it comes.

"If Caster finds evidence that Hands, or his deputy, committed a crime, you lose it. The state will take over. You sure you want us on board?"

Damn! Damn it. I thought about it, and the more I did, the more unsure I became. In the end, though, I didn't have much of a choice. If I wanted to get to Hands, I had to get the state involved. *There's no evidence of any wrongdoing, just that he might be screwing around with very high-class hookers of questionable sexuality. If that were all it was....*

"Yes, Michael. I want you on board."

"Good, because the wheels are already turning. Stay in

touch, Harry. My ass is on the line with you, and I don't like it."

Click.

He'd disconnected.

Damn and blast. I'd better call Kate.

She answered on the second ring. "What's up, Harry?"

"You'd better get down here. We have a lot to talk about. When can you get here?"

"Thirty, maybe forty minutes. I'm in the middle of a meeting."

"Good. Soon as you can."

Chapter Twenty-Six

There was more that needed to be done before Kate arrived. I needed to know more about that damned website, and I knew just who to turn to. He was at his oracle, typing like a man possessed; he didn't even hear me walk in.

"Hey, Tim." I put a hand on his shoulder, and he almost leaped out of his skin.

"Jeez, don't do that. You scared the hell out of me."

"Sorry, sorry. Look, we need to know who's running the Kalliste website. Can you backdoor it?"

He looked up at me, one eyebrow raised. "Give me a couple of minutes."

It took him forty-five. Kate arrived a few minutes before he finished, and we went to my office. I brought her up-to-date about my conversation with Condon. Most of it she already knew by virtue of a long conversation with Chief

Johnston. Apparently the man was boiling. Ready to explode.

"I got it, boss." Tim was talking as he walked, the open laptop in the crook of his arm.

"Okay," I said. "Just hold on a minute while I get coffee. Kate, you want some? Tim?"

They both shook their heads. I fetched one for myself, at least, and returned to my seat.

"Let's have it, Tim."

"The Kalliste website," he said, cuddling the laptop in his left arm, "is running on a dedicated private server owned by a company called Artax Enterprises. Artax is an offshore shell corporation owned by Zeus and Associates, another shell company. The trail ends with Zeus. Exactly who is operating the website, I don't know, and can't find out; there are no principles or associates listed for Artax, which is not unusual for some shadow in a back room somewhere in the Bahamas. Zeus, however, is a different story. It's part of a limited partnership, one we've run into before. It's owned by Nickajack Investments, which is—"

"No way. The Harper Foundation. You're kidding me." I looked at Kate. Her eyes were wide; her mouth was open. She was as shocked as I was.

"No, I'm not. And there's more, much more. The more I thought about all of the Kalliste connections to Belle Edmondson—especially Mason Jones.... Well, I ran an in-depth search of the companies listed under the Nickajack umbrella, and Nickajack also owns Destrex Security. Old man Harper used them extensively until he went down."

Sheesh. Rösche. It made sense.

"How do they get paid?" I asked.

"I don't know. Cash, I assume. There's no record of credit card payments, or any other kind of payments."

"Okay, Tim. Good work."

"Now for the icing on the cake.... Oh you're gonna like this." He was grinning like a damn baboon. "Sheriff Hands is Little Billy Harper's first cousin."

"Get outta here."

Two years before, I had been instrumental in putting Congressman Gordon "Little Billy" Harper away for fifteen years. The charges ranged from accessory to murder to political corruption to money laundering.

"So who's running the foundation now that Little Billy's out of circulation?" I asked.

"Out of circulation he might be; out of the William J. Harper Foundation? No sir. As far as I can tell, he's still running things through his daughter, Kathryn Greene."

"Kathryn Greene...? I think I know her. Check to see if she's a member of the country club, Tim."

"I don't have to. She is."

"What do we know about her?"

"She the middle daughter of three. Thirty-seven years old, married to Jonathan Greene, lawyer and lobbyist extraordinaire. She has a Master's in political science from Harvard. Greene, her husband, is handling Little Billy's appeal.

"Wow," I said. I was absolutely flabbergasted. "Little Billy Harper."

"It's not really so surprising if you think about it," Tim said. "He was, still is I suppose, into all kinds of shady enterprises, even though he's in jail: Stanwood, Goodwin, Nickajack, Green Tree, and the list goes on, many of them local ventures. This one, Kalliste, is right up his ally."

I nodded. "That it is, and it ties right in with his other enterprise, Mystica. We closed that down, but the corruption involved ran deep, all the way to Washington."

My thoughts began to wander. *How's Linda doing, I wonder. Haven't heard from her in more than a year.*

I'd followed Senator Linda Michaels' career with more than passing interest, but.... I dragged my thoughts back to the subject at hand.

"What do we know about the Greenes?" I asked.

"Not much. He's one of those really mysterious people, a shadow man, someone you don't see coming until he has you by the balls. He took an active role in Harper's defense, and was directly responsible for him getting off as lightly as he did. Fifteen years in a white-collar facility... well, if it had been you or me...."

"If she's running things now, we need to go see Mrs. Greene. Where can I find her?"

"She, or I should say they, have taken over Harper's suite of offices in the Tower Building."

"That figures. I think we'll pay them a visit. Kate, you'll need to take the lead. You up for it?"

She looked up, blinked, then shook her head, obviously stunned by what she'd heard. "Damn. Who'd have believed this? Yeah, I'm up for it. We'd better take Lonnie with us. When do you want to do it?"

"Good idea. The more the merrier. As soon as we can, but we can't go in there half-cocked. We need to figure out our approach first. And then there's the sheriff to consider. Where does he fit into all this? I guarantee that the minute we approach the Greenes, he'll know about it."

We talked about it for the next twenty minutes or so, and we got nowhere. The depth of the new situation was virtually unfathomable. The Harper Foundation was a cavern of murky dealings and shadow companies, corruption, bribery, blackmail, and God only knew what else. Why the Feds hadn't shut it down was beyond me. Eventually we decided the best approach was the simplest one. We would appear unannounced on their doorstep, and hit them hard. I couldn't think of any other way.

If past experience was anything to go by, and if Kathryn Greene was anything like her father, she wasn't to be underestimated, and that, so I assumed, would apply to her husband as well.

"No time like the present," I said, glancing at Kate. "Where's Lonnie?"

"I left him at the office. I'll call him, get him to meet us at the Tower Building in fifteen minutes."

I nodded and stood up. "Tim. You hold down the fort here. Kate, if you'll give me a minute, I'd like to change clothes."

I went to my bathroom, where I kept a full wardrobe of clothes for all occasions. This one I wanted to look good for. I changed into a pair of light tan brushed-cotton pants, and a navy, long-sleeved sport shirt by the same designer, then returned to my office, where Kate was waiting.

"I see," she said, smiling.

I didn't answer. I slipped into my shoulder rig, checked the M&P9, cranked the slide and put one into the chamber, slid it back into its holster. Then I went to the closet, grabbed my black leather jacket and put it on. It hid the rig nicely.

"Here," I said, opening the desk drawer. "Use this." I gave her the small digital recorder.

She nodded and slipped it into the breast pocket of her blazer.

"You ready?" I asked.

She didn't answer, just rose to her feet and walked out the door.

Chapter Twenty-Seven

Lonnie was already waiting for us when we arrived at the Tower. The old shit-eating grin was back. Lonnie was a confrontational type of police officer, never happier than when he was in a "situation," as he called it, and he looked like he was really looking forward to this one.

We took the elevator to the top floor and, as we travelled upward, I couldn't help but remember similar rides of a time now long past, and it was the same when I pushed open the outer door to what had once been the heart of Congressman Gordon "Little Billy" Harper's empire.

The décor was different, but the reception desk was the same. Terry Hamlin, Harper's receptionist, had been replaced by a beautiful young lady.

Kate, followed by Lonnie, took the lead. She flashed her badge and asked to see Kathryn Greene.

"Do you have an appointment, Lieutenant?"

"Please just tell her we're here."

The young lady rose from behind the desk, knocked on the inner door, opened it, and went inside.

She returned a minute or so later. "Mrs. Greene will see you. Please enter."

And enter we did.

She was standing behind her desk, flanked by two men, one on either side, who stood with their arms folded and their backs to the wall. Her feet were apart; her hands, curled into fists, were knuckles-down on the transparent desktop, causing her to lean forward slightly. She was lovely. Billy must have been proud of her.

She wasn't as tall as Kate. I put her at about five foot nine, but she couldn't have weighed more than 125. Yeah, she was slim, but her figure was full and alluring under the navy business suit. Her dark brown hair was cut very short at the back, almost like a man's, but the sides were longer, layered and shaped to frame her oval face. Her eyes were brown with long black lashes and accentuated by pale pink eye shadow. The lips were full and the pink lipstick she wore matched the eye shadow.

"Hello, Harry," she said, looking up at me through her eyelashes. "I can't say I'm glad to see you, but I was anxious to meet you. I've been hoping to run into you at the club, where I could throw a glass of something special in your face, acid, maybe. But you were never around. Now here you are, and accompanied by the inimitable Kate Gazzara."

She looked at Kate and did something with her face. It wasn't so much a smile as a baring of teeth. "Oh yes," she said, "I know who you are. I've been waiting to meet you too, for a long time. And now here you are. They do say that everything comes to she who waits." She glanced at Lonnie. "Who's the suit?"

For a long time I thought Lonnie was a dumbass, but I was wrong. His apparent stupidity was a persona he'd built for himself over many years. He was deceptively slow, both physically and mentally. The extra weight he'd once carried did indeed slow him down, but not anymore, and those bursts of brilliance he was so famous for were the mere tip of the iceberg.

"Detective Sergeant Lonnie Guest, at your service ma'am."

I almost laughed. *Damn, right out of Mayberry.*

"Hmmm," she said. "So, Harry. What brings you to my world.... Oh, I'm sorry. I should introduce you to my husband: Harry Starke, Jonathan Greene."

She looked around at the man standing behind her and to her right.

I'd already known who he was. I'd seen him talking to my father on several occasions at the club, her too, but I'd never thought anything of it.

He was sharp. A typical high-dollar defense lawyer. The suit, a weird shade of medium gray, must have cost at least five grand, and with his arms folded the way they were he was able show off a solid gold Rolex Yachtmaster.

I grinned at him. The vacant look in his eyes was something I was sure he'd cultivated, but I was also sure that his brain was in overdrive.

"Hello, John," I said as I gave him the deadeye. He didn't answer. In fact, he might well have been frozen in place. I'd known men like him before: powerful and corrupt. I've had to deal with them almost since the day I graduated college. Men like her father, Little Billy Harper, who have the ability to hide the truth, manipulate those they come in contact with, and make people disappear....

I looked at the other guy. This one was different. His eyes were dead, dark pools devoid of expression, and he was big, six foot two and maybe 250 pounds. A gorilla: muscle— protection—if ever I'd ever seen it.

She turned, looked at Gorilla, and nodded.

He took a step toward me.

"Whoa," I said, taking a half step back as he reached out to pat me down. "Back off. You don't touch me unless I invite you to, and that ain't happening."

We stood for a long moment, eyeball to eyeball. It was one of those "he who blinks first, loses" moments. I won.

He turned and looked at Kathryn, who nodded again, and then he backed away and looked at Kate.

"Don't even think about it," she said, her voice low and threatening. At her side, Lonnie tilted his head and smiled at him, very benignly.

Gorilla slowly backed away across the room, until he was standing against the wall behind her desk again, then he folded his arms and stared at us.

"Well, that was entertaining," Kathryn said dryly. "But I don't have time to fool with you, Starke, so let's get on with it, shall we? What do you want?"

I turned and looked at Kate. She didn't give me so much as a sideways glance, but she knew.

"Tell us about Zeus," she said, "...and Kalliste."

The color drained from Kathryn's face, and she sank slowly into her chair.

I grabbed two chairs and brought them forward, one for me, one for Kate. Lonnie grabbed another for himself. And so we sat and watched as she... well, she almost panicked.

"W—what?" she said. Then silence.

"You heard me the first time." Kate's voice was low, threatening. John Greene shifted against the wall.

Then she seemed to gather new strength. "What the hell are you talking about?" Now she was angry. "Zeus, Kalle —what?"

"Not good enough, Kathryn," Kate replied. "You gave it away. We know that both companies are part of one of your father's enterprises, Nickajack Investments. I'm surprised that's still going. I'd have thought it would have collapsed by now."

Jonathan Greene stepped forward, "My wife will not be answering any more questions. The affairs of the William J. Harper Foundation, which I represent as attorney of record, are confidential. And to answer your question, Lieutenant, I have no idea what you're talking about either. Now, we have things to do, so please," he gestured languidly with his right hand toward the door.

"I see. So that's how it is," I said as I rose to my feet. I took a couple of steps toward the open door, then I did the Colombo thing. I stopped, as if I'd had a sudden thought, and turned and looked at her.

"By the way, Kathryn. How's your cousin, Israel?" I asked. "Staying on the straight and narrow, I hope. It would be a shame to send him off to join your dad."

Again, the color left her face. I smiled and, one behind the other, Lonnie leading, followed by Kate, and finally by me, we filed out through the reception area where, once her office door closed, we all burst out laughing.

Was it funny? No, not really, but we had what we'd come for, and the look on Kathryn Greene's face when I mentioned the sheriff was priceless. Now all we had to do was figure out how it all fit together, if at all.

Still smiling, I looked at Kate, then Lonnie. "Let's go get some lunch."

We grabbed a table at the Flatiron Grill on Walnut Street. Kate had a burger; Lonnie, bless him, settled for a cob salad, and I wasn't hungry, so I just had coffee.

"Okay," I said, once we'd all more or less finished. "So now we know. But does it really matter? How does it affect our case? As far as we know, the Greenes, and the foundation, are clean. Maybe there's money laundering going on still, but we don't know that. There's nothing illegal about Kalliste—that we know of. Maybe Hands is covering up for the Greenes, Kalliste, whatever, but we don't know that, and we certainly can't prove it with what we have now."

I looked at each of them, but neither of them had any answers. Neither did I. It was going to be a long day. Hell, it was going to be a long weekend.

Chapter Twenty-Eight

Jacque was the only one at the office when I walked in. I looked at Bob's empty desk as I passed, and I had one of those moments. You know the ones, when your heart seems to drop into the pit of your stomach. I shook my head, grabbed some Dark Italian Roast from the Keurig, went to my office, and plonked myself down in one of the easy chairs in front of the fireplace. I felt like crap.

We need more, I thought. *A whole lot more. We need to talk to some of those girls....*

"Jacque," I called, too lazy to get up.

The door opened and she came in. "Yes, *boss?*" she asked sarcastically.

I just grinned at her. "C'mere. Sit down."

She did. She took the easy chair next to me. Looked at me expectantly.

"So tell me about Wendy," I said.

She was immediately on her guard. "Tell you what?"

"Does she know who you are?"

There was a long pause, then, "Ye-es."

"How much does she know?"

"What's going on? Why do you want to know?"

Hell, I could only be honest with her. "I need to talk to her, about Kalliste, and... well, I need some answers. She's the quickest and easiest source... sorry, Jacque."

"I damn well bet you are," she snapped. "I asked you not to screw this up for me, Harry."

"Okay. Look. You know her, at least a little. If you told her who you are, what you do and... why you met with her last night, do you think she would.... Christ, I don't know. You tell me. If you think she'd blow up in your face, forget it. We'll find another way."

"I already told her all that. She was not happy, but she appreciated my tellin' her." The accent was strong, which meant she was pissed. She jumped to her feet and walked out of the office, slamming the door behind her. I sighed, lay back in my chair, and closed my eyes.

Life's a bitch and then.... Damn it!

Five minutes later, the door opened again and she stuck her head in.

"A'll be back. Answer duh damned phones while A'm gone."

She was gone for almost an hour. When she walked back into my office, she wasn't alone.

"Wendy Tanner, meet my boss, Harry Starke."

I rose quickly and shook her hand. To say I was surprised would be more than an understatement. They made a great-looking pair. And Wendy, in the flesh.... No wonder Jacque had fallen for her. And, from the way Wendy looked at her, the attraction was mutual. She truly was a goddess in every sense of the word.

She was wearing jeans and a pale blue short-sleeve shirt. The long blonde hair, still in ringlets, fell over her shoulders almost to her breasts. She wore no makeup except a hint of pale pink lipstick.

"Oh my," I said. "This, I was not expecting."

I looked at Jacque. "Wendy has agreed to talk to you. Why I don't know." She wasn't smiling. I wasn't sure I blamed her.

"Well, please, sit down. Jacque?"

"I'm stayin'."

I put my hands up.

The both sat together on the sofa. Jacque, I could tell, was very uncomfortable; Wendy, not so much. She sat with her hands together in her lap, her knees together, feet crossed at the ankles.

"Wendy," I began. "I can imagine how difficult this must be for you, and I thank you for it."

She nodded. "I know who you are, Mr. Starke. You're quite famous. I also know that Jacque trusts you, so I trust you too. What do you want to know?"

"I want to know how Kalliste works, who runs it, and how, but first I want to know about you. What makes a woman like you do... do... what you do?"

"You mean why am I a hooker? Oh don't look so put out, Jacque. It is what it is. I hate it. I don't do it by choice. I do it because I'm forced to. I'm only thankful that I only have to deal with women... most of the time. Kalliste is a lesbian site. That's what I am." She shrugged.

"How old are you, Wendy?"

"I'm twenty-seven. And your next question is how I get involved with Kalliste, right?"

I nodded.

"At Belle Edmondson, of course. I thought when I graduated four years ago that they would let me go. Hah, that was a wild dream. They still have me firmly under their thumbs."

"They?"

"I'm not entirely sure... the chancellor. She was the one who made me become a member, not that I had a choice. Someone recorded me with another student. It was quite... graphic, shall we say? I am a very active and hungry lover,

Mr. Starke. She came to me one day, Chancellor Mason-Jones, and showed me the footage, and then she told me what was going to happen."

"Go on," I said.

"It's actually not as bad as you might think. The women are all well-to-do, wealthy, clean, nice-looking... most of them." She lowered her eyes and looked coyly at Jacque. "And, as I said, I don't have to deal with crass, uncouth men, and their groping, and their filthy body parts...." She sounded very bitter, and she was holding something back.

"So," I said. "Jones coerced you into the system. Who shot the compromising video, do you know?"

"No, but I can guess. The damned cockroach."

"You mean Captain Rösche?"

"Yes. The son of a bitch was—is—everywhere, during the day, at night, when we were there, when we weren't. He has master keys to every room. You have no idea how much of my underwear went missing during my four years there."

"Who else is involved?"

"With the blackmail or Kalliste?"

"Both."

"Rösche, for sure. We have minders when we go on dates. Protection, it's called. His men do that. One of them always accompanies us. Sometimes it's one of his guards, sometimes it's a sheriff's deputy...."

"What?" I couldn't believe what I was hearing. "The sheriff's department is involved?"

"Oh yeah," she said bitterly. "Hands is an appropriate name for that nasty son of a bitch. Him, Detectives Hart, and McLeish, and the cockroach. There's rarely a night goes by that they're not screwing one of the girls. Hell, even some of the guards are getting in on it." She shuddered, looked fearfully at Jacque. Jacque took her hand and squeezed it.

"Don't worry, Wendy," she said to her quietly. "It won't be for much longer." Then she turned to look at me. "Will it, Harry." There was ice in her voice.

"No, not much longer." I meant it. "Do you know of anyone else?"

"Not for sure. Mason-Jones, Rösche, the sheriff, a few underlings, and the girls of course, but that's about it. Oh, and there's a lawyer, Greene, his name is. He's been using some of the girls lately, so I've been told. He just hasn't gotten around to me yet."

Well I'll be damned. Why am I not surprised?

"What about the money, Wendy? How do they get paid, and how do you get paid?"

"Cash. Cash only. If you can't afford cash, you can't afford to play. They pay me in cash too. I get 30 percent of the fee. I deduct it from what the client pays. I put the remainder in a UPS Store drop box. Everything else is done by phone, disposable phones."

"And where would that drop box be?"

She told me, and I made a note of the address and number.

I'll get Bob to check that out, I thought, and then, *shit. No. How could I have forgotten?*

"How about your clients? Are they all local?" I knew the answer to that one, but I needed to hear it from her.

"Local? Oh no. They come from all over the United States and Canada, some even further than that."

"Wendy," I said. "Do you remember the two girls that went missing while you were at Belle Edmondson? Their names were Angela Young and Marcy Grove."

"Yes. I knew them both. They were sweet girls. Both of them were members of Kalliste. In fact, I knew Angela very well. I always wondered... what happened to them."

Well, that answers that question.

"Mr. Starke," Wendy said. She was now holding Jacque's hand in both of her own. "Do you think I'll ever be able to get out of this mess?"

I pursed my lips, tightly, slowly nodded, and said, grimly, "You can count on it."

Her eyes filled with tears, but she wasn't crying, she was smiling.

"One thing, though, Wendy. I—that is, we—will need you to testify about what has happened to you, in court. Would you be willing to do that?"

She nodded. "Damned right I will," she said through her teeth. "I want to see that filthy animal behind bars for what he's done to us; her too."

It didn't take a whole lot of imagination to figure out who she was referring to.

"Good," I said. "Lieutenant Kate Gazzara will be in touch with you shortly. She'll want you to make a statement and swear out a complaint. And that, I think will do it. At the very least, Mason-Jones is a pimp. But if this thing is inter-state, if you girls are traveling across state lines.... Did you?"

She nodded. "Only once, but some of the others travel all over. Florida, New York, Washington...."

"That makes it federal. The law states that anyone who coerces anyone to travel interstate to engage in prostitution, or in any other sexual activity, can be fined and/or impris-oned for up to twenty years. That's human trafficking, and these people are deep into that, and maybe murder too."

I rose to my feet; they did too.

"Thanks, Wendy. You've been a great help. We'll get you out of it. I promise."

She took a step forward, wrapped her arms around my neck, and hugged me. Afterward Jacque stepped in and hugged me too.

"I'm sorry, Harry," she whispered. Another first.

I hugged her back. "There's no need for that," I said. "Now

get outta here. Take her home. And... congratulations. She's lovely."

And they left, leaving me alone with my thoughts, wondering what the hell to do next.

First things first: call Kate, and bring her up to speed about Wendy and what needed to be done with her. And then I had to get out of there. I was closing on the new house at five o'clock.

Chapter Twenty-Nine

It was a little after six thirty when I arrived home, and I was in one of those moods. Even after I'd talked to Kate, even after I'd closed on the house, something about that meeting with Jacque and Wendy was sticking with me. They seemed to be so much in in love, and after only a couple of days. How could that be? I'd heard about such things, of course, but....

I thought about them, and then I thought about Amanda, and then I smiled to myself. I parked the Maxima next to hers in my garage, went up upstairs and found her in the kitchen, bottle of Laphroaig in hand. She smiled as I entered.

"The garage door, right?" I smiled.

She nodded and handed the glass to me. She'd poured a good three fingers and topped it off with a single cube of ice, just the way I like it. I took it, held it to my nose, breathed deeply, then closed my eyes and sipped. Life was good.

"Hey," I said. "Guess what. I closed on the house a few minutes ago."

She smiled, but didn't answer. I sipped again, relished the scotch as it coursed down my throat, then I set the glass on the countertop, slipped my arms around her waist, and pulled her to me. I held her tightly for a moment, savoring every curve of her body pressed against mine: her thighs, the gentle mound of her belly, the firm swell of her breasts against my chest. I kissed her, gently, and for what seemed to be an eternity. I don't think I'd ever felt the way I did in that moment: love? Maybe. Sadness? A little. Joy? Oh yes. I was a bucketful of mingled emotions. Even my damned eyes were watering.

"Hey," she whispered, pushing gently back and looking up into my eyes. "What's wrong?" She laid the back of her forefinger against my eye and wiped away the moisture.

"Not a thing. Not a damned thing. I'm taking the weekend off. Let's go to bed."

"But, Harry. It's not even seven o'clock.... Oh what the hell." She disentangled herself from my arms, took my hand, and led me into the bedroom.

We rose early the next morning and breakfasted lightly on scrambled eggs and toast, and then went to Erlanger to see Bob. I felt a whole lot better when we walked into his room and found him sitting up in bed.

"Well, look what the cat dragged in," he said, as Amanda leaned down and kissed him on the cheek.

"Bob," she said. "You look wonderful, but you need a shave in the worst way."

"Yeah, that I do," he said rubbing his chin ruefully. "But it's good to see you both. Sit yourselves down. Did you bring me anything to eat? One, no two, of those Hardies biscuits with egg and sausage would go down a treat right now. Do you guys know what they give us for breakfast in this sorry place?"

"Bob, shut the hell up," I said, grinning. "How you feeling, man?"

"Like shit. I got shot, damn it. How d'you think I feel? Harry, see if you can find my clothes. I gotta get outta this damn place. They're starving me to death."

"Can't do it, Bob. You're not ready yet. You need rest. Five or six more days and maybe—"

"Six more days? Are you out of your mind? I won't last that long."

"Yeah, you will. That tube has to stay in until your lung can stay inflated on its own. Another couple of days, maybe. Even then, you'll need rest, and you have no one to.... Yeah, you do. You'll come stay with me until you're fit enough to be on your own. I have a spare room, if I can get Amanda to clear all her clothes out of it."

"Harry," he said, "I can't do that."

"Sure you can," I said. "No arguments."

"I had Heart and Sole in here yesterday," he said sleepily. "What a pair of assholes they are. Wanted to question me, so they did. Nurse tossed 'em out on their ears. They'll be back. Couple of damned rats is what they are."

He sighed and looked at Amanda, who smiled at him and nodded. He shrugged, settled back into the pillows, and closed his eyes. I guess the anesthetic was still in his system. We rose quietly to our feet.

"Close the damned door on your way out," he growled.

We arrived at the club early that Saturday. Amanda and I had lunch with my father and stepmother, as we did most weekends.

August Starke, my father, is one of those larger-than-life figures that dominate any room they happen to be in, be it a lounge or a courtroom, and it's not just because of his looks, although even I have to admit he's a handsome old man. He's one of the country's top lawyers, specializing in tort. He loves taking on the pharmaceutical companies. To date, he has won almost a billion dollars for his clients, and he takes his cut of that. He's a very wealthy man. And that brings me to my stepmother. Rose is twenty years younger than he is, just three years older than me. She's a very beautiful woman: tall, blond, perfect skin, perfect figure. She's the quintessential "trophy wife," but actually, she's not. She a very caring person and loves my old man dearly, and I, in turn, love her for it.

They arrived just a few minutes after we did. He was, as usual, full of piss and vinegar. She was smiling indulgently at the outrageous remarks he made to one and all.

"Hello, you two," he said, plonking himself down on the window seat next to Amanda and waving a hand in the general direction of the waiter, who was already hurrying over to him. "Has he asked you yet?"

"Asked me what?" she asked, her face turning pink.

"To marry him, of course, To marry him. No? Damned fool. Wish I was twenty years younger. Oops, sorry, dear." Rose just smiled at him, winked at me, and leaned across the table and patted Amanda's hand.

"Take no notice of him. He's just kidding."

"Kidding my ass. What the hell's the matter with you, boy? Snap the girl up, before someone else does."

And then the moment passed, and he was off on another tangent. One after another his friends stopped by our table, said hello, offered to buy him a drink, patted him on the shoulder, kissed Rose on the cheek.

Lunch came and went, and finally he settled down a little. It was then that I asked him about the Greenes.

The smile dropped away. "John and Kathryn Greene?" he asked. He stared at me for a long moment. "What about them?"

"Come on, Dad. Give."

"If you know enough about them to ask me, you already know enough."

"What? What kind of an answer is *that*?"

He shook his head. "She's Billy Harper's little girl, and a chip off the old block. No. Billy is nowhere near as devious as she is. John Greene is a snake. I've run up against him twice, beaten him both times—barely. He'll shake your hand with his right and cut your throat with his left. Be careful, son. You're good, but.... Well, I'll be. Speak of the devil. Here they are."

"Hello, August," John Greene said, offering his hand. August looked at it, then at his other hand—I smiled; the old man believed his own BS—and then he rose and shook his hand.

"John, Kathryn." He nodded at one then the other. "Can I buy you a drink?"

"No, thank you, August. It was actually Harry I wanted a word with." He turned to me. No handshake was offered.

"I understand that you and Lieutenant Gazzara visited with my clients Victoria Mason-Jones and Conrad Rösche yesterday, and that Captain Rösche suffered actual bodily harm at the hands of the lieutenant. He won't be pressing charges, but from now on I must ask that you refrain from talking to either of them unless I am there to represent them. Understood?"

"Understood, Councilor. How are his nuts, by the way?"

He blinked at me, and kept staring. "Don't let it happen again."

I jumped to my feet. "Now listen to me, you piece of shit."

Kathryn stepped forward, but he held out his arm and stopped her. "You were saying?" he asked quietly.

"First, it's Mr. Starke to you. Only my friends call me Harry. Second, my friend here," I waved a hand in Amanda's direction, "had her blouse ripped from her body by one of Rösche's goons, and third, one of my employees is lying half-dead in the hospital because that crazy bastard is running a private army up there. You tell that son of a bitch, and the bitch he works for, that they are going down, both of them, and I'm going to make sure that they do. Now get out of my face. You're spoiling a good scotch whiskey with your presence."

He smiled. "You really are all they say you are, Harry. I'm sure we'll meet again soon. Kathryn?" And they left.

I sat down again; so did my father. His face was white.

"Damn it, Harry," he said. "Do you do that often?"

I grinned at him. "Oh, just now and then, when the need arises."

I picked up my glass, sniffed, sipped, smiled. *Not spoiled at all.*

One thing I was sure of, though: I wasn't finished with the Greenes just yet. Not by a long shot.

Chapter Thirty

The rest of the weekend passed quickly, and when I woke Monday morning it was to a bright, cheery dawn, with a watery golden disc rising above the tree line to the east. It was going to be a beautiful day, and in more ways than one, so I hoped.

The ride to the office was, as usual, something of a nightmare. Traffic on Thrasher Bridge was heavy, and downtown it was almost at a standstill.

I arrived at the office at a little after eight thirty, tardy. Everyone was at their desks, working. Normally I would have felt a little guilty, but not today. I had a feeling that things were about to break in a big way.

I grabbed some coffee, called the hospital, and talked to Bob. That done, I felt even better. He was doing well.

It must have been an hour later when my phone rang.

"Harry," Kate said. "I just heard from Caster. He's on his

way. I asked him to meet us at your office. He said he'd be there by noon."

I looked at my watch. It was almost ten o'clock.

"That's fine, but listen. I need you to come over here, and bring the burner phone we found in Emily's hidey hole. Can you do that?"

She said that she could. She arrived thirty minutes later. She had her hair tied back in a ponytail and was wearing lightweight black pants, black shoes with flat heels, and a maroon blazer over a white blouse. As always, she looked both professional and, well, gorgeous.

"I interviewed Wendy Tanner on Saturday," she said, as she sat down in one of the guest chairs in front of my desk. "She laid it all out: Rösche, Mason-Jones—and she implicated Hands, McLeish, and Hart. She also gave us a bonus. When I met with her, she had a friend with her. Aphrodite, or Alexa Rushton, as she's known in real life. She also unloaded. Better yet, she has a voicemail the chancellor left on her iPhone making threats. I have copies of both of their statements, written and on camera. Those two, along with Jessica's, should be enough to close them down and put them away."

I slipped the thumb drive into my laptop, and together we watched the interviews. She was right. Rösche and Jones were toast. Hands and his cronies, I wasn't so sure about. Other than a cover-up and coerced sex, they didn't seem to be involved in Kalliste. They were providing protection for some of the women, but that wasn't a big deal. Most cops moonlight as security these days.

Hands had demanded, and received, sex from all three women. So had the two detectives, and Rösche. Coercion? Maybe, but would it stand up? These women were, after all, technically hookers, and they weren't crying rape.

"Okay," I said, when the videos were done running. "Rösche and Jones are a given. Hands and his crew... not so much. All three of them were screwing our three girls, and probably the rest of the population of Kalliste as well. What that gets us, I dunno."

"Maybe so," she said, "but I'd say that when this gets out, his chances at reelection are slim to none. I suppose you'll hand it all over to Amanda, right?"

"She almost got killed up there. She deserves a little pay back, don't you think?"

"I suppose, but you need to be careful. We don't need to screw up this late in the game."

I just looked at her.

"I know, I know," she said, and rolled her eyes. "You know better than that. Just be careful, is all I'm saying."

I nodded. She was right. The Kalliste case was about done, but... we still were no closer to solving the two recent murders, much less the other two.

"What about Emily, Kate? We still have nothing, and I don't see how or why Jones or Rösche or anyone else connected to

Kalliste could have killed her, or Padgett. It makes no sense. They're all in it for the money. Why kill the golden geese?"

She had no answers.

I sighed, then asked, "Did you bring Emily's burner?"

She handed it to me, and I programed the four encoded numbers into it, and slipped it into my jacket pocket. She looked at me questioningly.

"Just a thought. You'll see."

They arrived right at noon: TBI's finest. Special Agents Gordon Caster and Sergio Mendez.

They were an impressive pair. Caster was typical of the brand. He could well have been FBI; he had it stamped all over him, from the dark gray suit to the heavy black shoes. Mendez was smaller by a couple of inches, and a little heavier, and dressed in jeans and a leather jacket.

Introductions were made, coffee was poured, and Kate and I did our best to bring them up to speed. It took longer than I expected, and I was surprised to hear that they were already familiar with Kalliste and had, in fact, been investigating the site for more than a year. The TBI has a very active human trafficking unit. These two were part of it.

They already knew about the connection to the college and to the Harper Foundation, and it was soon apparent that they had come down from Knoxville with every intention of taking the case away from us. My only question was why hadn't they closed it all down long ago. The answer was simple: no solid evidence.

Anyway, they spoke little, listened a lot, and finally they stood, took possession of the thumb drive and the paper printouts, and we followed their black Chevy Suburban to the Sheriff's Department on Walnut. It was almost five o'clock when we arrived.

Now you might think I was upset at the takeover of the case by the TBI, but I wasn't. As far as I was concerned, we were done with it anyway. My only concern at that point was to discover the connection between Emily and the sheriff, and I was already pretty sure that it was little more than sexual: he was charging for protection, and taking his pay in kind.

He wasn't expecting us. Nobody, so it seemed, had thought it worth informing him that he was under investigation.

"TBI?" he asked. "What? Why? And what the hell are you doing here, Starke?"

I didn't answer.

"I think we need to go somewhere a little more private," Caster said. "Your conference room, perhaps... and if you could ask Detectives Hart and McLeish to join us...."

"Hart and McLeish? What...? Yeah, sure, okay, but he goes," he pointed at me, "and her."

Kate smiled at him.

"They stay," Caster said quietly.

Hands grumbled angrily, but called Hart on his cell phone
and then led the way down the hall to the conference room,
where the two worried-looking detectives were already
waiting. He opened the door and politely held it open for
everyone, then he closed it, locked it, and took a seat at the
head of the table.

"So," he said, leaning forward on his elbows, hands clasped
together. "What's this about?"

I could see he was desperately trying to act unconcerned,
but it wasn't quite working. His face was red, accentuating
the scar on his chin. He had a tick at the corner of his right
eye that twitched, as if he were constantly winking at us.
Sheriff Hands was a worried man.

Caster opened his laptop, inserted the thumb drive, opened
one of the files—Wendy Tanner's—hit play, and then sat
back as the sheriff and his two officers watched,
mesmerized.

The video ended, and Hands began to bluster. Caster said
nothing. He spun the laptop toward him, opened the second
file, and again hit play.

"So?" Hands asked, when the video finished playing. "We
provided a little security once in a while is all. There's no
crime in that."

"If that's all it was, you would be right," Caster said. "But it
isn't, is it? These young women allege that you demanded
sexual favors in return for your not arresting them for prostitution."

"Nonsense. It was all consensual," Hands said, but his words lacked confidence. I watched the tick go wild.

"You know better than that, Sheriff. The statute says, and I quote: 'Consent cannot be given when it is the result of coercion, intimidation, force, or threat of harm.' That's what you did. You coerced them into providing sexual favors. You and your two detectives abused your authority. Coercion, Sheriff. That's rape. Sexual battery by an authority figure. Oh, and by the way, we have a third complainant. All three are willing to testify in court."

Hands had gone white, as had Hart and McLeish. They were done for, and they knew it.

"I need to call my attorney," Hands said. It was almost a whisper. He didn't even move to stand.

It was time. Surreptitiously, I slipped Emily's burner phone from my jacket pocket, went to contacts, and tapped the number from the coded Apate short list. After a few seconds, the iPhone on the table in front of Hands began to vibrate. He picked it up, looked at the screen, and the color drained from his face. He touched the screen and the phone went quiet. He placed it back on the table.

I grinned at him, then touched the screen again with my thumb. Again, the phone of the desk began to vibrate.

Hands stared at the phone, hypnotized. He was Mowgli to the phone's Kaa.

"Someone you know?" I asked. "Why don't you answer it?"

"It's... it's just a wrong number."

"Oh, I don't think so. Go on. Answer it."

Reluctantly, he picked it up and put it to his ear. "Hello?"

With my eyes locked on his, I slowly put the burner phone to my ear. "Hello, Israel," I said gently.

He slammed the phone down on the desktop so hard it was a wonder it didn't smash.

"Where did you get that from?" he asked.

"The question, Israel, is why did Emily Johnston have your private cell phone number, heavily encrypted, in her journal? Did you kill her, Israel?"

"I need to call my attorney, now."

"Agent Mendez," Caster said. "Please place these three men under arrest and read them their rights. Then Sheriff Hands may call his attorney. Following that, they will be taken to Bradley County Jail, where they will be held until they go before a judge."

He turned to me and Kate and continued. "Thank you, Lieutenant, and you, Mr. Starke. You should know that a team of agents are already on their way to the college to arrest Captain Rösche and Chancellor Mason-Jones. They, too, will be charged with coercion, along with several other charges related to human trafficking.

"Now, if you'll excuse us. We have a sheriff to look after." He said it with a smile, but there was steel in his eyes. "The

Harper Foundation," he continued, "is another story. Little Billy did a good job when he set it up. It's almost impenetrable. Almost, but that's for another day. Then again, who knows what we'll be able to dig out of this little mess. Immunity is an amazing and extremely useful tool."

It was almost six thirty when I dropped Kate off at her car and then headed home. Amanda was waiting for me in the kitchen, glass in hand. I accepted it gratefully.

"The TBI has arrested the sheriff and two of his detectives," I told her.

She sat down on one of the bar stools with thud. To say she was surprised, well, the word "understatement" comes to mind, but it would be inadequate. She was stunned. I stood by the bar and sipped on the drink.

"Well...? Are you going to tell me or not?"

I laughed. "Sure. Sure. It all started, as you know, with—"

"Whoa. Hold on a minute." She ran off, and came back a few second later with a digital recorder. She turned it on and set it on the bar in front of me. "There, now go. I'll transcribe and edit it later."

And so I told her. It took more than an hour, but when I'd finished, she had the bones of her story... well, part of it anyway. There was still Emily's murder to solve. And I still had a lot of thinking to do.

Chapter Thirty-One

The following morning, Tuesday, the airwaves were once again alive. Channel 7 and Amanda took the lead at seven; she had left me in bed and gone into the office at five o'clock. Hell, I didn't know there was such an hour.

The story of the arrest of Sheriff Hands took over the news channels for two hours. Amanda had woven a tale of intrigue and corruption the likes of which our city had never known. Needless to say, I figured prominently in her coverage. By eleven o'clock that morning, she had turned up at my office with Charlie in tow and interviewed everyone in the office. Well, most of them. I gave her what she needed, as promised, but I insisted she leave Jacque out of it, along with Wendy, Alexa, and Jessica.

From there she went to Cleveland and the Bradley County Jail and somehow managed to get footage of the three musketeers—Hands, Hart, and McLeish—as they were hauled before a judge and arraigned for a whole litany of crimes, some I'd not even heard of. The news that evening would be sensational.

So the Kalliste thing was just about wrapped up, with the exception of its connection to the Harper Foundation. But connection or not, that damned foundation was not going away, and neither were the Greenes. There was nothing illegal about running a website, and there was no way to connect them to Jones and Rösche's activities, or even the sheriff, unless one of them spilled their guts. And that, I was pretty sure, was not going to happen. What we had from Wendy about Greene using the girls... it was nothing more than hearsay.

It was already after eleven, but way too early for lunch. I called Kate. She answered, but was busy tying up loose ends. Kalliste was in the past, and I was suffering, just a little, from depression.

There I was: that case was closed, but I was still no closer to solving Emily's murder. I was at an impasse. I had three viable suspects. Mason-Jones and Rösche? Maybe, but I didn't think so. There were still those missing five days. Neither of them had the means to keep her hidden away for that long. Jessica Henderson? Nope, and for the same reason.

I sat at my desk, feet up, closed my eyes, and dozed. Well, that was what I intended, but something was bothering me.

Maybe they did do it, Mason-Jones or Rösche, or both.

Maybe there was somewhere on that campus—a shed, a disused storage building—but why would they kill the girls and Padgett? They wouldn't. The three girls were the golden geese, and Erika? I didn't think so. Her only connection to Kalliste was as a client, and that connection was tenuous at best. The girls were just a tiny part of the whole, and as far as we knew, they knew little of the inner workings and nothing of the principles besides the chancellor. No. It had to be something else, but what?

The more I thought about it, the more it made no sense. And then there were the murders themselves. There was so much anger in the way Emily and Erika had been killed, especially Erika. What was it that generated such anger? Only two things came readily came to mind: revenge and jealousy. And that was what kept niggling at me. Who would be jealous of Emily and Erika? Jessica? Maybe, but she couldn't have hidden Emily, not for five hours, let alone five days. There was no way. No. It wasn't Jessica.

Who the hell was that shadowy figure in the Sorbonne? Mason-Jones? Nah. Well, okay, so, white hairs, white paint, mold... mold.... dog hair.... Whoa! The neighbor! "Collins," she told me. "Lindsey Collins, and it's miss." She's single. Lives alone, right next door. Has a dog, a white Jack Russell. Damn! It could be. It just could be.... But how could she have held Emily right next door to Padgett without her knowing? Adam and Eve on a raft, my brain hurts.

In the end, I had to give it up. *Jeez, what the hell am I missing?*

I decided to go back to the beginning, to the day when they found Emily. I let my mind wander. Detail after detail flooded back through my mind. Some of it I could have done without, but it was no good. There weren't any answers there. The nagging tick at the back of my mind was still as elusive as ever, and the more I tried to grasp it the more elusive it became.

For some reason, my mind kept returning to that morning up on Wicker Road, the crime scene, Emily's dump site, whatever. There was something I'd missed, and it was bugging the hell out of me. In the end, I gave it up went and made myself a cup of Dark Italian Roast. It was close to noon anyway.

"Hold my calls, please, Jacque," I told her. I went back into my office and closed the door. I dropped into my throne and sat sipping silently, savoring the full-bodied flavor. There are many things in life I can live without. Coffee wasn't one of them.

I thought some more, finished the coffee, scribbled some notes on a legal pad, stared at them, tapped my teeth with the pen. I picked up the papers that Tim had left with me. The ones with initials and dates.

I need to talk to Jones, and to Jessica again. And how about Lindsey Collins? Hmmm.... Wicker Road, Wicker Road.... There's something about that morning I'm not getting. Jeez. And where the hell are those two cell phones?

I sat there for a long moment, remembering that morning, remembering the people I'd talked to. *Kim Watson,* I thought suddenly. *The woman who found the body. Maybe she can help.*

But first I called Doc Sheddon, asked him a couple of questions, and then I called Mike Willis, asked him several more, and then....

Aha. Oh yeah. That's it. I got it!

I grabbed another cup of coffee, sat back down at my desk, and opened my laptop. I went to the Kalliste website and clicked slowly through the first half dozen pages, looking carefully at each model. *Damn. I could have sworn....*

I flipped through the paperwork, found the number I was looking for, then picked up phone and tapped in the number.

Jessica answered on the third ring. By now she was well aware of the unfolding events, but she was still willing to talk, bless her. I asked her several questions and got answers, but not the ones I wanted.

So I made the third call. "Hello Miss Watson. This is Harry Starke. We met the other day, if you remember."

She said that she did.

"Great. Listen, something's been bothering me for a couple of days. Something about that morning when you found Emily. I think that you may be able to help me figure it out. I have to visit the college this afternoon and I was wondering if I might drop by for a quick word? It won't take but a minute. Well, maybe a couple of minutes. I want to show you something; see if it stirs your memory."

She paused, then suggested two thirty.

"Okay, thank you, Miss Watson. I'll see you then." I disconnected, sat back in my seat, put my hands behind my neck, and stared up at the chandelier. All I could see was the stark white shape of Emily's body lying face down in the depths of the forest.

Chapter Thirty-Two

It was a quarter after two—I was a little early—when I arrived. I parked the Maxima at the side of the house, walked to the door, and knocked.

I heard noises inside, someone walking and a dog barking, and then the door opened a crack.

"Hi, Miss Watson," I said. "It's me, Harry Starke."

She smiled, and opened the door a little wider. "Hi. Come on in."

I walked past her, and was immediately struck by a blinding flash of white light. Everything went black.

When I woke I was in the center of some sort of room and sitting with my ankles tied to the legs of a chair. A big wooden chair, with arms. I was leaning sideways over one of them; it was all that was keeping me from falling out of it.

My hands were tied behind my back, between me and the chair back.

I guess the chair's too wide to get my arms around it, I thought woozily. Blistering pain coursed through my head when I tried to sit up. *What the hell did she hit me with?*

I made it upright, and tried to look around. It was quite dark, which was good, because I had the mother and father of all headaches. What little light there was came in through a small window set high up in the wall, and I could tell I was in an unfinished area of the house. Probably the basement.

I looked down at my feet. My ankles were tied to the chair with plastic cable ties.

The lights came on. "Ah, you're awake, good," she said as she came down the stairs. She stood in front of me, twisting a nasty-looking boning knife in her hands.

Jesus Christ.

She was even bigger than I remembered.

Must work out a lot. Damn. The strangest things go through your mind at the strangest times. Who the hell cares if she works out?

"I always knew you'd come back, Mr. Starke," she said. "You're smart. When I met you that day on the road, when they found Emily, I knew that if anyone would figure it out, it would be you. What was it? What gave me away?"

She pulled up a chair and sat down in front of me, far

enough away so I couldn't reach her. Not that I could have, with my hands tied behind my back.

"You did, when you whacked me over the head." She blinked, but said nothing. "Oh, I had my suspicions, but that's all they were. I had nothing concrete. But I'd also been thinking about those two girls. The ones on bikes, remember? I needed an excuse to talk to you. I thought that would work. I thought that if I could show you some photographs of some of the girls from the college, maybe you'd recognize the two girls you saw on bikes. Either way, I'd be able to talk to you again without arousing suspicion. But the mind of a killer works in mysterious ways, most often driven by guilt and anxiety, as was yours. You had to fix it, but there was nothing to fix. Yes, I did have my suspicions. Your initials are in her journal, along with a list of dates. I assume those were the dates she met with you. That was what got me thinking. You were one of her clients, right?"

She stared at me, but didn't answer.

"And then there were the dog hairs. There were hairs from a Jack Russell terrier on Emily's body, and on Erika Padgett's. They say that criminals always leave something behind at a crime scene, and they always take something away. Where's Emily's phone, Kim?"

Her mouth twitched, but her eyes never left mine.

"Merry's a Jack Russell, right? You have her hairs all over you. I can see them from here.

"You want to know something really funny? Erika Padgett's

next-door neighbor also has a Jack Russell. His name is Harris. He's a cute little thing. He and Merry would make a great couple."

"So what? There are thousands of Jack Russells around here. Good God, man. I can name at least six, maybe more. It proves nothing. Neither do my initials. K. W. Damn it. There must ten thousand people in Hamilton county with the same ones."

"Well, of course you're right. It's all circumstantial. The initials. The dog hairs. They could have come from anywhere. There was tissue under Emily's nails, so we had DNA. But there was no one to match it to, until now, so you would have been off the hook, except...."

"Except what? You just said you can't prove anything."

"You're right. I couldn't. Not until you whacked me over the head and tied me up. It's funny how things work out, don't you think? All you had to do was talk to me, look at the photographs, answer a couple of questions, and I'd probably have been on my way."

She stared at me, open-mouthed. I think she suddenly understood what she'd done, and it horrified her.

I decided to turn the screw a little. "You know, she was my next in line, Erika's neighbor, after I'd finished with you. If I didn't get what I needed here, I'd planned on visiting her. She lived right next door, alone, with a Jack Russell, and plenty of room to keep Emily hidden away." I looked around the room. "Just like you have here. This is where you kept her, right. Yep, there it is. The swing, over there in the corner. Jeez, I bet you enjoyed yourself."

She was getting angry.

"And then.... Well, you thought you could fix what wasn't broken. I thank you for that, Kim."

"It won't do you a damned bit of good. You're not going to tell anyone."

"You going to kill me too?"

She didn't answer, but I could see the insane light in her eyes. She wasn't planning on letting me go, that was for sure.

"Why did you kill her, Kim?"

She didn't answer right away. Then, eventually, she shrugged. "She didn't love me. I loved her, but...."

I waited for her to continue, but she seemed to have retreated into another world.

"Well go on," I said.

"We met through the Kalliste website. Have you heard of it?

I nodded.

"I thought so. I figured it was bound to come out sooner or later. I did my best to keep myself out of it, but..." She shrugged again, and tapped the knife blade on the seat of the chair between her legs, staring absently at the floor. "Well, I changed phones often, used disposables, prepaids, but there's always something. Anyway, that's how I met her. She was into BDSM, like me, but it went beyond that. We became friends. She'd come here sometimes, stay with me, to get away. We were lovers. Well, I loved her. Then she told me it was over, that she was leaving me for that goddamn vet. Broadening her horizons. Bitch!"

She paused; I wriggled; she continued. "I followed her that Saturday night. I went everywhere she did. She ended up in that sleazy downtown bar, and that bitch was there. They didn't see me.... What?"

She'd spotted the look I was giving her.

"So that was you, in the bar, all alone in the corner. You were on the security footage, but it was too dark. Damn it. No wonder you looked familiar."

"I was wearing a ball cap, dummy. How do you think you would have been able to recognize me if Emily and that group of morons couldn't, as close as they were to me?"

She stared at me, smiling. It wasn't pretty.

"You were saying," I said.

"Yeah, well. They hooked up and left. I followed them to that bitch's home on Constitution. Would you believe she stayed the whole damned night? Didn't leave until almost seven in the morning?"

Her eyes were vacant. She seemed to be staring at me, but if she was, she wasn't seeing me. Maybe she was reliving it all.

For several minutes, she sat there, her hands together in her lap, holding the knife.

"Go on," I said.

She blinked, startled. "What? Oh! So they came out together. They got in that bitch's car and she took Emily back to the college. I followed. She dropped her off outside the block and left. Emily went inside and I called her, asked her to come out and talk to me. She didn't want to, but... well, she did. She got in the car with me. I kissed her; it was nice. For me, not for her."

She shrugged, smiled to herself—she was reliving it—then continued. "I asked her if she'd let me cook breakfast for her one last time. She didn't want to, I could tell, but she said okay, and I drove her back here. The rest, as they say, is history."

"You want to tell me about it?"

"No, not really. I made scrambled eggs and bacon for her... and coffee." She smiled at the thought. "A few drops of Ketamine, and she was all mine."

She stopped talking, staring at something on the floor I couldn't see, then looked up at me, tears streaming down her face.

"Why?" she asked. "Why did she do it? I kept her here, where you are. I tried to persuade her. I was so nice to her. I made her all her favorite dishes. I held her, cuddled her, told her how much I loved her, that we could be together, always, if only... but she wouldn't listen, kept crying, kept.... In the end I just gave up. She didn't suffer. I loved her."

"Then what."

"I put Emily in the little valley. It's so pretty there, what with the wild flowers and all. It was difficult, she was all stiff, you see. Then I went straight to that bitch vet's place and I strangled the shit out of her, literally. The cow!"

I waited, but I sensed that she was done, and that she was about to turn her attention to me.

"They weren't the only ones, Emily and the vet, were they?" I didn't use Erika's name because I had a feeling it might set her off.

"You mean Angela and Marcy."

"Yes."

"They were much the same, really. I never was very lucky in love. I met them both on the website. I fell for them, as I usually do. I had maybe a dozen or so dates with Angela. I thought it was going to last, but it didn't. Marcy? She was a bitch too. Lovely, but a bitch. She drove me wild. Made promises and never kept them. God, how that girl could turn me on.... They're both out back. The big flowerbed... oh, you haven't seen it, have you? Pity. Now you never will."

Shit. It's now or never.

I rose quickly to my feet, not easy when they were fastened to a chair. She began to rise too. I leaned forward, almost double, raised my arms as far as they would go behind me and brought my wrists down as hard as I could against my backside—it's a trick anyone with self-defense training knows. And it worked.

The cable tie snapped with a *crack*, leaving my arms free. And then she lunged forward, the knife aimed for my gut. I twisted sideways, leaned back a little, and punched her hard in the side of her neck with the knuckles of my right hand. She went down choking; the knife flew out of her hand, spinning. I had no choice. I reached up and caught it. Talk about dropped bread always landing buttered side down. I grabbed the thing by its blade, and felt my palm split open. No pain, but that wouldn't last.

I transferred the knife to my left hand and looked down at her, the knife at the ready. There was no need. She was done. She rolled over onto her back, coughed twice, and then passed out.

I collapsed back down onto the chair and took a deep breath. My palm was cut from the thumb joint all the way across to the base of my little finger; I was bleeding like a stuck pig, and it was beginning to hurt.

I bent down, cut the ties around my ankles, stood up, took a step forward and stretched. How long I'd been there I didn't know, but I sure as hell was stiff.

I found a piece of cloth on the draining board by the sink, and wrapped it around my hand; it wasn't much, but it would have to do. Then I found more cable ties on top of a pile of cardboard boxes. I used one to secure Kim's hands behind her back, another to secure her ankles, and then I sat down again and breathed quietly for a few moments. She began to stir. She was a big woman, and I began to wonder if she knew the cable tie trick. I went back and made sure that even if she did she would stay secure, by adding a second tie over the first.

That should do it.

I went upstairs, found my pistol and my phone. I called Kate first, then 911, then I settled down to wait.

And wait I did. Things move much more slowly in the county than they do in the city.

While I was waiting, I had a thought. I walked back into the house and hit the speed dial for Emily's number, put the phone to my ear, and listened. It began to ring. I took the phone away from my ear and smiled. Down in the basement, I heard it. I hung up, punched in Erika's number, and again was rewarded.

I found the two phones, along with several others, in an old dresser drawer. More physical evidence. I left them where they were, but photographed them, then went back outside to wait for the authorities.

A sheriff's cruiser was the first to arrive, followed by an ambulance, then a friggin' fire truck, and then another, and then, finally, Kate arrived with Lonnie.

The deputies took Kim into custody, sealed the house, and... well, it was over. I had to go to the hospital, because my hand would need some serious stitches, but it would heal. They always do.

I turned to get into the passenger side of my car—Kate would drive—but for some reason I stopped and turned to look up at the living room window. A little white face with a sharp pointy nose and a big brown patch over one eye was looking back at me. I hesitated for a moment, then looked again. She was still there. There was something about that face I just couldn't resist, so I went back up the steps. She was there by the door when I opened it, the stub of her tail vibrating wildly.

"Come on, Merry." I picked her up. She licked my ear. "You're going to need a new home."

Chapter Thirty-Three

I t was after nine o'clock when I got home that evening. I spent an hour at the hospital having my hand stitched—have you ever had the palm of your hand stitched? No? You don't want to. It was more painful than the cut.

I'd called Amanda during the ride down the mountain, so she was waiting for me at the hospital when they'd finished putting the stitches in. We dropped in on Bob, said hello and goodbye, and made a promise to drop by in the morning. Then it was away to the police department on Amnicola.

I spent two more hours making statements and explaining everything. Kim Watson was in a cell in Hamilton County Jail under suicide watch. Apparently she'd retreated into some quiet world all her own. She just sat there on the edge of her bed, staring at the wall, rocking back and forth.

Wes Johnston had left a message at the front desk saying he

wanted to see me. The paperwork completed, I tapped on his office door and pushed it open. He was seated behind his desk, staring out over the motor pool. He looked up, then waved a hand at the chair in front of his desk. It was a tired gesture, half-hearted.

"Hey, Harry." He continued to stare out of the window. "How's your hand?"

I shrugged. I wasn't sure if he was really interested or just being polite. "It's okay."

For a long moment we sat there, neither one of us willing to say the first word.

Finally, he turned away from the window and looked me in the eye, "Thanks," he said. His face was drawn. He looked tired. He was a changed man; something was missing, and it showed. That edge he'd had was gone.

I shook my head, slowly. "There's no need to thank me, Wes."

"Yes there is. You and I both know that if it had been left to Hands and his crew, it wouldn't have happened; the case would have gone cold. She would have been forgotten. You changed that, Harry. I'll be forever in your debt."

"Come on, Wes...."

"No," he interrupted me, "I owe you. That's the end of it." And it was. The next thing he said was: "Go home, Harry. Get some rest. We'll talk again."

He turned again to the window. I waited a few more

minutes, opened my mouth to speak, but the words wouldn't come, so I left him there to deal with his demons alone. All I wanted to do was go home and drink some of Scotland's best. And that was what I did.

Amanda and I sat together on the sofa in front of big windows—not for much longer, I hoped. I dozed a little, watched the reflections of the lights from Thrasher Bridge flicker and undulate. The night was clear and it seemed to me that the river was on fire: beautiful. I was feeling better... well, a little.

"So," she said. "Are you going to tell me or not?"

I looked sideways at her. She really was beautiful.

"How did I figure it was Watson, you mean?"

She nodded.

"To paraphrase Sherlock Holmes: Eliminate the impossible and whatever remains, no matter how improbable, must be the answer.

"First, I had no doubt that the two deaths were linked. That being so, I was positive the answer lay in those five missing days. Where was she? Who had the means to keep her hidden like that? It was impossible for Jessica to have done so. She only had a dorm room. The same went for Mason-Jones. Her apartment was big, but very public. Rösche? The same, unless he had some sort of hideaway on campus, but there was no profit for him in Emily's disappearance. I even considered the next-door neighbor. What was her name, Collins? She lived alone, and she had a Jack Russell, but she was no lesbian. Did you see the way she came onto me that day? Okay, don't answer that. So, who did that leave? The sheriff? He's corrupt as hell, but he's no killer. I even considered Jepson, the vet. I had Danny run a check on him, but he wasn't even here when Emily went missing. He was on some island in the Caribbean. So that left me with... nobody."

She looked at me over the rim of her glass. "Okay smartass," she said. "I'll bite. How did you figure it out?"

"I went back to basics, of course. How the hell I let it get past me... well, I guess it was because it was Emily, and I was so upset. Then Bob, and... ah, hell. I screwed up. Think about murder and prime suspects. They are?"

She looked at me, quizzically, "The spouse—husband or wife—a close relative, brother, sister...? The person who...."

I nodded.

"Found the body," she breathed.

"You've got it, and so did I, eventually. When I did, it was so damned obvious I could have kicked myself. She was the figure in the bar, in the ball cap. Had to be. I looked for her on Kalliste, but she wasn't there. And then I got that too. She wasn't there because she was a client. Then there were the dog hairs."

I put my hand down and tickled Merry's ears.

"And that damned great old house practically right next to the dump site? The motive was jealousy, just as I'd always thought. Kim Watson was obsessed with Emily, but Emily had found a new love with Erika, so both of them had to die. I figured I had the answer, but I couldn't prove it."

I leaned back in my chair, grinning, and took a sip of wine. I savored it. It was well worth the two hundred dollars I'd paid for it.

"So what to do? I decided to talk to her, but I didn't want to spook her. I had to have a reason. I figured the two girls on the bikes might work; she'd brought them up. I'd show her photos of Emily's friends, and twist her nose a little, figuratively speaking. The problem was, I underestimated her. I did not expect her to hit me in the head the minute I walked in the door. But that worked out fine. That attack and the subsequent conversation, which I recorded via my CIA watch, the two phones—Emily and Erika's—and the dog hairs, along with the paint chips, the mold, and the dust, all microscopically identical to what was found in her basement, put it away. Her DNA will clinch it: the tissue we found under Emily's fingernails. It's cut-and-dried. Another one for the books."

I sat back and savored the moment.

"By the way, I know we talked about this already, but Bob gets out in a couple of days, and I told him he's coming here until he can cope on his own. That's okay with you, right?"

She nodded. "Of course it is. I've already cleared my stuff out of the spare room...."

I took her hand, squeezed it, put her palm to my lips, kissed it, and stared out over the glittering waters of the Tennessee.

"So what now?" she asked.

"What do you mean?"

"Well. It's over. What's next?"

I didn't know what she was getting at. She was staring at me.

"The house, I suppose, and we'll have Bob here for a while...."

"Oh, Harry. I know all that. That's not what I meant. What about us?"

"Us? Us...?"

Suddenly I could hear my old man, whispering in my ear, *What the hell's the matter with you, boy? Snap the girl up, before someone else does.* And I almost did it. I almost asked her. But the words wouldn't come, not yet.

I put my arm around her and.... Well, that's a story for another day.

And More:

Thank you.

Thank you for taking the time to read *Gone*. If you enjoyed it, please consider telling your friends or posting a short review on Amazon (just a sentence will do). Word of mouth is an author's best friend and much appreciated. Thank you. —Blair Howard.

Reviews are so very important. I don't have the backing of a major New York publisher. I can't afford take out ads in the newspapers and on TV, but you can help get the word out.

To those many of my readers who have already posted reviews to this and my other novels, thank you for your past and continued support.

If you have comments or questions, you can contact me by email at blair@blairhoward.com, and you can visit my website http://www.blairhoward.com.

This story was book 5 in the Harry Starke series. Here's a Sneak Peek at Family Matters, Book 6 in the Harry Starke Series:

Family Matters

A Harry Starke Novel

By

Blair Howard

Family Matters Chapter 1

※☆※

A heavy mist hung over the narrow streets like a damp velvet shroud. The hour was a little after midnight, and all was quiet as Annie hurried homeward through the dark. Her soft slippers made no sound against the cobblestones. Her skirt reached almost to the ground, but the heavy fabric barely whispered against her legs. Even the rats that usually infested the gutters and alleyways seemed to be in hiding.

She'd spent the evening as usual, drinking at the Ten Bells and servicing her clients; just two tonight, but the extra sixpence would come in handy. Maybe she'd buy herself a half dozen eggs, maybe a pound of sausages to go with them. The thought was a pleasant one. Dinner in her ratty little room at Mrs. Crossingham's lodging house on Dorset Street.

She walked quickly, fearful of not only what might lie ahead, but also of what might be lurking in the alleys that separated the dank, decaying tenements on either side of her. Something was wrong. She knew it instinctively. Her skin crawled. She shuddered and looked back over her shoulder, but there was nothing there, only the mist that swirled and seemed to close in around her.

She drew her shawl more tightly around her neck and shoulders, tucked her chin down into her coat, and hurried onward through the darkness.

A gas lantern flickered faintly at the end of the street, casting weird, moving shadows. They grew to monstrous proportions, then shrank again as the night breeze bent and folded the wavering yellow flame. A dreadful feeling that she was being followed began to grow inside her.

She began to run toward the dim light, now seemingly far away in the distance. She had gone no more than a few steps when she heard it: a voice, whispering, as if borne on the mist.

"Annieeee."

Her eyes widened. She stopped, backed into the dark shadow of a shop doorway, and peered back down the street into the darkness. A shadow emerged, walking quickly toward her.

"Annie, there's no need to run. It's only me. I have sixpence for you." It was no more than a whisper, but she knew that voice. She'd been talking to him earlier, in the Bells. Now she was terrified.

"Annie, please don't run away from me. I want you oh so much."

She pressed herself back against the shop door, her hands held out in front of her.

The shadow stopped. "That's nice, Annie." She felt the words rather than heard them.

"No. Please. Please don't," she whispered.

And then the shadow was upon her. She opened her mouth to scream, but her voice wouldn't come. She began to choke. She put her hands to her neck. She knew then that she was dying. Her throat was a gaping hole. She gurgled, unable to get the words out. Blood sprayed from the gaping wound as she sank slowly to the ground.

The shadow gave a low laugh as it gently drew the blade down her face, laying her cheek open to the bone.

"Pretty Annie," the shadow whispered as the knifepoint pierced her chest. She tipped forward, landing on her face between the shadow's feet. "Goodnight, Annie. Sleep tight," he said, and then began to strip the clothes from her body.

Chapter 2

I t was a cold day in late May. Spring, the weatherman had said many times over the past several weeks, had sprung, and summer was just around the corner. But you wouldn't have known it. It was one of those rainy days when it's good to be at home in front of a log fire with a glass of scotch whisky and some good company; I had both.

My name is Harry Starke. I'm a private investigator based in Chattanooga. You may have heard of me. I've been in the news several times lately, sometimes for things that were not very flattering, but that's the way it is in my business. Most of us PIs have reputations akin to that of sleazy used car dealers. Most, but not me, thank heaven. I do very well. Have ever since I decided I'd had enough of the political infighting and turned in my resignation to the Chattanooga PD more than ten years ago. Since then, as the song says, "I've done it my way."

These days I live on the East Brow of Lookout Mountain. I

used to have a condo on the river, not far from the golf club, but after Mary Hartwell took it upon herself to try to kill me —she shot out the floor-to-ceiling windows in the process—it just wasn't the same. So I sold the condo and moved up to the crest of Chattanooga's Mount Olympus, up among the gods.... Well, the city's movers and shakers.

It's a quiet world up there on the mountain, a world where old money still reigns supreme among those they regard as the nouveau riche. It's also a world where the ghosts of America's Civil War still walk the heights, perhaps reliving, in their own ethereal way, the horrors of the Battle Among the Clouds.

The homes on the mountain are, for the most part, of a bygone age: old world, and very expensive. My new home is no exception.

I'll turn forty-four in a few weeks, and lately have become more than a little aware of my own mortality. I was still fit and healthy, standing six foot two in my socks and weighing in at 220 pounds. I still worked out for an hour every day, a ritual made easy by the fact I now had my own in-house gym, but the years were beginning to catch up, although I wouldn't admit that to anyone but myself. My mind was as sharp as ever, but my reactions were just a little bit slower, and that bothered me a lot. Three times during the past two years my chosen profession had brought the grim reaper knocking on my door. It was the Hartwell affair that finally brought it home to me with a bang—literally. And not just one bang, but several of them. The erstwhile Ms. Hartwell had opened up on my home with an AR15 assault rifle. If it hadn't been for my quick reactions, Amanda would have died that day.... But that was last June, almost a year ago, and I decided it was time to move on, and here I am.

My new home is an old place, built in the 1930s on almost two acres of Tennessee's most expensive real estate. A rambling, five-bedroom rancher complete with a pool and seemingly endless rock gardens, among which tiny pathways meander down the slopes for more than a hundred yards. I spent a fortune buying the place, and another bringing it into the twenty-first century, but it was worth it.

Anyway, it was a Friday afternoon, raining, and up here among the clouds the view was... well, misty. It was quiet times at my office, so I'd taken the afternoon off. Amanda wasn't working that night either, so we'd been out to lunch, and were relaxing, enjoying the solitude, feeling no pain. She had her knees up on the sofa and both hands wrapped around a glass of red. Me? I was sipping contentedly on three fingers of what I consider to be the nectar of the gods: twelve-year-old Laphroaig, Scotland's best, and my favorite. All was well with the world. At least, I thought it was.

"Harry, I need to talk to you about something," Amanda said. "I've had some news. Good news, I suppose, but... well, you might not think so."

Amanda is the love of my life, an inordinately beautiful woman, tall, strawberry blonde, with an amazing personality, a crazy sense of humor, and a huge soft heart. She was one of the stars at Channel 7 TV; the camera loved her, and so did her audience.

I say she's the love of my life, but that's a recent thing. There was a time when I... well, hated her guts would not have been too strong a way of putting it. But that's all in the past. Funny how life plays tricks on us. Now she spends more time at my place than she does hers.

I looked at her quizzically. "So tell me about it."

"You're not going to like it."

"Why not?"

"I may have to leave Chattanooga, for good."

She was damned right. I didn't like it.

"Go on...."

"My grandmother died a couple of days ago. Her funeral is on Sunday. I'll have to go. She's the only living relative I had, other than a distant cousin, who's at least four times removed and lives in Australia. Anyway, it seems I've inherited, among other things... well, a hotel. In Maine."

Okay, this is not good. I stared at her, speechless.

"Harry, talk to me."

"What the hell am I supposed to say? You just dropped a bomb. You're planning on leaving. How do I respond to that?"

"It might not happen. If it does, you could...."

"I could what, come with you?" I wasn't so much angry as I was hurt. Don't ask me to explain; I can't. "I have a company to run. Almost a dozen people rely on me for their livings. I can't just up and leave. Damn."

"Let's take it one step at a time, okay?" she said. "I didn't even know the old biddy owned a hotel, much less one in Maine. I have to go see her lawyers in Atlanta. I'd like it if you came with me."

"You know I will. When?"

"Well, as I said, the funeral is on Sunday. I need to be there for that. If you come with me, we could stay the night in Atlanta, and then go see the lawyer on Monday. Can we do that? The quicker, the better, and the sooner we'll know something.... Look, Harry, I don't want to go live in Maine. I don't want to leave my job at Channel 7, and I hate the cold. I know my grandmother didn't live up there. She lived in Macon. She must have had a manager run the place. Maybe... well, maybe that's the answer. If it worked for her, maybe it could work just as well for me."

I sighed, shook my head. She was right. I didn't like it, but there was nothing I could do about it except play along and see what happened.

"Go ahead," I told her, "give 'em a call. See if you can set something up."

She dug around inside her clutch, pulled out a folded letter and her iPhone. Punched in the number and put the phone on the table, on speaker. Then we waited. Someone picked up on the second ring.

"Duckworthy and Donald law offices. How can I help you?"

If I hadn't been so damned upset, I would have burst out laughing. "If they put that around the other way, it would be Donald Duckworthy," I whispered in Amanda's ear. She elbowed me in the ribs.

"I'd like to make an appointment to see—" she looked at the letter—"Mr. Duckworthy, please. Monday morning if possible."

"One moment please. I'll check if Mr. Duckworthy can see you then."

He could, and an appointment was set for eleven o'clock that Monday.

"You're not really thinking of moving to Maine, are you?" I asked. Hell, she can't be. She has a good life here. Success, popularity, and me. Me!

"I don't know. I might have to. I might.... Harry, I don't know. We'll have to wait and see what the meeting with Duckworthy brings. I don't *want* to go and live in Maine. I told you, I hate the cold, and it's cold up there all the time."

I didn't answer. I just sat and stared out into the gloom. The weather suited my mood perfectly. I got up and poured myself another three fingers of Laphroaig.

Amanda stretched out her glass. "Would you get me a refill too?" I did, and then returned to my seat beside her, but I was antsy. I couldn't sit still. I got up again and went outside, stood under the patio cover, and watched the mist swirling over the city below. It's very rare I feel out of control of any situation, but this.... I had no idea how to handle it, or even what to say to her. She was obviously upset, probably more so than me. I went back inside and rejoined her on the sofa.

"Do you have any idea at all what your grandmother had in mind?" I asked. "She must have spoken to you about her wishes."

"That's just it. She didn't. Never has. I truly think she thought she was going to live forever. I do know she was a wealthy old bird. The house she lived in must be worth... oh, I don't know, maybe a couple of million. A lot, for sure. Granddad made a lot of money. He was a stock broker." She paused, thought for a moment, and then said, "Wow. I suppose I'm suddenly quite well off. Now you can't say I want you only for your money." She smiled half-heartedly as she said it, but there was little humor in her voice.

"I never thought that, and you know it. Hell, Amanda. It's been only eighteen months or so; I was just getting used to having you around. Now I have to lose you?"

"No, silly. Of course not. We'll work it out somehow. I can always sell it all, can't I?"

One would think the answer to that question would be simple. I hoped it was. But that weekend turned out to be one of the longest of my life.

.   .   .

You CAN GRAB A COPY OF FAMILY MATTERS HERE:
My Book